1/50

Nine Lies

Robert M. Marchese

First printing

This is a work of fiction. Names, characters, businesses, places, events and incidents are either the products of the author's imagination or used in a fictitious manner. Any resemblance to actual persons, living or dead, or actual events is purely coincidental.

ISBN: 978-1-61296-450-8

PUBLISHED BY BLACK ROSE WRITING

www.blackrosewriting.com

Printed in the United States of America

Suggested retail price $16.95

Nine Lies is printed in Gentium Book Basic

For the Boys

Acknowledgements

I would like to express a heartfelt thank you to my sweet and lovely Allison for giving me space and time to write and think and be strange. I would also like to thank my parents for their love and support and for being honest readers. To Riley, my flower, and Robbie, my fire, thank you for the constant flow of beautiful inspiration – let me know what you think of it someday. To my grandparents, I love and miss you.

Thanks to Denise Earles for turning my cover design idea into something even sweeter. To Mary Helen Braceland and Lisa Landa, thanks for the early feedback and candor. Thanks to Jon Pardo and Phil Rosati for the cop scenarios and jargon. To Malcolm Watts, my ultra-professional photographer, thank you for the wonderful picture.

Nine Lies

Chapter 1: The Gunman

*"A wise man does not waste so good a commodity
as lying for naught."*
- Mark Twain

Before this past Tuesday, the last time I dealt with the police was ten years ago. My Uncle Alex killed my father only a few hours after my grandpa's funeral. We later found out that it was premeditated. He had been planning it since the previous winter—ever since Donato became seriously ill. Alex's plan, we discovered soon after, was to attend the funeral, allow his children and wife to see him mourn, go halves with my father on a big meal at an agreed upon Italian restaurant, and then, in front of family and friends, empty a five shooter into his brother's chest before killing himself. All of it came to fruition except the suicide. Though he reloaded the weapon and put it to his temple, he balked. He ended up whipping it across L'allegria's parking lot, sitting on the ground in front of my cousin Jeannine's new blue Volkswagen, lighting up one of his menthol cigarettes, and waiting for the police.

I wasn't present for the actual killing. But naturally I heard the shots; we all did. They seemed to rattle every wine glass, every piece of silverware. On my way out of the restaurant, I encountered Jody, the pretty waitress I had admired just moments earlier. She still looked pretty, but now there was a grave uncertainty in her expression as she scrambled to learn what was happening. By the time I reached the parking lot, my father had already died. I lifted him onto me and lay with him while everyone around us screamed or ran for cover or pulled out their phones. He felt like a pile of wet blankets. I tried not to look at him, but I ended up catching a glimpse of his face; even in death he had that stern, inquisitive look I knew all too well. With the sun hanging low in the sky, and a pleasant early August breeze, I eyed Uncle Alex from across the parking lot. He leaned back against my cousin Jeannine's new blue Volkswagen and released perfect plumes of cigarette smoke into the air. We were a hundred or so feet apart, but I could see that his eyes were closed and that he had the faintest trace of a grin on his face.

My Nana never witnessed her oldest son murder his brother on the day she buried her husband of fifty-two years. For this we were grateful. My cousin Joe had driven her home after the cemetery service. She had complained of stomach cramps and forewent the meal at L'allegria's. There would be no question as to who would break the news to Nana. It would be me. To save face, my cousins half-heartedly announced that they would do it. As we gathered outside the police station at dusk, my Aunt Janice, Alex's wife, through bewildered tears and smudgy glasses, told them it would be best if Marcus was the messenger. Despite my new burden of being fatherless, no one protested. They all knew and understood my relationship with the old lady. It would have to be in the morning, I argued; best to let whatever dreams she was going to have that night be about Donato and his Italian serenades, or his impeccable wardrobe, or the endearing ways he had with young children.

The New Jersey State Police got full cooperation from Uncle Alex. He not only signed a detailed confession, but he willingly handed over the unused suicide note he had folded in his breast pocket. The note, handwritten on three sheets of yellow legal-pad paper, expounded on the matter. He had built-up resentment towards my father for living hours away in cushy Connecticut, while he, Alex, tended to the constant needs of their parents. He felt that my father was undeservedly hailed as the good son. He even went into the minutiae of their upbringing, citing case after case where he felt slighted or passed over.

Though they were hardly close in adulthood, the worst I ever heard my father say about his brother was that he was a conman, a loser, a classic underachiever. The two men merely tolerated one another. Only three years apart, they seemed to come from different families entirely. My uncle stayed close to Morristown, which is where he and my father grew up; there he raised a family, worked a myriad of modest blue collar jobs, and grew to detest his only sibling, who put himself through law school, thus becoming the family's most heralded success.

In his note, Alex admitted to planning the murder; yet he failed to mention why he chose such a stark occasion for it. My theory is that he saw the passing of his own father, who scrutinized his oldest son's every move, as the optimal time to exact his pathetic revenge; he was apparently less concerned with how the rest of us would view the tragedy. That he carried out his plan the day he buried Donato, and in front of the family, suggests his wanton need to grandstand for an audience, an idea he must have felt was monopolized by his accomplished kid brother.

It was also discovered, a week or so after the murder, that Uncle Alex had long ago been diagnosed with bipolar disorder. He managed to keep this, as well as his refusal to take his prescribed lithium, from the family. I never went to see him in the wake of the killing. My concern was Nana; I broke the news to her the following day. She retreated to her tiny sun porch with the white porcelain dog statue and overgrown fern tree; there she sat quietly with her eyes closed and her hands folded neatly in front of her face. I stayed with her on and off for most of the day. She was silent the entire time, except when she looked up, gazed out the window at the oncoming darkness and muttered, almost trancelike under her breath, "I miei ragazzi sono andati tutti." My Italian has always been spotty, but I knew this meant something about losing her boys.

I moved in with her for a few days, ordering in calzones and Chinese, cleaning the house, and dealing with the police investigation. Uncle Alex, I was told, was not only lacking any remorse, but in one of his statements said he felt nothing but relief. I never revealed his apathy to Nana.

When I went back to Connecticut a week after the killing, I buried my father in the plot adjacent to my mother, who died in a house fire when I was in elementary school. I was twenty-six years old and parentless.

My cousins and my Aunt Janice pleaded with me to keep in touch. They opined that we should spend holidays together and even meet up on occasion at their Crescent Lake cottage. I avoided them as long as I could, always quick with a reasonable excuse, but finally acquiesced to Thanksgiving two years after the murder. It proved too awkward—we all knew my presence was a futile gesture of obligation—and I left after an hour.

The years following saw fewer and fewer phone calls and birthday cards until all ties were tacitly severed forever. *Fuck it,* they probably thought; *we tried—Marcus is, what, in his thirties? He can take care of himself.* I was exactly thirty by then and taking care of not only myself, but of Nana as well. Since the murder, her health seemed to decline rapidly. She was in and out of the hospital, complaining of stomach cramps, dizziness, migraines. I was in regular contact with Dr. Robertson, her primary physician, not to mention a handful of specialists, all of whom always claimed the same thing: It was nothing serious. But whatever ailed her could not be detected, or even treated. Most weekends I would make the drive to Jersey to be with her.

"It's time to move," she told me one afternoon during a visit. "I'm tired of these walls."

There was a retirement community less than ten miles from her home in Morristown. A beautiful single story building, mostly in red brick and stucco, with wildflower gardens and a quaint blue bridge leading to a duck pond, the place accommodates over one hundred residents, offering plush little apartments with kitchenettes and carpet and full furnishings. Three of her good friends had been living there for some time and they were happy with their lifestyle.

"Besides," she said, "you need to move on, too. E troppo e troppo."

"Move on to what? What do you mean?"

The look she gave me was the exact look my father had given me most of my life when I perplexed him or when he wanted to intimidate me a bit. Lips pursed; eyes wide and unblinking; nostrils slightly flared.

"Don't be a smartass, Mister Teacher-man," she said. "You know what I mean. Una donna."

"I have a woman. Remember?"

Joanna and I had met several months earlier; she was a student teacher in the art department at Louis Sutherland High School, where I had, at that point, been teaching English for the past nine years. I had already told Nana all about her; how she always wore a paintbrush through the bun in her hair as she moved through the halls of LSHS; how she had that simple, unpretentious kind of beauty I liked so much; how on our first date we went on a whale watch, which was her idea.

"Anyone can meet someone," said Nana. "When will you marry this girl? Per l'amor di dio!"

Nana ended up moving to Blue Bridge Retirement Center that May; her arrangement went from independent living to assisted living in a matter of months. The next and final stage, which I dreaded, was called constant care.

Joanna and I married that same spring. It was a small ceremony, held in the backyard of her childhood home, where her parents continue to live. We've been married now for five years and we have a two year old son named Coleman, whose name comes from Joanna's side of the family. We live in East Stonyfield, which is on the Connecticut shoreline. Each of us grew up in neighboring towns, so we know the area well. East Stonyfield is an old town with a population of about six thousand; there are a few beaches, Many Flavors, the old fashioned ice cream parlor, a front street with a used book store, an art cinema, a takeout deli, and a sweet shop called Eve's Treats that has been there since the 1950s and is the closest thing we have to a tourist attraction.

We're both certified high school teachers, though Joanna is not currently working; she's been on hiatus this past year so she can ostensibly work on her paintings, which she sells locally. The real reason for the hiatus—and this has yet to be acknowledged by either of us—is so she can get pregnant again, becoming a full-time stay-at-home mother. I am not at all sold on this idea.

Our house is a beige Cape style with burgundy shutters; it's on a cul-de-sac on Blackbird Lane in a modest, sleepy neighborhood of working class families. We know the Sandstrom's across the street, and the Coyle's, who live next door. Both have teenage daughters who have babysat for our son. Cole seems to like the Sandstrom girl a bit better; she's more animated and outgoing, while the Coyle girl is pleasant enough, but a bit dull. Cole is a sweet boy. He looks like me, which is secretly thrilling. He has thick brown hair and long, pretty eyelashes; his lips are full and his eyes clear and curious.

My life moves at a steady, predictable pace. Its momentum—if it has any—has been forged by routine. Working and playing; shopping and eating; paying bills; thinking about the past; planning for the future. I've admitted to myself in private that I'm a lucky man—and I've admitted it to Joanna as well. And I believe this to be true. I also believe that luck is not to be taken lightly. It's the most wonderful kind of currency we have; it seems to spill forth from some unknown source when your eyes are closed during some flash of daydream or when you're driving along the downtown front street looking for a parking spot. Regardless, once it's recognized as luck, it must be thought of in the same delicate way priests contemplate the cosmos.

When I was a teenager, my father began asking me if I would rather be good or lucky. I can recall the way he used to phrase this. The word "good" rolled off his tongue in a quick, bold manner, while "lucky" was given a more languid treatment, as though there was some summery quality to its ambiguity, some bright and breezy manifestation that could use the occasional airing out. The very first time he presented this to me, I picked the wrong one. Naturally. "Good" was something I'd heard of; it was familiar and conventional. It made at least a modicum of sense to me. I was told to be good; I was praised for being good; I was encouraged to find the good in others. Luck, meanwhile, was mythologized. It only existed in platitudes or in ways to conceal envy. To me, my friend John was lucky he had an older brother; our neighbors were lucky they had a pool; movie stars and the very wealthy were lucky. I eventually caught on, adopting my father's philosophy on the good versus lucky paradigm. In no time at all we were scoffing together at anyone who would choose the former. My mother, he told me one day in unsolicited confidence, shared his view. I suppose then that there is a bit of dark irony in how each of my parents died.

On our third date, I posed the question to Joanna. She spent too little time thinking about it, and then, with an almost incredulous gasp, gave the wrong answer. When she asked me the same, I said "good." The matter was then dropped.

This past Tuesday, when I was surrounded by police officers, and answering an absurd amount of questions, I recalled this memory. Not so much the conversation Joanna and I had, or even the lie I told her, but how I never came clean about where I really stood on the matter. Not later that night; not on our next date; not after five years of marriage. I haven't yet worked out what this says about me as a husband—or what my proclivity for luck over goodness says about me as a man, a father, a teacher.

On Tuesdays, I bring Cole to daycare by myself. Joanna volunteers once a week for a local organization called A Better Chance, or ABC, which integrates gifted inner city kids into the local schools here in East Stonyfield, so she's out the door before me. My routine is therefore the same every Tuesday morning: I dress Cole in the outfit laid out by my wife, we watch cartoons for fifteen minutes while we eat hard boiled eggs and toast with apricot jam, then I take him to get a chocolate donut before bringing him to daycare. He attends a place called Children's World, which is ten minutes away in Old Brookview, just halfway between our house and LSHS. Located on a remote, woodsy lot with its closest neighbor being an ancient VFW lodge half a mile down the street, the place is in need of a new red paint job and some fresh landscaping. Its fine reputation, though, belies its appearance.

On that particular Tuesday, Cole and I were earlier than usual. We walked in the door at exactly 6:36 a.m., a detail I would have to later recount several times to a state cop named Officer Walsh. No other children had yet arrived. Lynn, the chubby and overly serious morning teacher, greeted us from her regular position at the head of a red rectangular crafts table where she sat with paperwork and her breakfast. We spoke for a minute or two. It was small talk as usual: the mild early April weather; the previous night's full moon; the upcoming annual food drive the daycare would be sponsoring. Because Lynn is a bit dull, and her voice is forgettable, I only half listen when we converse.

My mind was distracted. I found myself looking past her to a stainless steel sink, the inside of which was streaked with blue and yellow paint. It had the appearance of some exotic spider crawling out from the bowels of the thing. Cole was in my periphery, bouncing on his favorite toy, an inflatable green rocking horse he's dubbed Clopper. A Hemingway test I was giving to my period one class suddenly came to mind. It's a test I've given for the past nine years. I had been meaning to change it—add a few questions, omit the confusing one about his suicide—but I never got around to it.

After I gave Cole a kiss goodbye, I asked Lynn if I might use the restroom, where I went and sat for a few minutes with the lights off, something I was doing a lot of lately. I found that small, dark spaces helped restore my balance and soothe my head, which had begun hurting several months earlier. My primary physician, Dr. Carlson, was able to rule out a serious sinus infection, which she was rooting for since some of the alternatives are not particularly pleasant. So she put me in touch with Dr. Stewart, a neurosurgeon out of New Haven; I was scheduled for an MRI with him the following week.

After I cleared my head a bit, I urinated in the dark before stepping back into the daycare's main room; I then bid Lynn a good day and walked outside. The cool early morning air blew through the bare trees; sunlight fell through the branches, illuminating the dull grey and brown of the wilderness. I stood in the gravel parking lot for a moment, staring out into the deep woods behind the building. Closing my eyes, I listened to the sound of unbroken quiet. No cars. No voices. Nothing. Then, without a moment's hesitation, I wheeled back toward the school, ran to the door and burst back inside. Lynn was washing her hands at the sink and Cole had moved on to playing with a toy barbeque set. They both turned to me. Cole muttered something about making delicious food for Daddy; Lynn just glared at me, her mouth agape and a slight squint in her eyes.

"You need to call the police," I said. "Right now! There's a man in the woods with a gun—he says he's coming in here."

Officer Walsh, a Connecticut state cop, told me it was remarkable that I thought to call work to let them know I was going to be late. That's the word he used: remarkable.

"Pretty good instincts," he said, "given the circumstances."

"My boss is a woman," I said, smiling a little.

The truth is that Dot Logan, LSHS's principal, is no more intimidating to me than one of my own students. She's been on the brink of retiring for a number of years and therefore lets her much younger and willing VP run the show. Walsh stared at me and then took some notes in a thin brown leather book. Handsome and fit, with his blondish hair shaved close to his head, Officer Walsh and I seemed similar in age.

"The truth is," I said, "I pictured nearly two dozen seventeen-year-olds taking advantage of my absence and wreaking havoc. So I made the call."

"And tell me again where you made the call from."

This was a detail we had already gone over, but I told him again. Lynn, prior to the arrival of the authorities, had declared an immediate lockdown. She yelled for Cole and me to take cover under the red rectangular crafts table. Since I work in a school, I am familiar with such drills. The state mandates that we have a couple of practice lockdowns each year in preparation of a real emergency. We're required to bolt the door, kill the lights, draw the blinds, and demand silence.

One time—I believe it was my second year at LSHS—a student in my class farted so forcefully during a lockdown that he soiled himself. The rest of the kids could not stop from laughing; meanwhile, the kid—Pete Jaimeson was his name—insisted on leaving my room to clean himself up. He never returned and I was later reprimanded by Dan Zinser, the young hot shot vice principal, for allowing him to leave.

I told Walsh that it was from under the red rectangular crafts table where I fished out my phone and called Louis Sutherland High School's main number. Dorothy Disario, the cheerful secretary, answered. Dorothy has a slight lisp, and the kids like her because she gives away Dum Dum lollipops and she always checks the "Excused" box on late passes.

"What was your son doing during this phone call?" Officer Walsh asked, scribbling some more notes.

"I couldn't really say," I said. "Maybe Lynn—"

"We'll be formally interviewing Ms. Olsen shortly," he said, rolling his eyeballs up from his pad.

The scene at the daycare was intense. There were four cruisers, two local and two state—not to mention the SUV marked Major Crimes Squad—parked haphazardly in the gravel parking lot, all with their lights on. They arrived one after another, probably four or five minutes after Lynn phoned them. With their weapons drawn, they secured the perimeter of the daycare.

Earlier, when they arrived, Lynn and Cole and I emerged from hiding and watched from the window above the blue dinosaur shaped bench. Cole, his eyes wide and wondering, barely blinked. He didn't seem upset, but I put him on my lap and whispered into his ear that everything was okay. I was truly relieved that he didn't appear to be frightened. He even smiled once the police dog made an appearance.

The search took close to an hour. First the dog and its handler combed the woods on all sides of the building; then a handful of officers with vests and rifles poked around the area. A few parents arrived with their children; they were met in the parking lot by a female officer who spoke with them for a bit before they drove away. By the time we were given permission to exit the building, the Major Crimes Squad showed up on the scene, driving a gleaming Chevy sport utility vehicle, out of which emerged two serious looking middle-aged men with windbreakers and walkie-talkies. Lynn spotted a female officer she seemed to know and walked towards her. Officer Walsh was the first to approach me. He asked that I give a verbal statement first; he took copious notes as I spoke. Then he asked me to fill out a proper statement form. Cole, he assured me, would be taken care of while I was otherwise engaged.

"Please read the form carefully," he said, handing me a clipboard and a black ballpoint pen. "The fine print as well as your own statement."

I skimmed through the fine print first. It was mostly generic, commonsense jargon.

"I feel like one of my students," I said. "Does grammar count?"

"How long have you been a teacher, Mr. DiMatteo?"

"You can call me Marcus. This is my fourteenth year. How long have you been a police officer?"

He had me beat by a few years, he told me. Then he asked me again to write my statement. Leaning against Walsh's cruiser, this is what I wrote:

After dropping off my son at 6:36, I kissed him goodbye—after some small talk with his daycare provider—and exited the building at probably 6:42 or 6:43. I walked towards my car when I heard a faint rustling in the nearby woods. This rustling increased in its volume almost immediately. When I scanned the backwoods of the daycare facility, I saw a distant figure making its way out of the thicket; clearly a person, it was moving towards me. Pausing for a moment, I watched the figure approach. We were probably two-hundred feet away when I saw that it was a man. He was looking in my direction and we seemed to make eye contact. Though he was somewhat obstructed by trees and branches, I was able to discern his physical features. He appeared to be in his early forties. He was probably close to six feet tall and a hundred and eighty pounds. His hair was dark brown, straight, and unkempt. He wore a thick goatee that grew a little too much in both directions on his face. His attire was that of green Army pants and a black t-shirt. Draped over the black t-shirt was a gold chain with a large cross on it. As he closed in the distance between us, I saw that he was carrying a rifle—or perhaps a shotgun. Upon recognition of the firearm, I panicked for a moment, took a few steps away from my car, eyed the man more intently, and ran into the daycare building. As I ran, the gunman yelled that he was coming inside to open fire. His exact words, I believe, were "I'm coming, you peasant motherfucker!" His voice, other than being loud and forceful, was undistinguished.

As Walsh read over my statement, I vacillated between gauging his reaction to what I had written and checking on the wellbeing of my son. Cole was being held by Lynn who bounced him a little as she talked on her cell phone. He was turning his head in every direction, searching the area, probably looking for me. I told Officer Walsh that I needed to get back to my boy.

"This is well written," he said. "Not at all like the usual shit I get —misspellings, fragments, poor punctuation."

"I teach English."

"English was always a favorite subject of mine. My favorite teacher was Mr. Kooper. Senior English. 'Save the bullshit for the bedroom, kids,' he used to tell us. He was a character. He's still there. I check in with him every once in a while. I bet you have old students visit you, don't you?"

I nodded. Then I asked him again if I could go to my son. It suddenly became quiet. Walsh didn't answer for a few moments. He was looking straight at me, but he didn't speak. Then, after some time, he said something:

"You didn't call your wife during any of this."

There was a slight emphasis on the word "wife." I wasn't certain whether this was a question or a statement.

"No, I didn't."

Sniffing a little, Walsh pointed two fingers into his cheek and looked at me. He seemed to barely blink.

"I guess I didn't have much time to think."

He shook his head, agreeing that it would be difficult to form cogent thoughts in such dire times. That was the word he used: cogent. But then he made a sound like he was suddenly changing his mind. And then he said what he was thinking:

"You did, however, think to call your school to tell them you were going to be late."

"Well, like I said, I was fearful—"

"Of 'nearly two dozen seventeen-year-olds taking advantage of your absence and wreaking havoc,'" he said, looking at his notes.

I nodded my head. Then I called for Cole.

"I've got a little girl maybe a couple of years older than your boy. It's wonderful, isn't it?"

Though I was listening, my attention was on Cole, who was making his way towards me with Lynn close behind.

"The way they look at you at this age," he went on. "It won't last forever; that's for sure."

Walsh put my confession on the dashboard of his cruiser. Cole jumped into my arms and hugged me. Lynn told Walsh that as per his request she had phoned Deborah McKinnon, the owner of the daycare; Deborah had been visiting her sister in Massachusetts and was now on her way back to town. Then Lynn looked at me and said Deborah wasn't certain whether she would be open the following day and that she would be in touch that evening. I asked Walsh if I was free to go. He smiled at Cole and tousled his hair a little.

"We have your information. Someone will be in touch."

"Fine."

"That someone will probably be me."

Rather than head home, I brought Cole to work with me that morning. When I pulled into the parking lot, I called Joanna and asked her to drop what she was doing and pick up our boy at LSHS. I would explain, I told her, when she arrived.

When Cole and I went to my room, Dan Zinser was teaching my period three class. With his flawless blue shirt and yellow striped tie, he moved seamlessly around the room with his hands stuffed into his pants pockets, speaking with a delicate reserve one might find at a business seminar. He paid Cole and me no mind as we entered—despite the obvious distraction we caused for each of the nineteen students in the room, some of whom greeted us verbally. A row of three girls in the back of the room waved at Cole and whispered how sweet he was. Dan finished his thought before collecting his sport coat, which was draped over my chair, bid the students farewell, and walked towards the door. Brushing by me, he stepped out into the hallway; I turned and thanked him for covering my class.

"Classes," he said. "Plural."

"I appreciate it," I said.

Putting on his sport jacket, he smoothed the sleeves and looked down at Cole who was holding onto my leg. Without smiling, Dan looked back up at me and said I owed him one. I gave the class the rest of the period to read and study their vocabulary words for an upcoming quiz. And I let Cole watch cartoons on my computer. Joanna showed up by the time the bell rang for the next period, which I have free. She was wearing the black skirt and burgundy blouse I always liked on her; her hair and makeup were done up nicely, and she filled my room with the scent of that Japanese cherry blossom body spray I bought her for Valentine's Day. She looked lovely; yet this was belied by the heavy breathing and wide-eyed terror she made no effort to conceal. Cole ran to her and said that he saw a big dog at Debbie's house—that's what he called daycare: Debbie's house.

"I just spoke with Lynn," she said. "My God!"

"It's been a hell of a morning," I said.

"My God!"

"Everybody's okay."

Releasing Cole back to his cartoons, she asked me to start from the beginning. As I told her my story, she said the thing I predicted she would say:

"I should call my parents."

This was a statement she had popularized through the years. Will and Aimee Armstrong, Joanna's parents, live two towns over—

less than ten miles away—and are not only fixtures in our lives, but are constantly being enlisted by their daughter as problem solvers, advice givers, all-knowing confidants who apparently have such precious life experience to share. No matter is too big or small for Joanna—where to vacation, Hilton Head or Savannah, what car to buy, the Honda or Subaru. I recall one conversation she had with her father around the time Cole turned two; she asked him whether or not we should raise our son to be a vegetarian.

I never intervene. Will and Aimee may dote on their adult daughter far too much—not to mention their only grandchild—but they are intelligent people who are good to have on your side. We're lucky, I suppose, to have them in our lives; their presence certainly punctuates the looming absence of my own parents who I always imagined would have been politely exhausted by the Armstrong's occasional sanctimoniousness. As far as my own relationship with my in-laws, I believe they have at last accepted me. For years, though, it seems as if they have been tacitly administering tests on my behalf, tests to determine whether or not they feel I am suited for their daughter. They will engage me in discussions about politics and the economy and my financial ambitions. My answers always seem to draw a similar reaction, which is slow, methodical head nods and polite smiles.

"What are your parents going to do?" I asked her.

Joanna detests sarcasm, so in my personal life I try to avoid what has essentially become, as a high school teacher, my dominant language from 7:30 to 3:00.

"Was Cole scared?" she asked, ignoring my question and turning the boy's face up towards her own. "Were you scared, baby?"

He absently nodded his head, clearly ignorant of what she was talking about. Joanna and I agreed it would be best to keep him home for a few days—regardless of whether or not Deborah decided to temporarily close the place down.

Cole's show ended and I kissed him and Joanna goodbye before walking them to the corridor just down the hallway from my classroom. A boy I recognized from a study hall I'd had earlier in the year was sitting on the floor against the wall; he was quietly arguing with a pretty, red haired girl who stood in front of him in a short-cut yellow dress. They paused when they saw us. Joanna and Cole, a bit self-conscious of these spectators, waved to me before descending the stairs.

By the time I returned to my room, there was about twelve minutes left before my next class. Closing the door behind me, I turned off the lights and locked the deadbolt with my key. Then I sat at my desk in the dark and rubbed my temples in slow circular motions. I did this for some time. It felt good. I sat there and closed my eyes and listened to the faint sounds of Jim McArthur's class, which was adjacent to my own. The level of noise was perfect. Its low, distant hum was actually more peaceful than absolute silence. My aim was to clear my head, which was consumed with all that had happened in the past few hours. I wasn't up for sorting it out yet or asking myself some goddamn difficult questions like why I had done what I did. A sense of drowsiness came over me around the same time as the knock on my door. I ignored it, but it persisted. That's when I knew it was Hank Blanchard, LSHS's head custodian.

"Look who's in the neighborhood," I said, welcoming him into my room, "Blanch, my dearest friend and comrade."

"You better not be jacking off in here," he said, "because I'm not cleaning that shit up."

I assured him there was none of that going on. He sat on a student desk in the front row and rubbed his fingers against one of his sideburns. Blanch is a nice looking man, probably in his mid forties. He has a full head of curly brown hair with streaks of gray, a menacing smile, and the build of a former high school wrestler. He keeps an attractive pair of brown framed glasses folded over the collar of his shirt, and every so often puts them on to look at something in front of him.

We became friendly at the beginning of last year when he noticed I was staying late most days. I had begun teaching a bullshit remedial class I had never taught before and had to put in extra hours for lesson planning, something I hadn't done since I was a first-year teacher. Blanch would come into my room to empty the garbage and recyclables or vacuum the floor if it needed it; he'd always make small talk, and soon we were commiserating over our dislike of the administration, or agreeing that the girls' dress code had changed since we were in school.

Before long, I was invited on occasion to follow him in my car to Sidewalk Caesars, a pub in Soundview, which is one town over, and, conveniently, on my way home. There we would drink Guinness and Goldschlager, shoot pool, buy the occasional round for a group of locals who were mostly men in their sixties with bad teeth and dirty ball caps. Joanna, who had encouraged me for some time to make friends with my coworkers, was okay with this unwinding ritual I shared with Blanch. Yet she made me promise over and over to drink responsibly, reminding me I was a father and a professional.

Last May, Blanch and I were walking to our cars, feeling the buzz from the liquor, when he turned to me and asked if I wanted to get high. Then he pulled a nicely rolled joint from his breast pocket and held it up to my face. We ended up sitting in the cab of his truck, which he pulled around to the rear of the bar by some dumpsters, smoking and listening to the Rolling Stones, thus starting what has become a tradition. Blanch eventually offered me my own personal stash in case the need ever arose to smoke by myself. I told him I'd rather smoke with him, but he insisted, promising it would come in handy one of these days.

"What about Joanna?" he said. "Is she corruptible, that wife of yours?"

I merely nodded, avoiding telling him the truth, which was that my wife was as straight as they come. Blanch ended up rolling a nice looking number, which he hid in an old sunglasses case in my glove compartment.

"I've got something new in mind for tonight," he said last Tuesday, "if you're up for it."

"I'm not sure. It's already been one of those days."

I had no intention of telling him about the gunman incident. Blanch and I had grown close, but I wasn't interested in revealing a story that could very well cause a litany of questions I knew I was ill-equipped to answer.

"Then what I have in mind is exactly what you need. It'll be the perfect way to unwind after you deal with that dickless moron—what's his name?"

"Owen McAllister."

Blanch knew all about the boy. I had complained, on more than one occasion, how each day for me at LSHS ended the same way: sweating out my Period 6 American Literature class, which was dominated by Owen McAllister's brazen obnoxiousness—his homophobic innuendo, his sexism, his constant pleas for attention. Dan Zinser had met with the boy several times, but each meeting always ended with Dan's mild reprimand and Owen's bullshit promise to turn things around.

"Let's say 4:00," he said. "Phone that wife of yours and tell her you're going on an adventure with Uncle Hank."

Joanna, when I called her, said she didn't mind if I went out with Blanch for an hour after work.

"After this morning, I suppose you deserve a few drinks," she said.

I followed Blanch to The Cowgirl Club, a strip joint by the water in Soundview. The place is notorious. I had never been before, but stories of its wildness are well known to anyone on the shoreline. It is as infamous for its raids as it is for its lascivious after-hours goings-on. A few years back, I overheard a student in my class brag to a group of boys that his brother had been to a stag party at The Cowgirl Club; his brother, the boy whispered in a ridiculous fervor, swore that an orgy had broken out sometime after last call.

"It's still daylight out, for God's sake," I said, meeting Blanch at the front door of the place.

"Not in there it's not," he said, tucking his shirt into his blue jeans.

Strip clubs were never my thing. I hadn't been to one since college; even then it was a pointless novelty for me. Blanch handed me a couple of one dollar bills, smiled mischievously, and ushered me inside. The man at the door knew Blanch; they joked with one another for a bit before we ordered a pitcher of beer and pulled up seats in front one of the dancers, a petite, dark skinned black girl with white iridescent underwear and pink suede platform heels. The place was rustic and dimly lit; its Wild West décor meant there were wagon wheels, six shooters, lassos, steer heads, Wanted posters, and barbed wire garland hanging from the walls or on shelves behind the bar or suspended above the stage. The music, some awful techno and country hybrid, blared from every corner. A DJ announced whenever a new girl emerged from a little back room that was in the rear corner of the place; they all had stage names like Sapphire or Isis or Lake.

Blanch tossed a few bills on the stage and poured some beer in the plastic cups the waitress had given him. A black girl with small breasts and a pretty face put on her show for us, scooped up the money, and made her way towards a lone man sitting a few seats down from us; he had neatly arranged a handful of bills in front of him on the stage floor.

"They just follow the scent of cash," I said, leaning over to Blanch.

"These women are artists," he said, smiling and hanging his glasses back over his collar, "show some respect."

"It's like an assembly line in here," I said. "But nothing's being made."

"Not true," he said, "hard-ons are being made."

We finished off the pitcher and ordered another. More dancers made their way towards us when they saw the money Blanch was leaving. Most of them were young—probably in their early twenties —and beautiful. Some of them had studs in their bellybuttons, tattoos on their lower backs, and silicone implants, which creased up when they lay on their backs. Blanch was in his element; he was having fun with the girls. He talked to them about sports and beer and complimented them on their dance moves or attire. A lot of them laughed and touched his face or ran their fingers through his hair. Then they would turn to me and see the two or three dollar bills Blanch had forced out of my hand and onto the stage, and they would fulfill their duty before thanking me politely and moving on down the line. Blanch, who caught me looking at my watch, told me I was awkward.

"Let them do their job," he said. "You're fucking up their thing. Show them you want to be here. It excites them."

The truth of it was I enjoyed the people-watching aspect more than anything. There was the solitary man a few seats down; I noticed that he played with his moustache while receiving a dance. There was a man and woman across the stage from me and Blanch; the woman kept whispering to the man while they watched the girls take off their clothes. There was an elderly man who stood near the restrooms with a bottle of beer in his hand, nursing it and gazing mindlessly towards the stage.

And there was Blanch, whose comfort level in the place helped put me at ease. His confidence, or bravado, or stupidity—whatever it could be called—always seemed charming and ingenuous to me. I liked Blanch more than a lot of my colleagues in the English department; they were mostly veteran teachers who had been at it for close to thirty years and were exhausted with the life. Inspiration came to them only on payday; they drew a line between obsolescence and apathy, vacillating between the two, caring not one bit that they were the ones to abolish all other choices.

Blanch caught me looking at my watch again. It was past 6:00. I didn't mind telling him I wanted to see my son before he went down for the night.

"You sentimental bastard," he said, standing up and finishing the last of his beer.

"Thanks for taking me to the early bird special. What a treat."

"A little debauchery every now and then is good for the blood. That's a fact; don't forget it."

We walked to the door where Blanch stopped to talk again with the bouncer. As they ran down their list of hopefuls for the new baseball season, the DJ announced a new dancer. Callie Starz was her name; the DJ made it a point to say that it was spelled with a Z. She had strawberry blonde hair and a small, round face with a serious looking expression. A black lace garter slip hugged her figure, which was fit and lovely. She moved slowly, ignoring two other dancers who were exiting the stage, talking as they gathered their cash and clothes. The way she carried herself reminded me of a chanteuse from the 1940s on the verge of breaking into song. After a few moments, Blanch shook hands with the man and asked if I was interested in a nightcap in his truck.

"Rain check," I said, barely averting my eyes from the stage, "I need to use the head."

He warned me not to touch anything in the john and bid me a goodnight before walking out into the parking lot. I never used the bathroom; I just stood there for some time watching Callie Starz circle the stage, barely smiling, collecting a few dollars, putting on her show, which was slow and breezy and seemed in sync to her own music that might have been in her head. When she finished, she put on a short, black silk robe and sat at the bar and accepted a drink from the bartender. I watched her for a few more minutes; she didn't speak with anyone and she never let go of her glass. The bouncer glared at me on my way outside.

"I still can't believe you weren't scared," Joanna said when I returned home that evening. "I called my parents."

"And what did they have to say?"

"That we should look for a new place for Cole."

"Don't you think that's a bit rash?"

"Marcus, I don't want him going back there."

I told her we should sleep on it. She calmed down and agreed. Joanna fell asleep that night as we watched one of the home improvement shows she likes. I was wired. So I graded a few essays and listened to some of Joanna's Vivaldi, which always makes me tired.

I found myself walking around the house a bit, easing from one room to another, absorbing the inertia of the place. Joanna's studio, which is actually the fourth bedroom of the house, always has that rich aroma of oil paint and charcoal. Located in the rear of the house, adjacent to the garage, it had been an addition the former owners had added a year or so before they sold the place to us. The room, which is littered with canvases and easels and shelves of books on art, is one I seemed to avoid whenever possible. It confirms that Joanna is the artist of the family, and it leaves me cold and embarrassed that I abandoned my own literary interests.

I used to write short stories—I published one in some no-name, second-rate rag—and have even written the first four chapters of a novel I called *Mister Walker*. It's a magical realism story about a man named Bill Walker who finds himself in a world utterly devoid of art and artists. And though this is commonplace in Bill Walker's world, he happens upon a myriad of classic books and paintings and musical recordings he begins passing off as his own. He copies all of Shakespeare's plays and sonnets in his own hand and claims authorship; he hosts his own art shows, taking credit for works as diverse as Picasso's Mother and Child with Shawl to Jackson Pollock's No. 5, 1948. He produces recordings by Joe Pass and Django Reinhardt and invites critical reception. The idea for the story came to me one morning as I drove to work, ruminating over a George Bernard Shaw quote I was prepared to discuss that day: "Without art, the crudeness of reality would make the world unbearable." The quote was for a lesson I was teaching in my American Literature class; I never thought it would lead me to Bill Walker and his duplicity.

But that's no matter now; I let it all grow stale, losing my momentum after settling into domestic life. What is perhaps most disheartening to me is that Joanna, my own wife, never once tried to coax me back into writing. She seems okay that in a pathetic act of resignation I deserted the art form entirely. Nana, my only real champion, has been too busy suffering to continue asking me about it. Not that there is anything on which to report; aside from comments on high school kids' papers—comments they scarcely read—I haven't written a word in over two years.

With Joanna and Cole asleep that Tuesday evening, the room felt safer to me than if they had been awake. In private, I can study her paintings and drawings—mostly of children and oceans and angels—and not feel like a failure. I'm not forced to give flattery.

There's no one sidling up beside me to ask what I think of her latest creation.

At a little past 10:00, I headed upstairs to Cole's room. He was sound asleep, lying on his back, his arms splayed out on both sides of his pillow. His room, illuminated by nightlights at both ends, always has a warm, fresh laundry smell. Its walls are painted a deep denim blue and are covered with race car decals. My head always feels light and uncluttered in Cole's room, which makes it one of my favorite places in the house. Sitting on the edge of his bed, I watched him for a while. After some time, I picked him up and held him in my arms; he stirred a little, but didn't wake. The stillness of his room, my house, the neighborhood, was pleasant. The steady breathing of my boy, the soft, clean touch of his skin against my own, the fresh laundry smell—it was all enough to make me drowsy and begin to nod off. Just as I approached the edge of serious sleep, I was suddenly awoken by headlights beaming through Cole's window, which faces the cul-de-sac we live on. The lights, which made a slow sweep of the room, lingered for far too long; I tucked Cole back into bed and made my way to the window where I saw something I hadn't seen in all the years we've lived on Blackbird Lane: a police car slowly circle the cul-de-sac, creep by my house, and drive off up the street.

Chapter 2: The Drive

"Lies require commitment."
- Veronica Roth

I began spending summers with my grandparents in New Jersey shortly after my mother died. Years later, around the time I was approaching high school, my father confessed to me that he would reserve the summers to have a bit of a breakdown; he needed solitude, he told me, to cope with his demons. He went through the depression, the drinking, the anger, the gratuitous rebound affairs.

"I didn't want to unravel with you around," he admitted. "So I kept it together for ten months out of the year and then let myself go the other two. Damn good ratio if you ask me."

When he was free from it all, he told me, he felt he could be a fit parent on a full time basis. But the truth is I had fallen into a routine with Nana and Papa, and the summer arrangement had become something I looked forward to. Donato would take me golfing on a rundown course down the street from their house; there we would hack away at balls with his cheap, warped clubs, work on my Italian, and flirt with any ladies we came across. Nana, or Min as I sometimes called her, let me sleep late. She would bake biscotti and pumpkin-amaretto cheesecake in the afternoon, and in the cool evenings we'd play rummy and drink iced coffee on her sun porch. They had both retired early from Westinghouse and spent their time and pensions living the way they wanted to; I always had the impression that they were a little embarrassed by their contentment. They would occasionally shrug and say things like "Se solo avessi un milione di dollari..." But the truth of it is that they did not need a million dollars; they were happy with what they had.

Music always seemed to be playing in the house. Records by Dean Martin and Nat King Cole could be heard at all hours of the day. And Donato, who was not terribly demonstrative, would grab Nana on occasion and dance with her in the kitchen while she prepared supper. He was also known to goose her every so often and say things to her in Italian that I couldn't always understand, but that would make her blush and hit him lightly on the back of the head with her hand.

I was never made to get a job. It was not even a matter of discussion. Nana and Donato, augmenting the couple of hundred bucks my father gave me for the summer, provided me with an allowance of fifty dollars a week for doing chores like mowing the lawn and setting and cleaning the mouse traps in the garage. Aside from their pensions, Nana and Donato were able to generate more than a little income from their trips to Atlantic City. They went a few times a month, taking a senior tour bus, and always seemed to return in fine spirits, tossing me a fifty dollar bill and telling me it was nothing but dumb luck once again. One day, I caught Donato hollowing out some of Nana's romance novels where I discovered they were keeping their winnings. I pretended not to notice and we never spoke of it.

If my time at Nana and Papa's was characterized mostly by leisure, it would soon evolve into being known as much for strange adventure. This happened the summer I turned sixteen. It was the summer before my junior year in high school and it was when I first met Enid Dahler. Enid's hair, which she wore long and straight, was jet black and often covered one side of her face. Her lips always seemed to have a natural gloss to them, and her pale skin was flawless. The only makeup she wore was around her eyes, which considerably darkened the already honed femme fatale countenance she had working for her.

We met at a Fourth of July block party where the neighbors got together and barbequed and lit off fire works and got drunk off one another's liquor. Enid lived up the hill with her mother in a colossal white Victorian mansion. The house had been something of a mystery to me since my days with Nana and Papa, who would refer to it as manicomio, which means madhouse. The place was stately, but had a solemnity to it that was in contrast to the rest of the neighborhood. The grounds were overgrown with unkempt spruce trees and arborvitaes; the driveway was a pitted mess of broken tar clumps and divots; the house itself was old and weathered. With peeling paint, spindles missing from the front porch, and mismatched colored patches of roof, the place didn't quite look abandoned as it did neglected.

Enid and I hadn't met prior to the block party, yet I was familiar with her; I had seen her walking the neighborhood, often in a bikini, always barefoot and smoking cigarettes. She fought constantly with her mother, who was a petite, dark skinned woman with short black hair and a big, booming voice. Enid and her mother could occasionally be seen battling one another in the street in broad daylight; one would be storming after the other, shouting obscenities, threatening with violence, throwing things like rocks or sticks.

Enid first came to my attention that Fourth of July for obvious reasons: She was wearing a shiny black bikini and smoking Newports, which she kept tucked into the thin side string of her bottoms. Her mother was nowhere to be found, and the girl circled the crowd in a cool manner. Walking by me a few times, she seemed to almost go out of her way to blow smoke in my direction. The eye contact we made that night was something entirely new to me. It had desperation to it. It was apparent that she was more than just a face and body.

At around nightfall, I witnessed Enid being accosted by Mrs. Bull, an officious and heavyset woman who lived with her husband and three young daughters a few doors down from Nana and Papa; the woman claimed she had witnessed Enid spiking a cooler of pink lemonade. Enid didn't deny or confirm the accusation; she simply drew a fresh Newport from its pack and told Mrs. Bull that her name was anything but ironic. We ended up talking later that night and she invited me over the next day.

And so we began seeing a lot of one another—always at her place and never at Nana's and Papa's. In all my visits, I never actually made it *inside* Enid's house. There was an empty in-ground swimming pool in her backyard where she seemed to spend most of her time. She called it "the Bunker." It was replete with a couch and coffee table and a TV with an extension cord that ran all the way into a screened-in back porch. Aside from a small pile of brown leaves in one corner, the pool was clean and orderly with blue tarps spread across its surface. There Enid watched television, napped, smoked, and ate pot cookies she had learned to make from an ex-boyfriend she simply referred to as "much older." Her mother never seemed to be around.

Aside from our simple "lounging" as she liked to call it, we would walk the neighborhood, crossing over hot lawns in our bare feet, smoking Newports, and talk about sex and TV and music and the neighbors we thought were dull or strange.

"Your grandparents are sweet," she would say, to which I would nod, inspecting her tone for sincerity.

In Enid's garage was a 1975 orange Cadillac convertible. It was covered in dust, and the backseats were filled with overstuffed black garbage bags, inside of which was balled-up clothing. The car, which was so long that it spanned the entire length of the garage, had belonged to Enid's grandfather.

"It's a perfect symbol of the man himself," she once said, never explaining further.

We took to riding around in the Caddy, the top down, the ancient radio blasting whatever local stations would come in clearly. Venturing far beyond Morristown, we drove everywhere—to Newark and New York City, and once we even went to Atlantic City, where we picked up a young couple hitchhiking along the way.

Though I was seeing a lot of Enid that summer, I knew little about her besides her age; she told me she was eighteen. There were occasional comments made about ex-boyfriends; they could be held in high regard one minute for teaching her to drive or roll a joint, and then vilified the next for being too controlling and shallow. As for her mother, she described her as "unhealthy" and "clueless." That was it. I always got the sense that she preferred to remain somewhat enigmatic. I think it empowered her. So I rarely asked questions.

One evening in early August, Enid and I took the Caddy to an abandoned baseball field just outside of Morristown. It was a place where I assumed she spent a lot of time. There we drank some red wine we swiped from her mother as we walked the bases and looked up at the perfect summer stars. After an hour or so, she led me down into one of the dugouts, where we sat close together on a metal bench. Soon we began kissing and undressing one another. When we were half naked, Enid looked me in the eyes and told me this was the perfect place for her at the moment.

"I love being underground," she said.

With no idea how to respond, I unclasped her bra. We had sex, which I had not planned. It was my first time. It didn't last long, but it was not marred by clumsy, awkward gestures. It seemed rather peaceful and even organic. Afterwards, we lay there next to one another in the dugout, a few feet beneath the earth, and listened to the quiet sounds of our breathing.

The drive back was silent. With the Caddy's top down, we smoked cigarettes and drank the remaining alcohol. My head and body were lighter than ever before. The fresh air and wine and tobacco and sex had loosened me into something so malleable, so spry, that I felt like I could have slipped through the door of the Caddy and sprinted alongside it. Every so often, I would turn to look at Enid; with her head leaning back and her beautiful black hair whipping around her face, she seemed like some nightly apparition sitting there beside me.

When she pulled into my grandparents' driveway, I moved closer to her, asking if she wanted to see a movie the following day. Staring straight ahead, she didn't answer me. After some time, she turned her face towards me and I could see she had been crying.

"Are you okay," I asked. "Did I do something?"

She didn't answer. We sat there for a few minutes, the car's engine idling against the quiet of the neighborhood. I wasn't sure how to end the evening, so I opened my mouth and said the one thing I thought could have possibly been truer than anything else: I told her I loved her. She said nothing and I walked to the front door of Nana and Papa's house, convincing myself she didn't hear me over that damn Cadillac.

I didn't see Enid again for weeks. This is not to say I didn't call or stop over any number of times. The calls went unanswered and she was never in her bunker; once, when I tried the front door, her mother appeared wearing a half open bathrobe and asked who the hell I was. When I told her, she said she thought Enid went to stay with her father.

"Did she drive herself?" I asked.

She laughed, informing me that Enid did not have a driver's license. A couple of days before I was set to return to Connecticut, Enid finally paid me a visit. It was dusk. Nana and I were playing cards and drinking chocolate cappuccinos when Enid knocked on the door to the sun porch. Nana welcomed her inside and excused herself before bringing us some cassata and coffee.

"She's sweet," Enid said, sipping the steaming mug.

Looking at her, I realized it was the first time I had seen her in proper clothing. She was wearing a black low cut skirt and a white tank top. Her hair was pulled back from her head and caught up in a simple ponytail; she looked older than when I'd last seen her.

"How's your dad?" I asked.

"He's fine, I guess," she said.

"Where does he live?"

"Nantucket."

"Nice."

"It's better than here."

"I'll bet it is."

"Summer's ending, Marcus," she said.

"I know."

"I'm not good at these types of things."

"It's okay."

"It's not okay," she said, "I've been a total bitch."

"No you haven't."

"It's not like I'm without a reason. There *is* a reason."

"A reason for what?"

"I'm pregnant."

I recall that the exact moment she said this coincided with my realization that she was not wearing any shoes. My gaze was fixed on her feet, which I always thought were pretty and feminine looking. When I looked up, her eyes were fixed on me in unblinking scrutiny; she waited for a response. My mind reacted the way it always did when I heard confounding news: It braced itself for more while searching for something reasonable and intelligent to say. At that moment, I thought we would marry. I told myself that was what Enid had been doing during those three weeks—working out the details to our future life together. Jobs, an apartment, negotiating that orange Cadillac with her mother. By summer's official end, I thought, we would be married. This idea was even given additional gravity when my clumsy silence provoked her to say what she said next:

"How much money do you have?"

"I have a little."

"How much is a little?"

"I can get some."

She sank back into the wicker sofa and crossed her legs and sipped her hot coffee.

"How much can you get?"

"How much do we need?" I asked, imagining formula and diapers and monthly rent checks made payable to some shady landlord with bad skin and a knack for tackling every repair with duct tape.

She put her mug on the table and took a deep breath. Then she told me she needed around a thousand dollars.

"It's expensive," she said, "I looked into it."

The good news, she said, was that I did not have to accompany her to Nantucket for the procedure.

"Besides," she said, "you'll be back in school."

More clumsy silence on my part. My mind went again to that place of waiting. Enid said she confided in her father, who was far more reasonable than her mother.

"I'll probably live with him once it's over with," she said. "He lives on a little houseboat. It's not much, but it's better than here. I'd ask him for the money, but he's been broke since he split with my mom. She's a castrating bitch."

Sparing her my embarrassment over what I thought were her intentions, I told her I could have the money for her the following day. She started to say something, but suddenly stopped herself.

"Really?" she said after some time.

She kissed my cheek and told me to meet her in the bunker with the cash.

"8:00 p.m.," she said.

I managed to get the house to myself the following evening after convincing Donato to take Nana to the town diner for some dessert. I would stay behind, I told them, and begin packing for my return home the following afternoon. They had barely pulled out of the driveway in Donato's Duster before I was in their bedroom. Nana's many romance novels were neatly kept on a shelf that was built in to the headboard on their bed. The first one I opened, a book entitled *The Beautiful Troublemaker*, rained twenty dollar bills on their green and white duvet. So did the second one. I found that all of them—there were probably a few dozen, some paperback, some hardcover—held money in the center of their hollowed-out pages. Counting out an even one-thousand dollars, I replaced the books, smoothed the duvet, and headed out the door to meet Enid at the bunker.

The first week of school that year was marked by restlessness. Thoughts of Enid crept in at the oddest of times. I would be eating breakfast or driving to school or trying to fall asleep and I'd flashback to the summer. Crystal images of her flawless skin and feminine feet and reckless joyrides in that orange Caddy filled my mind. Yet she eventually became a phantom, and I soon questioned whether I had perhaps invented her out of the blue. This feeling was so strong that I told no one about my fling with the older, enigmatic temptress, for fear they would ask for proof of her existence.

Fantasies of a reunion soon surfaced. I envisioned showing up at the bunker and whisking her away to our baseball dugout. I might have been naive, but I knew for sure that she would never reach out to me. I imagined her storming the streets of Nantucket, still in that black bikini, smoking her Newports, in a state of constant mourning over her recent procedure, perhaps remembering Marcus DiMatteo, the feckless, inexperienced grandson of the elderly neighbors she thought were sweet.

My thoughts were not just on Enid; I figured it was a matter of time before my grandparents noticed the missing money. I felt sick over having stolen from them. When my guilt and embarrassment finally met up, they produced something caustic enough to provoke me into action. So on a Friday night when all of my friends were cheering on our high school football team, I was home eating leftovers and watching *Duck Soup* with my father, all the while trying to figure a way to break to him my summer's travails. There was no natural segue into what I had to tell him. My reticence finally prompted him to ask what was wrong; I muted the television and told him everything. He listened in his lawyerly way, which is to say intently and without judgment.

"Is that everything?" he asked when I stopped talking.

I nodded. He reached behind himself and produced his day-planner, which he flipped through, stopping on one page in particular and studying it for a moment. Then he asked me what I had planned for the following day.

"Nothing."

"Good. How about a road trip?"

The next morning, we went to the drive-through at his bank; he withdrew a thousand dollars the teller sealed in an envelope he stashed in the glove compartment. Then he waited until we were on the interstate, on our way to Jersey, to tell me he was positive I had been conned by Enid.

"How do you know?"

He smiled as he looked in the rearview mirror and made a lane change.

"Because I know."

"Lawyerly intuition?"

"Fatherly intuition," he said.

We stopped for breakfast at a diner about an hour from his parents' house. Dad called them and was relieved they were not at home.

"Maybe we can check the first part of our plan off the list nice and early," he said. "That would be good."

"What plan? You still haven't told me why we're even going."

"And you still haven't asked. You need to be more inquisitive, Marcus. Ask questions. It's the mark of an assertive man. I don't want to lecture you, but that might be part of the reason for your little predicament here. It sounds like you should have asked this girl more questions. And don't be satisfied with any old goddamn answer."

My instinct was to argue—to tell him that asking questions was his job, so naturally it came easy to him. But I kept my mouth shut until the moment receded.

"So what *is* the plan?" I finally said.

"I thought you'd never ask."

He told me to open the glove compartment and retrieve the envelope in there.

"You replace the dough and I'll do the rest," he said.

Fingering through the cash, I noticed it was all twenties and fifties. I mentioned that I was certain there had been some tens in the money I took.

"Their inventory is not that tight," he said. "Trust me."

We arrived at their house at a little after 1:00 p.m. Donato's Duster was gone and the house was empty. Dad used his key to unlock the door and let me inside.

"Go to it," he said. "And no fucking around. Just do what needs to be done. You've got the easy part."

He clapped me on the back before turning around and crossing the driveway towards the front lawn. I called after him, asking where he was going.

"To do the hard part," he yelled over his shoulder.

After I replaced the money, I sat in Donato's faded blue recliner and watched game shows for an hour. Then I fell asleep. By the time I awoke, I could hear voices in the kitchen. It was nearly 4:00

p.m. Nana and Papa greeted me with open arms. My father held a glass of beer in his hand and was talking on the phone. When he saw me, he winked and smiled.

We stayed for a few hours and ate raviolis and Italian sausage and soft, warm bread from a Greek bakery up the street. During the meal, I continued to look in my father's direction, hoping for eye contact and some indication of how he might have fared. He caught me doing this a few times and winked at me again before turning back to Papa to discuss boxing or law or who was a better singer, Nat King Cole or Frank Sinatra.

At around 8:00, we headed home. Nana and Papa asked us to stay the night, but my father told them we had early morning yard work to do, a completely arbitrary lie. I barely waited until we had backed out of the driveway before asking him what had happened.

"If there was an Olympics for playing head games," he said, "that girl's mother would be a fucking gold-medalist."

He then muttered something about how she should go into law.

"What happened?"

A lot, he said. She invited him inside her house, offered him a drink, took the most circuitous way of answering even the most direct question, drank a few drinks herself, asked him questions that were all too personal, drank some more, came on to him, shouted at him that she was a fine parent and that her daughter was a manipulator, a liar, a whore.

"Is that it?"

"This Nantucket business is bullshit," he said. "Her father lives out in Vancouver. She showed me some pictures."

Enid's mother, he said, turning to me with that austere quality he inherently had in him, certainly appeared to be a head case, but he believed what she told him—and she had no idea where Enid had run off to at summer's end. But the woman laughed aloud at the mention of her daughter being pregnant.

"I got the impression that she has pulled this pregnancy routine before. Several times, in fact. From what I gather, it seems to have served her quite well."

He cupped his hand around my neck and squeezed it a little.

Then he told me to get some rest. He wouldn't allow me to be embarrassed in front of him and I loved him for that. I closed my eyes. As I was drifting off, he said something to me I knew I'd always remember:

"The art of bullshit has never really been given its proper due. Because it truly is an art. I believe that. Just don't ever go making it your livelihood like I did."

My father never told Nana and Papa about the money. I half convinced myself that they somehow knew I had taken it, but had faith that I would do the right thing and someday return it. As for the Enid situation, it could never really achieve closure. My father and I both knew this. It was too full of mystery. So we would revisit it on occasion, speculating on the whys and the hows of Enid's machination. We even came to have a twisted sense of respect for the girl and her brazenness. Sometime we would joke about it, contriving absurd aftermaths—she fled to South America and with Nana and Papa's money began a pizza delivery business; or she hitchhiked out to the Ozarks where she became the first ever bikini-clad wildlife tour guide.

The incident seemed to bring me closer to my father. He let me into his world a bit. I think he believed I had passed some kind of test—that I had endured betrayal, and was now that much closer to knowing what those occasional stabs of real life felt like. He opened up about his suffering after my mother's passing, his excessive drinking, which was, at the point of our venture together, a thing of the past, his fickle relationships with other women. I was even able to finally meet some of them that year—Sydney, the dental assistant; Sophie, the actuary. Though at the time I wouldn't have been able to articulate it, I felt that the Enid incident, as well as my father's handling of it, put me a few steps closer to being a man.

So now, all these years later, I wonder why in the hell I feel like a little boy when I think about that summer. Perhaps I need my Daddy by my side, making light of it, telling me not to worry, that women often get the best of men and that it will happen again and again and again. Putting aside whatever mysteries there are about women, I can't get over how often I think about Enid. All these years later. She was but a mere fling. Granted, my time with her was marked by some memorable events, but it was over the course of a single summer. She is in fact the only girl I was ever with who never met my father.

True, she took my virginity and extorted a thousand dollars from me. Both, I suppose, are worthy of remembrance. But when I think about Enid, that's not what comes to mind. I think about what must have been her conviction to live life by the precarious tenets only she could have devised. Tenets that involved having vision and discipline and balls. When I think of Enid today, I think of that remarkable eye contact she made with me. It was perfect. Long enough to make me truly believe I had gotten in her head. And deep enough to make me think I would stay there forever. To me, it seemed she lived the life she wanted to; and even though a certain sadness pervaded her, I never got the sense that she wanted to be doing anything other than what she was doing at that moment. Enid lived underground, literally and figuratively, and that suited her in every way.

In all the years I've visited Jersey since that summer, I've stayed away from Enid's. There's something nearly sacred about the way I remember our time together; it has precluded me from driving up the hill to see what has become of her place and who might be living there. But a new inspiration has lately crept its way inside my head; it has convinced me that I might be missing something if I let more years pass without giving in to nostalgia.

So about a week after my episode with the police, I decide to drive to Jersey, following my 9:00 a.m. appointment with Dr. Stewart. My original plan was to teach my first class, head out for the MRI, and return to work. But instead I'll ask the secretary to find coverage for my remaining classes, explaining that there have been unforeseen circumstances. Telling Joanna about the trip will only elicit questions I don't yet feel equipped to answer.

"Be a good boy for Mommy," I tell Cole, kissing him on the

forehead as he sprawls out in our bed watching TV.

Since my statement to the police about the gunman, Cole has not been to Children's World. His days are spent at home with his mother, where he plays and naps and gets more attention than he probably knows what to do with.

He throws his arms around me and says he loves me. Joanna, standing in the doorway, hands me a thermos of hot coffee and offers a sad, forced smile.

"There's no question he should stay home for a few more days. Right?"

"Sure."

She wishes me luck at Dr. Stewart's, before asking for the third or fourth time this week if I want her to meet me at his office. I decline, telling her again that it's a simple MRI and that I will be fine.

When I arrive at work, I inform Dorothy about the unexpected coverage I will need for my classes.

"Can you see if Mr. Mann is available?" I said.

Mr. Mann, a twenty-something intern with broad shoulders and oily hair, is LSHS's in-house floating substitute. Dorothy mentions that he is not available; he is sitting in for Mr. Knight, LSHS's beloved Tech. Ed. teacher. But she will scramble, she says, and will find someone.

Half-heartedly, I teach my first period class, waiting for word of my day's replacement. At around 8:20, minutes before the bell, Dan Zinser walks into my room, a folded newspaper under his arm, and a drawn look on his cleanly shaven face. He regards the kids with polite reserve before approaching me at my desk. His silence tells me that he will be my coverage for the day.

It's been said that out of all the menial tasks the vice principal carries—issuing parking passes, desk and chair inventory—filling in for absent teachers is the least desirable. Perhaps it undermines their authority in the eyes of the kids; or maybe it reminds them why they've left teaching behind in favor of administration. I would think it's a nice way to get back to one's roots, to keep in touch with the kids, to show them what you know besides enforcing discipline. But this is clearly not the case with Dan Zinser, who taught middle school math for only three years before being fast-tracked to his current position. "The wunderkind" is what some of us call him behind his back.

"So what are we doing?" he said, his voice louder than necessary.

Some of the kids look up from the collage assignment they've been working on.

"I appreciate this. I've got a doctor's appointment."

"I know you do."

Handing him my lesson plans, I thank him again. Then I remind my class of their homework and tell them I will see them the following day.

"That would be wonderful."

When I look at him, he doesn't smile or offer to repeat himself. I thank him for the *third* time and head towards the door. But I suddenly stop myself before stepping into the hallway. Then I turn back and approach Dan who is now sitting in my chair reading his newspaper.

"What would be wonderful?"

"Excuse me?"

"You said 'that would be wonderful,' and I'm just wondering what would be wonderful."

Folding his sports section, he stands up and faces me. We are nearly identical in height. I can smell his cologne, which is woodsy and cheap smelling.

"You really want to do this here?"

"Do what?"

Dan turns to a couple of female students who have stopped working to watch us. They quickly resume their cutting and pasting while Dan puts his hand on my elbow and ushers me towards the door and out into the hallway.

"Every year, when Patty sends the 'Birthdays in April' email, I laugh a little to myself," he said.

Patty Whitman is the guidance secretary; for years she has taken it upon herself to send monthly group emails with a list of faculty birthdays.

"We're both on there," he said, "as I'm sure you've seen. You on the 22nd and me on the 29th. And it always strikes me—every year, in fact—that you're older than me. Did you know that? We're born in the same year, just seven days apart. It's not much, but still. And that strikes me."

All I can think of is how he must have looked in my file to learn the year I was born—that he somehow took this to be an important enough matter to do actual research.

"I guess what I'm saying, Marcus, is that where you and I are concerned, this seems to be rather symbolic. I would think that being an English teacher, you would like that very much."

I can hear Jim McArthur's class doing their Chaucer recitations next door. Andrew, the youngest on the custodial staff, rounds the corner carrying paper towel refills. He is a young, skinny kid with a shaved head and neck tattoo. He nods politely and walks past Dan and me.

"What's the symbolism exactly?"

With mock laughter, he backs away from me.

"Now that can't be how you teach your students. Is it? No, I'll bet you teach them to go after that symbolism and figure it out for themselves."

With that, he turns and walks back into my classroom, letting the door close behind him. Of course I'd love to follow him, and in front of my students tell him how embarrassed I am for him that he thinks he's gotten the better of me, and how absurd it is that he flatters himself the way he does. Sure, I'd add, I take issue that you really haven't paid your dues enough to earn a six figure salary, but I've never once thought about how similar we are in age. But since my life is not some ridiculous revenge movie, I head towards the stairs, half wondering if Dan is on to anything with his insights.

When I reach the corridor, I meet up with none other than Owen McAllister, the miscreant of my Period 6 American Literature class. Owen is tall and wiry with curly brown hair that I often witness him playing with in class. His teeth, which he seems to show off on purpose, are his best asset. My plan is to nod politely and walk past him, but he stops me in the hall, which he often does.

"Mr. DiMatteo, I read the first four chapters in *The Gay Gatsby*," he tells me, with slight emphasis the word *gay*. "Very interesting."

The books were handed out a few days ago, so this is doubtful.

"I'm glad," I said, ignoring the malapropism.

"It's a real page turner. I keep wondering if Nick and Gatsby are going to hook up."

"Would you like them to hook up?" I said, looking at my watch. "Would that make you happy?"

He flashes a crooked, arrogant grin that tells me he is pleased I've stooped to his level. Then he shakes his head and walks past me. The merit of my Jersey trip is reinforced further in that I will get a day off from Owen McAllister. It's true that I have other obnoxious kids in my classes—there's David Sperry in my Journalism class and Bill Donahue in my other American Literature class—but no one rivals Owen. The mark of his obnoxiousness is that unlike most kids his age, he doesn't always require an audience for his inane rhetoric; he's perfectly comfortable to stop me in the hall and warn me that he's particularly flatulent that day, or seek me out in the cafeteria to ask if Jim, the runaway slave, was actually a pedophile who had designs on Huckleberry Finn, or catch me coming out of the bathroom and ask if I ever fear that one of my own students might see my dick.

I sometimes think about calling his parents, but I never do. It's easy for me to imagine them as well-to-do burnouts who eschew discipline since they haven't the time to deal with their son. Despite being an asshole, Owen is well bred, well fed, and well clothed. Yet he must get the better of his poor parents. On the weekends, he probably steals a few bucks from them and goes to the mall where he harasses younger girls and gets thrown out of the same stores for loitering and causing a nuisance. Then he will walk home, where on the way he will contemplate just exactly how and when he will masturbate later in the day.

Over the years, there have been only a few students I can say I have disliked. Own McAllister is one of them. He has often inspired me to think of Cole and all I want for him. When it comes down to it, I suppose all I want is for him to be nothing like Owen McAllister. And that gets me thinking about whether I want Cole to be at all like me. It's hard to say. There's a part of me that feels temporary about myself. I think it must have to do with watching my own father get killed in front of me. Like I never fulfilled my own duty as a son. And there's another part of me that feels helplessly inadequate. I think it must also have to do with watching my own father get killed in front of me.

Between Dan and Owen, I'm already tense by the time I pull out of LSHS's parking lot. Then I remember what Blanch put in my glove compartment. Without hesitating, I pull into a convenience store for a book of matches as well as to buy a few things for Nana. Before turning onto the interstate, I light the joint.

I'm stoned by the time I reach Dr. Stewart's. Fearful that I might reek of the stuff, I spray myself with peach air freshener from the lobby restroom before entering the office. The secretary, a short, curly-haired woman with beady eyes and a slow, wrinkly smile, slides the glass window and accepts my insurance card and co-pay before handing me a clipboard and ballpoint pen.

There is one other patient in the waiting room—a paunchy, gray-haired man, several years older than me; he is staring blankly at a barely audible TV in the corner, which shows off the sunny weather report predicted for the next few days. The forms I'm to fill out ask me if I have claustrophobia, hearing sensitivity, or any metal implants. They also ask for family medical history. With as much focus as I can muster, I complete the forms and hand them back to the woman.

Then I take a seat and check my text messages—I have none— and read a short article on Jimmy Van Heusen, one of Frank Sinatra's songwriters. After about ten minutes, I am asked to follow a nurse into a small, windowless examination room. The nurse, a lovely young Latino woman named Gabriela, asks me to undress, slip into scrubs, and wait for Dr. Stewart.

It's bizarre to be stoned and away from the comfort of Blanch's truck where we always have plenty of music and food and privacy. Here in the doctor's office, where it's cold and sterile, my mind feels like some slick stretch of interstate that can't help but watch everything roll away as fast as it appears. Thoughts, ideas, misgivings. Just as I contemplate searching the cabinets for something to eat—an absurd notion—Dr. Stewart walks into the room. He is a tall man in his forties with thick brown hair that sweeps away from a broad forehead. His wire-rimmed glasses rest low on the bridge of his nose and he tilts his head down to get a look at me. We shake hands and talk a little about the procedure before he leads me to an adjacent room that houses the scanner, a ridiculous looking contraption that seems like it belongs in a Stanley Kubrick film. There are consent forms and pep talks and ear plugs given. At one point, Dr. Stewart pauses to sniff the air around me.

"Is that peach?" he said.

The scan takes about thirty minutes. Despite the close quarters and god awful clanging sounds, I feel myself able to relax. Being stoned, perhaps, has turned the experience into a safe adventure. Without the pot, I might have otherwise been fidgety or annoyed. When it's over, I get dressed and collect myself while Dr. Stewart checks to see that the pictures the machine took are usable.

"We'll be in touch from here," he said, shaking my hand.

Besides my sudden craving for pretzels and pink lemonade, all I can think about as I walk to my car is finishing the rest of that joint before making my way to Jersey.

Through the years, most of my visits to the Blue Bridge Retirement Center have been solo ventures. Joanna has accompanied me only two or three times, while Cole's only visit was this past winter. This is my choice. And it's a selfish one. To me, there's something between my Nana and I that I can't explain, let alone share. Perhaps it's due to the tragedy we've endured together, or maybe those years I took care of her. Either way, I feel more comfortable with her when we're alone. There's a tacit bond between us that holds within it my secrets of growing up and the pain of losing my father.

And that bond is the only real vestige I have to my old life. I feel a sense of guardedness over it. So Joanna sends her best wishes along with her cranberry lemon bread; and Cole will scribble outside the lines on a picture of some Disney character that Nana will happily post on her refrigerator.

My best visits with the old lady had always been unannounced. I show up either late in the morning or early afternoon and find her gardening in one of the many wildflower gardens or playing cards with friends in the common room or watching old Bob Hope movies on the flat screen TV I bought for her last birthday.

When she sees me, her mouth falls open and no words come for a while; it always looks like she's on the verge of tears. But soon she opens her arms to me and pulls me down to her, covering my face with kisses. And if she is in the company of others, she will usually introduce me as her baby's baby, which will make me wonder if they know her baby had been murdered years earlier. Then she will add, proudly, that I am an English teacher. I always have with me a bag full of gifts and groceries: new suede slippers, which she seems to lose on an almost weekly basis; a few new romance novels; lanyards for her glasses; anisette cookies; fresh fruit; Italian bread; and a certain pomegranate tea she can't find for sale anywhere near her.

Often we will cook a meal together in her apartment, or walk the grounds, her arm clasped in mine; unknowingly, she'd give me the same tour each time—the blue bridge, the duck pond, her favorite bench by some rose bushes, a nature trail with light posts and metal handrails. When it comes time for me to leave, she is often exhausted and will pull my hands to her face, kiss them, and bid me farewell in Italian.

When the visits are planned, they are not usually as pleasant. Nana will cook and clean obsessively prior to my arrival. By the time I get there, she is often asleep and I have to get one of the care staff to let me into her apartment. We pass the time by discussing her ailments—mostly her stomach—and the conversation invariably turns to how she misses my father and grandfather.

"You're just like them," she will say, assuming I understand exactly how.

We will sit in her small family room and flip through the channels for a bit. After a while, I'll walk around her place and take inventory of relics from her old life—that white porcelain dog statue, her hollowed out romance novels, as well as newly acquired possessions such as an oak mantel clock and a painting of an underwater ocean scene given to her by Joanna as a house warming gift.

Then we'll play cards before walking to the common room where I'll play piano for her on the beat up Samick I'm told was donated by one of the resident's daughters. By the time I get ready to leave, Nana will be in tears, swearing she will never see me again, that either she will succumb to her body and die in her sleep that night, or that for some reason I'll abandon her and never return. It can take upwards of an hour to calm her down.

The effects of the pot have pretty much dissipated by the time I reach Blue Bridge. I find Nana in her apartment; she's watching TV and eating from a plate of cookies that rests on a small table beside her chair. Her reaction to seeing me is a bit tamer than I'm used to. Though she smiles and extends her hands towards my face, the energy surrounding her is placid and drowsy. My last visit was about one month earlier when Grace, her friend down the hall, passed away in her sleep.

"I knew it," she said, her voice thin and frail sounding.

"You knew I was coming?"

Nodding, she turns back to the TV.

"You must have sensed me," I said, kissing her forehead.

As she watches her show, I unpack the shopping bag on her counter.

"How are you feeling?"

She doesn't answer.

"I brought you some oranges and pink lemonade."

By the time I finish putting everything away for her, there is a knock at her door. I open it to a young female nurse, whose nametag says Elsa. Introducing myself, I invite her inside. She has a cart beside her, on top of which is medication and a tray of food.

Wheeling it into the apartment, she asks Nana how she is feeling. Then she takes her blood pressure and checks her heart rate. Nana compliments Elsa on the way she smells.

"Are you still with that boy?" said Nana. "What's his name?"

"Dominic," she said. "Yes, we're still together."

"He must love the way you smell."

Elsa looks at me and smiles. When she's finished with her visit, she gently massages Nana's arms and tells her a woman named Samantha will be checking on her in a few hours. Nana lets Elsa know that Samantha's smell is not a particularly memorable one. The girl looks at me again and shows her amusement. I walk her to the door as Nana watches TV.

"How's she doing?"

"She has some pain we're trying to manage. But her diet has improved and she's fairly active."

"How far is she from constant care?"

"I couldn't say. You should speak with Dr. Robertson; he'll be able to tell you more."

Just as she's about to walk down the hall, she stops herself and turns to me.

"She's been talking a lot lately to Donato. Pretty much everyday. She sets a place for him at the table. She's even tried to order meals for him. That's pretty common, I think, but I thought you ought to know."

"Thank you."

"Also," she said, "who's Anthony?"

"Anthony's my father."

"She's been talking a lot about Anthony as well. It's Anthony this and Anthony that. She's awfully sweet."

Nana and I take a short walk together. The weather is sunny and mild. Two men playing chess at a picnic table say hello to Nana, as do several other residents who are walking by themselves or with family. Nana is pleasant enough, but doesn't take the time to stop and talk or even introduce me.

"How is that little boy of yours?"

"Cole is great. He's getting big. He'll be three this summer."

"July 7th."

"That's right."

Relaxing on one of the benches on the blue bridge, Nana and I sit in silence for a little while. Two ladies walk by us, waving and commenting on the sunshine.

"Any visitors lately?" I said.

"No."

We are of course referring to my cousins and my Aunt Janice, who, over the years, have withdrawn from Nana to the point where I considered intervening on the old lady's behalf. I tell Nana I can't bring myself to contact them—that it's all too complicated; she assures me it's not my responsibility.

"Ah, questa famiglia; che cosa mai successo a noi?" she said.

"What happened to this family is that my fucking uncle murdered my father," I said.

Swearing in front of Nana is not something I make a habit of doing. It's such an aberration that she lets it go. After some silence, she tells me she received a letter a few days ago from Alex in prison. It was the first time in all these years he had reached out to her. Laughing, she says it was more of a gesture than his wife or children had offered as of late. Yet it's nevertheless in vain.

By the time I take her back to her apartment, she seems exhausted.

"Un momento," she said, pulling one of her old romance novels from the bookcase and disappearing into her bedroom.

When she returns, she hands me a couple one hundred dollar bills and tells me to buy early birthday presents for Cole and myself.

"This is too much."

She waves her hand at me, telling me to put the money in my pocket, which I do. Then I help her into her bed and sit by her side for a while. It's approaching late afternoon. As she begins dozing, I find myself in need of something to tell her—something pleasant that might combat the implicit gloom that seems to pervade the day. So I blurt out that I'm back to work on my novel and that it's going well.

Nana was an early supporter of my writing; once an avid reader herself, she would encourage me and even read some awful stories I wrote as a younger man. I knew this would please her. And it does. She doesn't say anything, but before she nods off, she gives me an approving glance and mumbles something that sounds like *good for you.*

As I make my way into her living room, curiosity has put me face to face with the set of romance novels. Her reading days are over. What was once a simple act of pleasure now exacerbates her migraines and strains her eyesight. Naturally, thoughts of being a tactless teenager come rushing back to me as I'm about to reach for one of the books. Out of respect for Nana, as well as a sudden rush of that long forgotten fear I felt that summer day back when I was a sixteen, I resist.

Yet this doesn't stop me from walking around her place and looking things over. Not that there's much to look at. A small living room with a sofa, end table, chair, bookshelf. A few plants. A kitchenette with a table for two by a little bay window overlooking the building's rear courtyard. But something on a glass table in the foyer does catch my eye. It's an envelope with a return address that says New Jersey State Prison. Of course I read it.

Dear Ma,

It's been a long while since you and I have spoken. I suppose the last time was the day Daddy died. I don't know what to say about our lack of communication other than I think it's been best for everyone. For longer than you can imagine, I've had no means to convey all that I have to say about our family and my life and what I've done. But I am just now putting things in perspective. That's what this place does – it allows you to not only get your thoughts in order, but it allows you to figure out where those thoughts might have come from. I've found that giving a heading to each thought works well for me. It helps me to stay focused on that thought. So I'll be doing that in this letter, focusing on the three matters that have pretty much dominated my thinking for the past ten years: Strength, Forgiveness, and Revenge.

Strength:
I believe I've always had strength. But I think I needed to come to this place to truly discover it. You are able to discover a lot while being here. And the truth of it is that I would never have been able to survive all these years if it weren't for my strength. Moreover, I wouldn't have been able to do what I did to get in here without having a certain kind of strength. I know how that sounds. And I know I hurt you all with what I did, but you'll never know what I went through emotionally to do what I did. That leads me to forgiveness, which takes great strength to offer.

Forgiveness:
The Bible says "He has delivered us from the domain of darkness and transferred us to the kingdom of his beloved Son, in whom we have redemption, the forgiveness of sins." I like that. The Bible has not only been a true source of comfort to me over the years, but it has been a peerless guide as well. My good friend and spiritual advisor, Cal - yes, he's a fellow inmate - says the Bible tells the story of every man's life, but can only touch those who are open enough to all its wisdom. I have opened myself to God and let him in my life. I thought this might make you happy.

Revenge:
What I did to Tony was, simply put, out of revenge. Revenge for being a better man than I. Revenge for being a greater success than I. And, most importantly, revenge for making me feel the appalling emotion that is jealously. Revenge, I now know, is the lifeblood of the weak. The Bible says "You shall not take vengeance or bear a grudge against the sons of your own people, but you shall love your neighbor as yourself." I have also learned about the story of Cain and Abel, which I find absolutely spellbinding. I suppose that I was Cain and Tony was Abel. My act of vengeance spent me entirely. Once I realized that, I saw that I was now a new man, a different man, and hopefully a better man.

In writing this letter, my hope is that we may begin a new correspondence with one another.

Your son,
Alex

When I finish reading the letter, I am left with a sickening feeling in my gut. Such pathetic personal musings must have confounded the hell out of poor Nana—especially now. Maybe ten years ago, when her wounds were fresh and she was sharper, the letter might have prompted more of a headstrong reaction. But what could she do now besides whisper of its existence, shrug her shoulders, and fall fast asleep?

I count the first person pronouns he uses in the letter. There are fifty or so, as well as a handful of times he uses second person. Yet there's not *one* fucking occasion where he asks about his ailing mother or even wishes her well. Leaving the letter where I found it, I walk out of Nana's apartment and head toward the parking lot, my uncle's wayward didacticism and Biblical bullshit replaying over and over in my brain.

Driving past Nana and Papa's old house is a strange trip. Since they've lived there, a lamppost has been installed by the driveway, and the garage looks like it has been re-roofed. Besides that—as well as a new flower bed here and there—the place looks pretty much the same after all these years. With the sunlight in my eyes, I keep the car at a creeping speed of about ten miles an hour as I make my way up the hill towards Enid's place.

I can tell before I even reach the front of the house that all its crumbling decay has been restored to pristine grandeur. Its grounds are clean and attractive with a new stone wall and newly planted red maples. The driveway has been repaved, and the house itself had been repaired and painted a sort of deep beige color. All the mystery it once had, all of its sad, eerie splendor is gone. It is now simply a lovely suburban home that blends in to the rest of the neighborhood.

Parking the car in the street, I walk up the driveway and up on the front porch. Its floorboards have been replaced with an expensive composite material. There is a woven, straw colored welcome mat by the front door with a fancy capital M in its center. As if the renovations to the place are not enough, this tells me for certain that Enid's family no longer lives here. When I ring the bell, a young woman, probably in her late twenties, comes to the door;

she is pretty with big green eyes and short blonde hair that curls in perfect half moons at both sides of her small face. In her arms is a baby girl who can't be more than six or seven months old.

"Can I help you?"

She has a southern accent.

"I'm sorry to bother you."

Bouncing the baby a bit, she tells me it's no bother. The first thing I tell her is that my grandparents used to live down the street and that I spent many summers there. Then I segue into the story of Enid Dahler and her mother and their house, this house, and the swimming pool Enid would refer to as "the Bunker." It's been many years, I point out, but I'm trying to track them down. The woman's face takes on a staid expression before she looks at her baby girl and smiles.

"My husband and I moved up from North Carolina about seven years ago. R.J.'s with the government. We fell in love with this house right away. It needed a lot of work for sure, but we saw the potential."

She continues, telling me too many unnecessary details about her own life—her husband's job, uprooting from the south, the birth of their daughter, whose name is Liza—while eventually explaining what she knows about the Dahlers. Mrs. Dahler, she tells me, had to foreclose on the property.

"It was a regular Grey Gardens. She really let the place go. I guess the town got involved. The neighborhood, too. It seems that she—this Mrs. Dahler—had some problems."

The woman takes a deep breath and says that she had heard from her neighbors that Mrs. Dahler's problems—both financial and emotional—really began to escalate once her daughter had died.

"I gathered that it happened a year or two before we bought the place. I'm so sorry. What a terrible thing to lose a child."

She brings her baby closer to her and kisses her forehead.

"Would you like to come inside? I was just going to make some iced tea."

I'm still processing what she's just told me. It isn't shock I'm feeling. Shock would mean that I could only picture Enid thriving and living a healthy life as part of mainstream society, which is not the case. Enid was like a few of those students I invariably come across every couple of years at Louis Sutherland High School. Living on the fringe. Transient and elusive lifestyles. Dim looking futures.

It's definitely not shock I'm feeling. Maybe it's disappointment that Enid had succumbed to something bigger than her. In my mind, she looms large, unreasonably large—certainly larger than she ever deserved to appear. But how else could my memory produce the girl who was a con-woman at eighteen, smoked like a mob boss' wife, and put every ounce of her initiative into doing exactly what she wanted to do, which turned out to be not much of anything.

I politely decline the woman's invitation to go inside.

"Do you have children of your own?"

"Yes. A little boy. Coleman. My wife wants another."

Smiling at me, she adjusts the baby in her arms and extends her hand for me to shake, introducing herself as Jesse. Then she tells me again how sorry she is for the death of my friend.

"Do you happen to know where her mother moved off to?"

"Out west somewhere. From what I understand, she has a brother out west. I want to say Sausalito."

It hardly matters.

"Is there anything I can do for you?"

Thinking on this for a moment, I reach out and give my finger over to baby Liza who has been staring at me for some time.

"Would you mind if I took a quick look at your swimming pool?"

Like the rest of the property, the pool has been transformed into something scarcely resembling my memory if it. Gone are any signs of its once bohemian aura, its makeshift quality, its decked out, tripped out mess. Though it is concealed with a tautly drawn green cover, I imagine in a month or two it will be filled to the top with clear water that will show off a spanking blue liner. There's a surrounding patio of clean, grey pavers that is new to me, and the lush, green landscape, even in early April, is healthy and tasteful. It looks like something Enid would have scoffed at, reducing it to some awful suburban cliché.

As I drive away, I pretend for a moment that this is another of Enid's cons—that she has faked her own death to evade an ex-boyfriend or perhaps the IRS. Maybe it's all just a ruse and she's actually fine, living on the beaches of Costa Rica or out of her suitcase in cheap motels down south. But I know it's no ruse and that she's really dead. I try to picture how she might have died. Drugs perhaps. Maybe violence. Maybe something sudden and inexplicable due to years of hard, unconventional living. It takes me a bit of thinking to figure out what saddens me about her passing. Perhaps that I will never get the chance to flatter her with sentiments about being such a strange inspiration to me. And that I'll never get to tell her that for some reason I think of her every so often and even admire her. Admire her resilience and cunning. Admire her mystique and nonconformity. Admire the very chicanery that extorted a thousand dollars from me and caused me to steal from my own grandparents.

With my head teeming over thoughts of the past, I drive a little under an hour to a place I haven't seen in a decade. It's a place that will come up in conversation whenever I explain to someone how my father died. New Jersey State Prison is on 2nd Cass Street in Trenton. With its guard tower and coiled barbed wire, it looks like your average prison. Except for the painted mural on its exterior wall that runs nearly an entire city block. The mural, which depicts whimsical baseball images, is supposedly an homage to Trenton's Minor League team.

Parking in a lot across the street, I let the car idle for a while as I sit and stare out at the expansive compound. I imagine my uncle in his cell, reading Nietzsche and the New Testament, memorizing passages to quote to his brethren, a host of psychotic megalomaniacs. I imagine him writing out his thoughts on paper, sophomoric rants absurdly organized by theme.

The last time I spoke to him was at my grandfather's funeral. We exchanged a mere handful of words, mostly of condolence. If I saw him now, what would I have to say to him? It's difficult to know. On the one hand, he's a stranger to me, a grey specter from the past. But on the other, he's the person I think of as altering the course of my life, having forever changed who I am as a father and as a husband and as a man.

Such thoughts prompt me to call home, which I do. When Joanna answers, I tell her what a hectic day it's been—that my doctor's appointment threw off my rhythm, putting me behind in my work—and that I'll be home late, probably past 7:00, and to please eat without me. She asks if I'm going out with Blanch and I tell her I'm not. Satisfied, she asks about my visit with Dr. Stewart. I tell her it was fine and soon enough we'll know the results.

Then I ask to speak with Cole, who gets on the phone and tells me about his snacks and toys and cartoons. He asks when I'm coming home to him and tells me he loves me. The sinister sweep of the prison before me, combined with my son's adulation, nearly brings me to tears. In a choked up voice he's heard at odd times in his short life, I tell him I love him and that I'll be home soon.

Hanging up the phone, I check my text messages for the first time since Dr. Stewart's waiting room. There are two. One is from Joanna at 8:58 a.m.; it says *"Good luck with your doctor's appointment. See you tonight. Love Jo."* The second one takes me a moment to process. It reads, *"Let's meet to discuss a few things. I'll be in touch. Matthew Walsh."* By the time it takes for me to read it a second time, I realize it's from Officer Walsh. My stomach churns a little. Turning the radio on, I find something on the heavier side—some Black Sabbath—and turn the volume up higher than usual. Then I take in one last view of the prison before I put the car into gear and head towards the intersection.

Chapter 3: The Novel

"Deceiving others. That is what the world calls a romance."
- Oscar Wilde

The memories I have of my mother mostly involve us making something together. Pancakes. A bird house. A navy blue winter hat with a perfectly round pom-pom at its peak. She was, by all accounts, very handy. And she was equally skilled in finding a role for her young son in her many domestic projects. I can recall the feel of her strong yet slender hands holding mine as they helped me to flip the spatula, or the serious tone her voice would take on when she warned me about the dangers of jigsaws, or the absurd spells she would cast as she pretended her crocheting needles were magic wands.

There are these memories as well as the photographs I've probably studied hundreds of times. There's the Fenway Park one where I'm sleeping in the baby bjorn against her breast while she eats a hotdog; there's the Newport, Rhode Island one where she has affixed my eyes with her enormous sunglasses and then pressed the side of her face into mine; there's the Halloween one where we are both in superhero costumes, lying on the living room rug sorting out a pile of candy before us.

Her name was Angela and she died the fall I began third grade. A good friend of hers, a woman named Hannah Reeves, had just left her husband and had recently purchased a small home across town. The place was in shambles—that is until my mother agreed to help Hannah with the repairs. The two women worked the entire summer and into autumn, restoring the little bungalow themselves, replacing fixtures and flooring, painting walls and shutters, refacing cabinets and countertops.

On October 8th, towards the end of their renovations, the

women decided to celebrate their efforts with some pizza and wine. Too drunk to drive herself home, my mother opted to sleep over. Then, sometime around 2:15 a.m., the house caught fire, the flames apparently encasing its entire perimeter. By the time the fire department arrived, the roof had already collapsed and the house was folding in on itself. When the blaze was finally extinguished, both women were dead; my mother's body was found inside, just inches from the front door.

Foul play was not initially ruled out. For a while afterwards, Hannah's ex-husband, some local failed musician, was a suspect. The police brought him in for questioning on a number of occasions, but never had enough of a case to pursue it. The fire was therefore ruled an accident. I never asked him, but I always imagined that for the rest of his life, my father tortured himself for not offering to pick her up that night.

From the time of my mother's passing, my father became a silent curator of her memory. As a result, there were never any cathartic bouts of materialistic purging. No stuffing black garbage bags full of her things and leaving them to dampen in the basement or be sorted by some clerk at a secondhand store. He kept everything. Her car and clothes and recipes and even her collection of Red Sox memorabilia. There was nothing creepy or unnatural about it. He wouldn't knock off a bottle of tequila and pass out on the floor of her closet with her picture clutched to his chest. He simply wished to keep things the way they were. Yet he would, on the occasion of bringing a woman back to the house, rearrange the mantel photos or hide some particularly feminine artifact. I never held this against him. For Christ's sake, he was so young at the time of her death.

One day, when I was a senior in high school, he came to me and asked what must have been a difficult question.

"How well do you feel like you know your mother?"

I recall being secretly thrilled by the foreignness of what he had just asked. Though her memory was all around us, we hardly spoke of her. Initially, I probably even thought it was a trick question. Like maybe he was about to reveal that she was a master prankster and was not in fact dead, but had been hiding all these years in some exotic location like Panama or Morocco.

"I don't know," I said. "Pretty good, I guess. Why?"

My sense of security seemed at stake, so I became defensive.

"Do you know where she went to college? Or what she collected when she was little?"

I admitted to not knowing the answer to either question, as well as others that followed: What athletic record did she once hold at her high school? How did she once foil an attempted robbery at a diner she worked at? Where did she live for a spell during her early twenties?

Once the air of my ignorance receded, my father asked if I was interested in taking a week off from school.

"For what?"

"To find the answers to these questions. I suppose I could just tell you, but how much goddamn fun would that be?"

We would take a road trip, he explained. Our destination would be Ohio, my mother's home state. He would show me her childhood home, her alma maters, old haunts, and even locate a few long lost friends. When she was alive, we never traveled as a family to the Midwestern state. My mother, like me, was an only child, and she went when I was a baby, and that was to bury my grandmother who died after a long, drawn out battle with lung cancer. And her father, a career Naval Officer, died years earlier when the B-47 jet bomber he and three other men were flying during a test mission, slammed into the top of Wright Peak, in the Adirondack backcountry near Lake Placid.

"Yes or no?"

"Yes," I said, partly to appease him and partly out of my own genuine curiosity.

It had been close to ten years since she passed. Life had gone on in that time. It's true that I missed my mother, but the rhythms of my days were such that I was now used to being without her; any longing for her presence had eased with time.

My father, who ran most of his affairs with a strong sense of order, left much to the imagination on this trip. Where we ate and slept, when we stopped, how far we drove at a clip: These were all determined by the whimsical force that seemed present throughout the odd journey. And it *was* odd. My father, who quit smoking in college, took it up again during those few days. A nervous energy seemed to course through him as we toured the campus of Youngstown State University, and circled the parking lot of Rayen High School, and drove up the driveway of her parents' first house, a modest two bedroom place on West Wood Street. Most were sites he had once visited himself, but that was no matter. It was different this time. He was now with his son and there was the profound feeling that he did not want me to be disappointed.

"Very cool," I continued to say with as much enthusiasm as I could muster.

We knew one another well, my father and I. So there couldn't have been a doubt on his part that I was humoring him. It was important to him that the memories I had of my mother be fleshed out some. I'm not certain if they ever were. It's true that I learned that she once held her high school's track and field record for the 200-meter sprint, and that as a kid she collected harmonicas, amassing close to a hundred of them, and that she lived in Amsterdam for six months when she was twenty-two, but none of this had enough weight to revamp my image of her. Our time together, though short, was already rooted in a way that I knew and accepted.

If anything, the trip brought me closer to my father. He may not have known it, but I watched him a lot during the five days we spent on the road. I watched his grave expressions give way to contentment as we ate at The Bulwark, a diner my mother worked at for a few years, and I saw his melancholy charm work its way through a conversation with Rachel Arnett, one of my mother's closest childhood friends. I think I was able to further appreciate my father's loss. In its own strange way, it allowed me to see him once again as a family man—but it was now from the perspective of a teenager rather than as a young boy.

Of all I learned about my mother during that trip to Ohio, one thing has stuck with me more than the rest. It's something my father told me one night as we pulled onto the interstate after a late night meal at a diner somewhere in Pennsylvania. We were headed home. The highway was empty. He reached for a cigarette he swore would be one of his last ever—he did give up the habit as soon as life resumed again in Connecticut—and turned to me in the dark of the vehicle.

"We were going to have another baby," he said, lighting up. "Me and your mom. We were talking about it a lot that summer. We had waited long enough. Jesus, you were eight by then. It seemed like the right time. We were both ready."

There wasn't much for me to say. So I listened. I listened as he spoke of Alex, his own brother; he said sibling relationships were often complicated, but could at times be rewarding. It had always been his wish, he told me, that I have the type of sibling relationship he and Alex never had.

"Chances are you would have made a damn fine big brother," he said, flicking his barely smoked cigarette out the window into the air. "Anyway, I thought you should know."

Turning on the radio, he told me to get some sleep, and that he planned on driving through the night. This conversation, which seemed to serve as the coda for our trip, has come back to me a lot lately.

Joanna and I began negotiations for a second child when Cole was about six months old. Joanna was teaching then and it was making her miserable. She cried constantly, declaring that her place was at home with her son, not teaching brush strokes and art history to indifferent adolescents. Another baby, she argued, would warrant her early retirement from teaching. Promising me she would sell an average of one painting a month, she even presented me with a carefully outlined budget.

For me, it was not a matter of money. I did the math myself. It's true that things would be tight, but we could make it work. For me, it was something else. When I went over it in my mind, it amounted to the kind of father/son issues that any therapist would sink their teeth into. Firstly, I felt tremendous guilt that my own father was forever deprived of knowing his grandson. And vice versa. Having a second child might magnify this. Then there was the idea that, through having Cole, I managed to duplicate the very child/parent relationship I knew best. It seemed like it was meant to be. Having Cole seemed like an homage to my own father. Having another baby would destroy that balance.

These were thoughts I never told Joanna. Whenever the topic of a second child came up, I was able to placate her for the moment and defer the matter. I would point out things like the commitment her art career required, or my Nana's failing health.

But the time has now come. Cole is two, soon to be three. My days of stringing Joanna along are behind us. I can feel it. There's an almost palpable sense of real responsibility and obligation creeping into our life. We're now in our mid-thirties—I'll be thirty-six this month—and the past is behind us. We're adults. And we're now meant to act accordingly.

So this morning when Joanna brings up the subject over breakfast, prevaricating hardly seems an option.

"I feel ready," she said. "Cole is getting bigger. I think it's time."

For a moment, I'm tempted to mention that she's negated me from her equation. Pointless, though. She is focused.

"I understand," I said, forking some of my pancakes onto Cole's plate.

"Can't you just picture it? The two of them."

The daycare incident has brought about something of a new trend in Joanna; she now envisions the world as suddenly darker and more dangerous. It has become a place where a protective sibling is now a requirement. There's no one to share in the bleak irony of this absurd cause and effect I have inspired.

Since the incident, I've listened to her talk passionately about all the things our children will do for one another—and for us for that matter. She's mentioned holidays and old age and hard times that will come. Two children, she reasons, will make life more balanced, more diverse, more whole.

When I look at Cole, he smiles at me and laughs a little; smears of maple syrup are on his chin and cheeks.

"Have you thought of names?" she said.

"Not really."

"I have."

"I'll bet."

She begins to talk about names she likes. Some are girls and some are boys. Some I remember from when she was carrying Cole. There's Christopher and Ryan and Emma and Madeline. She ranks them according to preference, expounding on why, and even telling me the ones her parents favor. This goes on for a while. I begin to tune her out. As I look at Cole and watch him eat his third strip of bacon, I suddenly remember the text message I received just a few days earlier from Officer Walsh. He said he would be in touch. It was logical to assume that it would be today, Saturday, when he would call. In my head, I begin to go over what he might need to discuss. Maybe it's just to verify a few small details. What else could it be?

"What do you think?" Joanna asks.

"I'm not sure."

"Let's wait for the summer to talk more about it. We've waited *this* long. Maybe we can try then—in the nice, relaxing months of a long summer. It might be fun."

Part of me wants her to be impetuous and entitled about the matter; this will embolden me to put it off further. But she breaks my goddamn heart with her selflessness and practicality.

"Okay."

I don't want to lie to her by saying anything else. When I look over at Cole, he is using syrup to fix a piece of bacon to his lip, wearing it like a meat moustache. Joanna and I both laugh at this, which makes Cole laugh.

Officer Walsh ends up getting in touch with me the following morning at a little before 10:00 a.m. He texts me. With a cup of hot coffee and a stack of mostly terrible essays on *A Farewell to Arms*, I am alone at the kitchen table when I receive the message. It simply reads *"How does this afternoon work for you? Maybe around 1:00. You pick location. Somewhere with food. Walsh."* I allow myself to grade four papers before responding. All I say is *"Let's make it 1:30. How about we meet at Vic's Hideaway in Westville. It's on Roosevelt. Marcus DiMatteo."* Within seconds, he responds with *"See you there."* He doesn't sign his name this time.

With Cole napping and Joanna painting, I leave to meet Officer Walsh, pretending I am off to pick up some forgotten groceries. During the drive over, I notice I am fidgeting a lot. I switch the radio on for a moment before turning it off in a flash. Then I put the window down and then back up and then down again. And then there's my hair, which I keep fixing in the rearview mirror.

Vic's, known for its famous cornbread and coffee combo, is just off the interstate in a small tucked away plaza in Westville. They open early, so on occasion I'll stop in the morning on my way to work.

The parking lot is half full. I pull into a space in front and sit in my car for a few minutes, the engine idling, the radio softly playing a Dusty Springfield song. It's 1:13. Figuring I'll get a jump on Walsh, I shut off the ignition and head into the restaurant. The place is a cross between a diner and a deli. There's a counter with a handful of swivel stools, a small to-go coffee bar, a fresh bakery case, and about a dozen and a half tables and booths. To my surprise, the moment I walk inside, I spot Walsh. Sitting in a corner booth by a window, he's drinking from an oversized mug and looking in my direction. Our eyes lock for a moment before he finally waves me over. He's wearing blue jeans and a black v-neck t-shirt. A thin brown leather book is on the table, open and face down.

"Waiting long?"

"Ten minutes or so. Not a problem. There're a few things I want to review with you? So I appreciate you meeting with me."

"I was surprised to hear from you. I'm not sure what else I can tell you."

Walsh is about to respond when he must have sensed the

waitress approaching our table. With her pad and pen ready, she gives me a smile and asks if I want to hear the specials. She's young and plain looking, but has lovely skin and a nice figure. Declining on the specials, I tell her I'll just have the coffee and cornbread combo. As she begins to walk away, I add that I want the cornbread to go.

"It's for my son," I said, turning to Walsh.

"How *is* your little boy? Is he adjusting okay after what happened?"

"He's doing well."

Walsh drinks from his mug before setting it aside. Reading from his book, he clears his throat a little, but doesn't speak. We sit there for a few moments in silence, listening to an elderly couple at a nearby table talk about leg cramps. The man appears to be the one with the cramps. The woman is getting worked up that her husband is too stubborn to see a specialist.

"You got a good look at him, didn't you?"

"At who?" I said, knowing full well who he means.

"The alleged gunman."

"Of course. I'm sorry. Yeah, I suppose I saw him pretty well."

The waitress returns with my coffee and a brown box with the cornbread. The box has a whimsical cartoon drawing of Vic's face, which is the same image that adorns the menus and the sign out front.

"Why do you suppose he didn't enter the facility? He told you he was going to, right? His exact words, according to the statement you gave were 'I'm coming, you peasant motherfucker!'"

He says this loud enough for the elderly couple to turn in our direction. As I smile apologetically at the woman, I can feel Walsh staring at me. Taking a sip of my coffee, I think for a moment.

"Why do you suppose he had a change of heart?"

"He must have heard you guys coming and got spooked."

Walsh doesn't miss a beat. Referring to his notes, he mentions that my statement indicates that I spotted the alleged gunman at 6:43, called the police at 6:45, and they were in the vicinity at 6:52. That's close to ten minutes, Walsh said. A generous window of time.

"A lot of damage could have occurred in that ten minutes," he said.

"I'm glad as hell it didn't."

He nods. Then he twists his mug on the table for a few moments, all the while looking at me with unblinking concentration.

"Officer Walsh, I can't rationalize the behavior of a total stranger. Let alone some local madman. It's impossible. He didn't enter because he balked. Or maybe he never planned on entering; I don't know. Again, I can't speak on behalf of a madman."

"But you thought you were in real danger? You and your son and Ms. Olsen? You thought the three of you were in real danger?"

"Of course."

Inhaling for a moment, Walsh regards me with the sort of wry smile forged out of artifice and impatience. We each sip our coffee and wait for the other to say something.

"You never thought to ask about our meeting," Walsh says.

"I'm not sure what you mean."

"I mean you never once asked me about why I wanted to meet with you on a Sunday. And at a restaurant of all places."

"Because you're just as much of a sucker for Vic's cornbread as my two-year-old. That's why."

"It's because I thought you'd be more comfortable in a public place like a restaurant. And less inhibited than in a place like a police station. Police stations can be intimidating for some people. The truth is I thought you'd be cooperative in a place like this."

"Am I not being cooperative?"

"I'll bet you don't even know if I'm sanctioned to be here with you right now—meeting with a witness like this. You never thought to ask."

"I suppose I have faith in the State Police."

"Well, I'm glad to hear that. Especially given how delicate a thing like faith is. It's hard earned, that's for sure."

His voice changes a little when he says this. Its pitch seems to elevate. This makes it difficult to detect whether or not he's being sincere. Nodding my head, I toss a few one dollar bills on the table.

Then I stand up.

"We all want to have faith," he continues, remaining in his seat and looking up at me. "You want to have faith in my professionalism just as much as I want to have faith in this statement you've given me. Right?"

He adds a few more dollars to the pile before rising and walking outside with me. He puts on a pair of sunglasses and uses his key remote to unlock the door of a burgundy Ford pickup that's pulling a small two-toned blue fishing boat on a trailer.

"You fish?" he asked.

"No."

"I'm selling this to a friend of mine," he said, slapping the side of the boat. "I'm buying a thirty-footer next week."

"Very Hemingway," I said, not knowing how else to respond.

"He did like to fish, didn't he?" Walsh said. "I recall that."

I mention how just this morning I was grading student essays on the author's work.

"How'd the kids like him?"

"They tolerate him. I think they recognize there's something profound there, but they don't necessarily grasp what it is."

"No special effects in literature, right?"

"Right."

"I was always more partial to Shakespeare. I loved that stuff. Murder, treason, bloodshed. High drama, right? *Othello, Hamlet, Macbeth. Macbeth* is probably my favorite, though."

Officer Walsh braces himself a little and takes off his sunglasses. Squinting his eyes ever so slightly, as though he is on the verge of discovering something fresh and vital, he begins reciting *Macbeth* from memory.

"There's no art to find the mind's construction in the face."

He's working hard to remember. That's plain to see. He has a little more in him, too.

"Look like the innocent flower, but be the serpent under it."

He's finished. Putting his sunglasses back on, he shrugs as if to deflect praise that I never offer.

"Mr. Kooper thought that memorizing Shakespeare would help

some of us impress the girls," Walsh said.

"Did it?"

"I don't think so. But it came in pretty handy right now, didn't it?"

"What do you mean?"

I said this with more defensiveness than I ought to have.

"I mean it must have impressed *you*, Mr. English teacher. Not bad for a cop, right?"

Extending my hand towards Officer Walsh, I admit that I'm not sure what we accomplished this afternoon.

"More than you know."

I wish him luck on the sale of his boat and bid him a pleasant day.

"Aren't you curious about *anything*?" he said.

"Like what?"

"Like about what was accomplished this afternoon? Like about whether I'm within my jurisdiction to be here with you right now? Or about my complex views on faith? Or simply my intentions, Mr. DiMatteo. Don't you ask questions?"

We stand face to face for a moment before he turns from me and climbs inside his truck. I'm tempted to tell him about Oedipus and how his quest for answers didn't end so well. But another thought trumps this.

"Officer Walsh," I said, just as he is about to shut the door, "should I look into getting a lawyer or something?"

Peeling off his glasses again, he flashes a little grin and turns his head slightly to the side.

"Now he starts with the questions."

A few days later, on a Wednesday, it's my birthday. I am thirty-six. Joanna gives me a choice between reservations at Consiglio's, one of our favorite Italian restaurants, or a home cooked meal of my choice. Knowing that Blanch has planned a little debauchery for me after work, I choose Consiglio's, which isn't too far from The

Cowgirl Club. Blanch, I tell her, is planning on buying me a beer or two at Sidewalk Caesars. So it makes the most sense for me to meet her and Cole and her parents at the restaurant.

My birthdays are usually devoid of any emotional fanfare. I'm not the type to get contemplative or poetic in the face of another year gone by. This one is unusual, though. I can feel something physically different. My body has a heaviness to it that seems foreign. And my thoughts feel inscrutable. The only ones I can identify are about Cole, who I call a couple of times in the morning. Joanna, declaring that my devotion to our son is endearing, puts him on the phone both times. I say little more than 'I love you,' to which he says the same, but it somehow helps me fight through the absurdity of my sentimentality. Each instant I hang up the phone, I am able to face a sea of teenagers with a strange sense of renewal.

During my lunch period, I call Dr. Robertson, Nana's physician. He isn't available. His nurse takes my name and cell number and tells me he will get back to me later in the day. I ask if she has any information on Nana, but she says I will need to speak with the doctor. Just as the call ends, Blanch enters my room. He is grinning like a court jester.

"I know what you're thinking about," I said. "It's written all over your face."

"Right now it's on my face, but in a few hours it'll be written somewhere else entirely."

Blanch always proves a good distraction for me. His bawdy humor allows me to put the burdens of work and home aside and regress to a place where grown men can behave like idiots. It often amuses me to consider how my students would react if they became privy to the innuendo between Blanch and me. It's all liquor, naked women, and weed.

"You're depraved."

"I don't know all your fancy English teacher words, but if that means looking forward to seeing some ass, then yes, I'm *depraved*."

I tell him about my reservation at Consiglio's. He warns me that

I might smell like a strip joint for my birthday dinner. The bell rings and within a few moments my next class begins to arrive. Blanch steps aside from the doorway and smiles politely at the students who enter the room.

"Enjoy," he said, saluting me. "The celebration kicks off at 4:30."

He starts to turn around and then suddenly stops. Reaching into his pocket, he pulls out a white envelope and throws it on my desk, wishing me a happy birthday. The envelope isn't sealed, and I can see that it contains a generous stack of one dollar bills. With a sweeping motion, I drag it into my desk drawer, which I open almost immediately. None of the kids seem to notice.

The rest of the day wears on with languid, nondescript energy. I'm glad to see it end. It's nearing 4:00 when my phone rings. It's Dr. Robertson. We've spoken on numerous occasions through the years. And we've met a few times in person. He's a pleasant man with a mild manner. It's become habit for him to ask me about my family, sharing with me that his son is studying premed at Northeastern and his daughter is in Central Africa working for UNICEF. Aside from being gregarious and professional, Dr. Robertson is candid when he speaks of medical matters. This call is no exception.

"I think we're going to need to keep a closer eye on your grandmother."

He urges me to increase her level of care at Blue Bridge to the next and final tier. We speak for a while about Nana's diet and some recent blood work and her stomach cramps and migraines and dizzy spells. Dr. Robertson is also worried about her falling. And there's the matter of her mental health, he says, which seems to be in steady decline. There are days when she remains in bed from sunup to sundown.

"A few of her friends have passed away in recent months," I said. "I think that's taken its toll."

He agrees. Then he urges me to make the arrangements for

Nana to have Constant Care as soon as possible. We end the call with my assurance that I'll be making the drive down to Jersey as soon as I can get away.

The Cowgirl Club is awash with a lazy, dusky sort of gloom when Blanch and I walk through its doors at a little before 5:00. There are only six or seven other customers in the place. It seems darker than the last time we were there. And the music, which is some jangly pop guitar tune I half recognize, is not nearly as manic. There's only one dancer on the stage. She's topless with high heels and a red bikini bottom. Her back is to a pole, which she slides up and down in a seamless motion, staring off into the distance at nothing or no one in particular. She's Hispanic, and though approaching being plump, she's attractive.

When Blanch and I take our seats, I scan the place and notice that everyone seems to be whispering to one another. A man across the bar is whispering to one of the dancers, a bleached blonde sitting beside him, probably propositioning him for a backroom dance. The bartender, an older woman with a low cut shirt and a large chest, is whispering to a man with an unlit cigar, who might be one of the owners. And the bouncer by the door, who shook Blanch's hand when we entered, is whispering to a girl who looks about ready to climb on stage.

Blanch reminds me of the envelope he has given me. I take it out while he orders us a couple of beers.

"It's the kid's birthday," he tells the bartender. "So put a ribbon on it."

She smiles and wishes me a happy birthday. Blanch and I sit and drink for a while. He buys every round and won't hear of me paying.

"Let Uncle Hank take care of the beer," he said, dipping into the envelope and tossing a handful of ones onto the stage, "you're having a hard enough time managing your money."

The truth is that I don't need to; Blanch has been consistent at reaching into the envelope, counting out three or four ones, and fanning them out on the stage, usually in front of me. When a dancer approaches, Blanch introduces the two of us and tells them it's my birthday. Then they collect the bills and embarrass me by pulling my head into their breasts and thrusting their ass in my face. It amuses the hell out of Blanch who coaches me through each time with quips like "Take it all in," "Smell that youth," and "Don't fall in love." He always says these loud enough for them to hear.

By the time the envelope thins out and we have each drunk five or six beers apiece, a new girl appears on stage. I recognize her from my last visit to The Cowgirl Club. The DJ introduces her as Callie Starz, adding that it is spelled with a "z." The crowd, which has increased to probably a dozen and a half, cheers for the girl, who begins her slow stroll around the stage. An upbeat country song plays, to which she begins to undress.

"You like that one?" Blanch said, probably noticing that she has consumed my attention more than the others.

"She seems very devoted to her craft," I joke, adding that Blanch has just reduced her to the likes of a menu item.

He scoffs at this, assuring me he has more respect for these girls than anyone. To prove it, he said, he will call her over and settle the matter right now. So he empties the white envelope onto the stage —it has seven one dollar bills in it—and waves at Callie Starz, who has already been heading in our direction. When she stops in front of the cash, she stands with her hands on her hips and looks down at us. There's the slightest trace of a beguiling grin forming on her face.

"Please accept this for all your hard work," Blanch said, "we want nothing in return."

She looks between us both, probably waiting for the catch.

"I have nothing but respect for what you do," Blanch continues. "Not to mention how you do it."

He turns to me with a prideful beam in his smile. Callie Starz moves in towards us before crouching down to pick up the bills. I feel myself staring at her, which she must notice. Her breasts are exposed; they are not large, but they appear natural. Her features, especially up close, are beautiful. Her eyes are so light that they look almost clear.

"Such a selfless gesture, gentlemen. Seven dollars."

Her voice is the perfect marriage of childlike playfulness and sexy nonchalance. It has a lilting quality that doesn't demand attention, yet seems to rise above all the other noise in the club. She sits down in front of us on the stage. The music changes from one country song to another.

"But this is not how it's done," she said, fanning me with the money. "I'm supposed to earn this."

"You must recognize me," Blanch said, "I'm in here a lot. And that makes me qualified to say that you have absolutely earned it. You earned it, and then some, before we even entered the door."

"Explain yourself," she said, a wry little grin turning her lips into something exotic and new.

Blanch improvises. The man is quick on his feet, and has charm to spare, so he doesn't come off as offensive or condescending. There are even moments when I think he actually means what he's saying. He talks about the risks she is taking by being on stage and how she's vulnerable in front of so many and forced to maintain confidence, even if it *is* pretense; he tells her she give that very confidence back to countless men, whom she tantalizes with her beauty, making them feel invincible, if only for a brief moment. When he's finished with his dissertation, he calls over the bartender, remarking to Callie and I that honesty always makes him thirsty.

"Wow, we don't get a lot of poets in here," she said. "I'm speechless. That was beautiful. And completely original."

"I put myself out there," he said, turning to me, "and this is the thanks I get."

"How much thanks does a true poet need?" she said. "It's a rather selfless endeavor from what I understand."

Blanch looks at me, probably taken aback by her willingness to be so playful.

"Though I do consider myself a sensitive man," he said with

mock self-flattery, "a man of passion and feeling, *he's* more the poet type."

Blanch waves his finger at me and pretends to sneer.

"Mr. English teacher," he goes on, "uses all sorts of fancy words like *depraved*. Do I look *depraved* to you?"

Now Callie is focused on me. Something Blanch said seems to strike her.

"Are you really an English teacher?"

"Yes," I said, annoyed that Blanch has given up my real identity in a place like this.

"Go ahead," Blanch said, "quote her some goddamn Robert Frost or something. She'll love it."

The bartender appears and Blanch orders two more beers. Then he looks at Callie and tells her it's my birthday. She asks the bartender to put the drinks on her tab.

"There's a lot of giving going on here tonight," said Blanch. "It's making me very tingly."

"What grade do you teach?" she asks.

"High school," I said, knowing she is young enough to be a former student.

"Literature, grammar—that kind of stuff?"

"Mostly literature."

"Give me some specifics."

"You want specifics?"

"Name some authors."

She sits there in front of me, half naked, and listens intently to the list, nodding in what seems like either recognition or approval. Then she tries to match up the work I probably teach with its corresponding author. She's right on every one of them. She even has a suggestion for me.

"Instead of *Animal Farm*," she says, "you should do *Coming Up for Air*. It's not as well known, but it's a much more important work. It derides the whole capitalist thing before it was en vogue to do so. You should read it."

"How do you know I haven't?"

"Have either of you read *The Tremendous Fucking Buzz Kill*?"

Blanch said.

"I'm sorry," Callie said, "are we leaving you out of the conversation?"

The bartender comes back with the drinks. Blanch takes his and stands up.

"You two get better acquainted and I'll just amuse myself with Pete over there."

He's pointing to the doorman, who is slouched against a wall studying his phone. Before Blanch leaves, he reaches into his pocket and pulls out a few twenty dollar bills, which he throws down next to my glass of beer.

"All I ask is that you go easy on him. He has to work in the morning."

When Blanch walks away, Callie puts her clothes on and climbs off the stage and sits in Blanch's seat. She asks if it's really my birthday. I tell her it is and we make some small talk. No matter how hard I try to keep the focus off of me, it seems we always end up back there again. Callie wants to know all about my teaching. Her questions are eclectic. They're about my students and the school's English curriculum and what my favorite titles are to teach. She even asks where I attended college.

"What about you?" I keep saying, plying her with my own set of questions, only some of which she answers.

I discover that she is originally from the west coast, has two sisters, dropped out of the University of California, Santa Cruz, her freshman year, and owns a motorcycle. My back begins to stiffen a little from sitting so long in the metal slat backed chair. So when I adjust myself, Callie notices and suggests we get more comfortable in the VIP lounge.

"You're already paid in full," she said, stuffing Blanch's twenties between her cleavage.

Before I can decline the offer, she's dragging me from my seat and towards the VIP lounge, which is in the rear of the place. My protests along the way are feeble at best. Callie leads me up five stairs to a series of doors with keypads on them. After entering a code on one of the doors, it opens and we enter. The room is small and dimly lit. There's a leather loveseat, two large fern plants, and wall to wall shag carpeting that glows in the dark. Up-tempo instrumental music sounds from speakers that are built into the ceiling. The room smells like dessert.

"Make yourself comfortable," she said, leading me onto the loveseat.

"Thank you."

"Does your wife know you're here?"

"How do you know I'm married?"

"Because you're polite. Most of the polite ones are married."

"Why do you think that is?"

"Maybe you feel like you're performing all the time when you're married, and good manners is an extension of that."

"So good manners are a performance?"

"I think they are."

"Interesting theory."

"So, does she know you're here?"

"No."

"No?"

"My wife is very conventional."

This depiction strikes me; I believe it to be true, yet never before have I used it to convey a sense of Joanna.

"Then maybe we shouldn't do this," she said, straddling herself on top of me.

"What exactly are we going to *do*?"

With her arms in the air, she begins to gyrate her buttocks in slow, sensual circles.

"We're going to talk about *The Sound and the Fury*," she said, "and then look at its influence on subsequent southern novels like Flannery O'Connor's *Wise Blood*."

Smiling down at me, she runs her fingers through her strawberry blonde hair before stroking the side of my face with her open hand.

"Then I thought we could get into some Vonnegut," she said. "Maybe talk about the use of satire in his works and whether it was inspired more by his personal politics or other writers of his time like Mailer."

"You seem to like the American stuff. Maybe you should be a guest speaker in a couple of my classes. I bet some of my students would really take to you."

As I say this, I feel myself getting aroused. It doesn't faze Callie, who continues with her seduction. But I'm seized with an impulse to put an end to it all. So I start squirming underneath her, which only succeeds in bringing me to full arousal. When she perks up a bit over this, smiling and putting a hand coyly to her mouth, I call a timeout and ask her to please let me up. The expression on her face appears more pleased than embarrassed, as though she revels in bringing me to a sort of moral impasse. If I don't want a lap dance, she asks, then what am I after?

"I'm meeting my family in a little while," I tell her, "so let's just continue talking. Give me forty dollars worth of your best rhetoric on, say, Twain. What can I get for forty dollars on Twain?"

Sidling up beside me on the loveseat, she folds her legs into herself and tells me it will be the easiest forty dollars she will ever earn. Then she laughs a little before breaking into a rant about how underrated Twain's lesser known works are and how they are as equally influential on other regionalist authors. I wait for her to finish before asking about her fascination with literature. It seems like a reasonable question.

"My mother was a librarian. The biggest currency in our house was books. She used to bring home armfuls at a time. I devoured them from an early age."

Naturally, I have questions aimed at how Joyce and Camus led her to The Cowgirl Club in southern Connecticut, but I stop myself. She goes on, mentioning how books kept her out of trouble and how they provided solace at times. With mock sentimentality, she says I am lucky to make my living as a teacher. Then she says something I am not at all expecting, something that shoots me with a pang of wonder. In an earnest and unassuming voice, Callie tells me she has written a book. Any incredulity I might feel is instantly allayed with the expression on her face. It's mild and humble and even nervous, as though she wants to be taken seriously at the moment, but knows we are in exactly the wrong place for such beneficence.

"What kind of book are we talking about?"

"Fiction. It's a novel."

"Is that so?"

"Yes, that's so."

Her tone is a bit more aggressive than it had previously been.

"The inevitable question. What's it about?"

The novel, she tells me, is entitled *Me and Mr. Crowley*. She describes it as a surrealistic exploration of fate, luck, love, and death. The book, set in the 1930s, is about a man named Tennyson Roderick III who is hired to murder Aleister Crowley, famed occultist, after the latter performs a black magic ritual on W.B. Yeats, causing the poet to go deaf, dumb, and blind.

"It's in the vein of dark, absurdist humor. Similar maybe to Albee or Beckett."

Having finished the book within the last year, Callie said she is both editing it as well as shopping around for an agent. This is all said with such casualness that it makes publication seem imminent. The inevitable questions are asked. How long is the manuscript? How long did it take to write? What inspired the idea? More casual answers. It's as though we're at a signing in some local ma and pa book store rather than some dimly lit sex cubicle in the rear of a strip club.

Her confidence begins to annoy me. I imagine, in a sheer display of strange irony, that the book is outstanding and will in fact see the light of day. There's something about not only the girl, but in the graceful way she extols her passion, that seems more than just a mere suggestion that she has something to be proud of. I look at my watch.

"Running late for your birthday bash?"

My family, I tell her, is meeting me at a restaurant. It's time to get going. But not before I leave her with some news of my own. Very coincidental news at that, I remark. I have a novel of my own. *Mister Walker*. And it is currently in the hands of one Gavin Murphy, a publisher out of Virginia, who is finalizing the deal. As Callie listens to me discuss the particulars of the novel, its storyline, its revisions, its ultimate fate, which I tell her rest in the hands of Mr. Murphy, she seems more amused than impressed.

"What a coincidence. Especially in a place like this."

Her tone is new to me. It's brighter and full of wiry sounding syllables. If I knew her better, I might have been able to discern its implications.

"Not to mention both our books have the word 'Mister' in their titles. But I suppose stranger things have happened. Maybe it's an omen."

I stand up to leave. Callie remains in the loveseat, stroking her bare legs in what seems like an effort to warm them. As I make my way towards the door, I tell her we should swap stories and give one another feedback.

"Sounds like you're beyond the 'getting feedback from a stranger' phase," she said.

"Is that what we are? Strangers? Really? After all the profundity we shared on the classics?"

"Writers are the worst people to read one another's work," she said. "Which is why I suppose there are agents and editors and publishers. Fellow writers are the enemy. They will for sure hate what they read; either it will be shit, and their hatred will be justified, or else it will be better than what they've written, and their hatred will be justified."

Though she wears a blithe expression when she says this, it's evident she means it.

"Happy birthday."

"Thanks for a lovely evening," I said, a glint of mockery somewhere in there.

Blowing me a kiss, she commends me once again for my politeness.

The rest of the evening wears on in a slow blue haze. I feel self-conscious and exposed, like I'm being filmed by a movie crew wherever I go. Maybe it's the alcohol Blanch and I drank so much of, or maybe it's the feeling of being humbled by a stripper.

When I meet my family at Consiglio's, they have already been there for close to half an hour. Joanna cuts me a break and says nothing about my lateness. Instead, she orders me a Black and Tan and makes a toast. Her parents, who have Cole sitting between them, a coloring book and some crayons splayed out in front of them on the table, seem annoyed that I kept them waiting. My father-in-law even makes a comment about how I seem a little drunk. Joanna comes to my defense and her mother asks her to keep her voice down.

I'm only half listening to everyone. My mind is going over the plot of Callie's novel. Admittedly, I know next to nothing about Aleister Crowley, and probably even less about Yeats. Yet I'm intrigued. And I know it has little to do with her macabre storyline and more to do with the story of Callie Starz.

Here is a small town stripper who knows the classics, discusses them eagerly, and wrote a fucking novel that seems as quirky and fresh as her own attitudes. But it isn't simply the striking contrast of the young woman that floors me—the nimble transformation she must make daily from erotic dancer to disciplined author—but rather the way she seems to fully embrace both roles with such peerless conviction. It's easy to imagine her at a family reunion, confounding her own relatives as they stare at her from afar while guessing who the hell she truly is and what she might do next.

Despite all the alcohol I've drunk this evening, I'm wired by the time we return home. Joanna puts Cole down for the night and then falls asleep with the bedroom TV on. I'm bouncing from room to room, searching through dusty bins that are stored in closets, turning over bureau and desk drawers, leafing through stacks of old bills and papers and magazines. Finally, in the hall closet by the laundry room, I find what I'm looking for inside a weathered orange Nike shoebox.

There are a hundred-and-eight typed pages in all. Four complete chapters. It's been so long since I held the manuscript in my hand that I barely recognize its first sentence, which reads,

When Bill Walker forged his own conscience, he did so in a way that left enough room for the magic and madness of life. After reading this several times, I begin to remember my protagonist and who he is and what he's after. I read the second sentence. And the third. Soon, I find myself sitting on the floor in the hallway, rereading all four chapters. By the time I finish, it's close to 2:00 a.m. With the manuscript strewn across the floor, I hurry to find a pen and paper. When I do, I return to the hallway and stretch out on the hardwood floor underneath a single recessed light that splashes my yellow legal pad with a perfectly round pool of illumination.

After a few moments, I begin to write, slowly and with caution, as though the words I'm producing in sharp black ink might somehow be catapulted from the page and into infinity. But then something happens; a neuron must have fired because my pace increases. The words begin to come forth rapidly and with greater ease. Sentence after sentence fills the page, which I flip up before moving on to the next one. It's all visceral. There's no way to tell for sure where my story is going or if what I'm writing is any good. I like it this way.

The soft distant sounds of the bedroom television play as I continue to write. Thoughts of Cole begin to fill my mind. I want to check on him while he sleeps. Hell, I want to wake him up and tell him, "Look, baby, Daddy's writing again. After all this time, Daddy is actually writing. Hallelujah!" But I let him sleep. And I continue writing, absorbed in the notion of not knowing what I'm doing. I like the not knowing. The mystery of it gives my brain a fresh thrill. And it seems too damn long since I've had anything in my life resembling a fresh thrill.

Chapter 4: The Prognosis

"Man is not what he thinks he is: he is what he hides."
- Andre Malraux

When my father was murdered, I was left with the task of cleaning out his house. Five years prior to his death, he had sold my childhood home and purchased a raised ranch not quite two miles away in a secluded residential neighborhood with ancient elms and a faded picket fence. The house was smaller and easier to maintain. To say he lived like a bohemian would be understating it. Every room appeared to be an office of sorts, littered with red milk crates of books and papers and dated issues of law journals. Much of his furniture had been sold off at yard sales and he never bothered to replace a lot of it. My mother's belongings, now stored neatly in a dozen or more W.B. Mason boxes, were stacked neatly against the far wall of a spare bedroom.

I spent the better part of a weekend going through everything. Some items I gave to Big Brothers Big Sisters; some I donated to a local consignment store; some, like all of his work-related things, I threw away. And some I took home with me. Like the set of professional chef knives. And a first edition Wallace Stevens I bought him one year for Father's Day. And a hardbound maroon book I scarcely remembered from my childhood. It was this book that turned out to be my most interesting find. It was a journal he kept, chronicling his fatherly exploits. On the inside cover, it read, in meticulous black print, "Careful Considerations on Fatherhood, Manhood, Childhood, and The Job I Think I'm Doing – For Marcus When He Himself Becomes A Man, Or Father, Whichever May Come First."

Except for a handful of pages at the end, the book was entirely filled. Sitting there in his house, the dusk entering in heavy blue slabs of fog and shadow, I began reading it. It spanned most of my life, beginning the day I was born, and ending at my early twenties. All the entries were addressed to me personally. And they were all dated and ranging in length from just a few lines to a full page. His sentiments were not at all maudlin. They were scattered musings, some filled with humble wisdom or hardnosed angst or lucid memories.

An entry written when I was ten months old reads as follows:

Dear Marcus,
You're starting to walk a little. What a racket. Your mother and I can't wait to see where you're headed.
Love,
Daddy

One written on Christmas Eve, just a few months after my mother died reads as follows:

Dear Marcus,
Sometimes I think you're too damn smart for your own good. Today, when we passed each other on the stairs, you looked at me with such a doleful expression and said nothing. You have this ability to drain language from my mouth and render it completely useless. What could I say to you anyway? I'm sorry. I'm sorry. I'm sorry. That hardly seems like it's worth a fuck.
I do love you, my boy, but I am wishing right now that I was childless. And not just for my own sake so I can go off on a bender and behave like a goddamn grieving fool, but for your sake as well. We both know I'm no fucking good for you right now.
Maybe you'll have a boy of your own someday and get my meaning. There will be times when you'll give to him all that you possibly can. And to him it will be the world. And when you look at each other, you will both recognize the vitality of the moment. And then there will be times when

you're lucky if you can summon the courage to look him in the eye.

I want to say Merry Christmas to you, but it's a foolish thing to say right now.

Love,
Daddy

Another one, written on my eighteenth birthday, reads as follows:

Dear Marcus,
Today you turn eighteen. The law says you're a man. But I'll be the one to let you know when that actually happens. You're damn close. It's impossible to believe that we've both made it this far. You'll be leaving me in the fall, which will be good for you, I suppose.

I'm on a Paul Simon kick lately. I keep listening to that song of his, "Slip Slidin' Away." Wonderful lines: "And I know a father who had a son. He longed to tell him all the reasons for the things he'd done. He came a long way just to explain. He kissed his boy as he lay sleeping. Then he turned around and headed home again." The funny thing is I still don't consider myself sentimental.

Eighteen is a good age. Enjoy it.
Love,
Dad

The very last entry, dated just days before he was slain, reads as follows:

Dear Marcus,
Donato's condition is worsening. It's just a matter of time now. I hate all this saying goodbye shit. How do you know when you're supposed to lay down all that heavy, burdensome emotion, or when you're supposed to hold tight to it and wait it out? I want to say it only <u>once</u>. The redundancy might make it sound insincere. These are strange thoughts to be having right now, but my mind is in a different space lately.

I'm going to miss the old man for sure. It's impossible to think that we will never again have another talk about music or boxing or have another argument about my drinking.

He loved your mother and you very much. It's important that you know that. Be glad as hell you had all your summers with him. You two bonded easily. Partly because you had one common enemy. Me. Someday, if you have a boy, you will know how this feels. We're going to run circles around you.

Love,
Dad

Cleaning out the house of someone who has died is a strangely thrilling experience. Grief occasionally subsides and makes way for hope, which enters, slow and exasperated, as if it's been beaten along the way by blunt, protruding memories. It's the hope that there will be some miraculous discovery among the bins and boxes and spare bedrooms. A discovery that will illuminate a fresh revelation about the dead. And, perhaps, all the mysteries they've taken with them to the grave.

Reading this journal taught me nothing new about my father. I was okay with this. In some way it was a relief. It was just nice to hear from him after he was gone. It did sadden me that he didn't live to give the book to me himself. I imagine he was waiting for me to embark on the enterprise of fatherhood before handing it over. He would have done so in that cool, dignified way he had about him, saying something like, "Just some bullshit I threw together over the years—consider it light bathroom reading if you will."

I never showed the journal to Joanna. It would have felt like a betrayal to my father. So I brought it to my classroom where I keep it in my bottom desk drawer under a stack of old grade books. Each time I look at it, I feel guilty for not doing the same thing for Cole. My intentions were to carry on the tradition. The idea of waiting for his twenty-fourth or twenty-fifth birthday to hand over several hundred cleanly typed and bound pages always fills me with the sort of mock pride that comes from an unrealized ambition. In giving it to him, I would be as cavalier as I knew my own father would have been. And Cole would treasure the damn thing, sharing some with his wife and children, keeping some only for himself, laughing over nearly forgotten reminiscences, resigning to confusion over the inscrutable musings on the dramatic follies of my life.

My intention is always to start a journal in the near future. I tell myself that I'll wait until Cole hits a landmark age. One month. Six months. A year. But then I put it off some more. And though it's hardly too late to start it now—he's not quite three, for God's sake—I know I never will. This is not for lack of material. There's plenty to say. There's just something daunting about committing all of those truths to the page. Maybe it's the English teacher in me, or maybe it's the skeptic, but I'm too damn conscious of creating a persona that might make me into some one-dimensional halfwit that my son will either loathe or pity in years to come.

It seems as though some stories are just beyond the telling. Like the one about Cole's first night home from the hospital. It was a Sunday night and we lost power due to a lightning storm. Joanna was running through the house in a panic, collecting candles and closing windows. The oncoming darkness, she convinced herself, was potentially harmful to a newborn. It took some doing, but I was able to keep her from calling her parents. She eventually calmed down and we began to have a pleasant evening. With the house ablaze in candlelight, we drank virgin daiquiris and feasted on the chicken cacciatore our neighbors brought us earlier in the day. Then we sat at the kitchen table, full and satisfied, and passed our baby back and forth to one another.

It was close to 10:00 p.m.—I remember Joanna commenting on how our boy was almost exactly seventy-two hours old—and we were looking at one another over thin wisps of black smoke that rose from the scented candle jars on the table. Cole was asleep in my arms. The house was cool and quiet. Something struck me at once. It was a fierce kind of sorrow that seemed to be instantly born out of the delicateness of the moment. What I ended up saying was not planned, but it was not impulsive, either. It was one of those things you say, knowing it will take hold and be regarded as strange and even shocking, yet there's the hope that it might be understood, and even, God willing, appreciated. I was not looking to be a poet or a prophet when I looked down at my newborn son and mused how I could not believe that someday he would be dead.

It's impossible to forget the look my wife gave me at this moment. The antipathy in her expression should be reserved only for the most vulgar of criminals.

"What's the matter with you?" Joanna said.

The regret I felt was immediate. But not because I didn't mean what I had said. I did mean it. I was having strong feelings about my son—feelings of love and fear and bewilderment—and that's how they came out. The regret I felt was over my wife having no understanding of any of this. Joanna, shaking her head, circled the kitchen table, lifted Cole out of my arms, and walked down the hall, leaving me alone in the near dark, speechless and embarrassed.

Then there's the story of Del Russo, a former colleague of mine who was a science teacher at LSHS. Del, when I knew him, was in his late forties. He was a thin man with sandy colored hair and a friendly, modest smile. He coached the girls' basketball team and drove an old Mustang in the warm weather and won district teacher of the year on two separate occasions during his tenure.

Del and I, for much of the time we were colleagues, rarely spoke to one another. He was always a veteran teacher to me and we seemed to have few reasons to get acquainted. Yet we were pleasant enough to each other; we would nod if we passed in the halls, or make idle banter in the copy room about it finally being Friday.

Then, during a faculty meeting one afternoon, my department announced that Joanna was expecting our first child. This was followed by a brief burst of applause. When the meeting ended, Del approached me and offered his personal congratulations. In the weeks that followed, he would make a point whenever he saw me to ask about Joanna. Besides this, he would ask about me and whether I was excited or nervous. It was easy to see that he was sincere. Before long, I asked if he had any children.

"Two," he told me, locating some pictures on his phone. "He's in the Coast Guard, stationed in Cape May. She's a junior in high school."

His son's name was Timothy and he knew he was military bound since the fourth grade. With bright, confident eyes and a face chiseled out of the 1950s, he looked focused and serious. Isabelle was his daughter; she was dark haired and athletic looking. She played basketball and was interested in becoming a veterinarian. This became the bond Del Russo and I shared: our children.

Cole was born and I found myself giving Del updates each time we saw each other. I reported on sleeping and eating habits, ear infections, what made Cole laugh. Conversations were never one-sided; I always asked about Timothy and Isabelle.

There was something about how Del talked about his children, some awkward charm he had that humanized them to me and made him appear as a sort of Atticus Finch, flawed, rebellious, proud. Del was a natural storyteller. He favored brevity, too. There were many times I'd walk away from our exchanges secretly wishing for an invitation to his house so I could finally meet Isabelle and hear her side of the story, and maybe get a look into Timothy's room where there was probably a wall of wrestling and baseball trophies with gold and bronze medals draped around them in a careful display.

Del's wife, Leigh, came up on occasion, but it was his children who dominated these talks that I came to value. Del, unbeknownst to him, became something of a mentor to me. There was no pretense about him, no design to edify or preach. He was just an average man who seemed to understand perfectly the blunders and triumphs of parenthood.

Last March, on a cold and rainy Thursday, LSHS had a teacher development day. It was to be a day filled with workshops and team building activities and a guest speaker who was driving in from Rhode Island. I entered the building at a little before 8:30 a.m. and went straight to the cafeteria where bagels and coffee were being served. The usual levity that resulted in the absence of the entire student population on such days was nowhere to be found. Instead, I found my colleagues in a near silent state. Many of them were sitting together in small circles, staring at the floor, picking at their breakfast, or holding their head in their hands. Others were crying and hugging and offering barely audible words of solace. Probably noticing my late arrival, not to mention my confusion, Frank Nichols, a veteran member of the Social Studies Department, approached me and told me what had happened.

The previous evening, Del Russo had driven his wife to the airport for a flight to Pittsburg to visit family. Isabelle stayed home alone. Upon his return, Del discovered his daughter hanging in the garage. She was already dead by the time he cut down her body.

There were no workshops or team building activities that day. The guest speaker was cancelled. Our principal, Dot Logan, announced to the faculty what had happened. She invited everyone to spend the day how they pleased. I retreated to my classroom and locked the door. At around 10:00 a.m., I took a nap in my chair. Waking at around noon, I graded papers and listened to soft music. A few colleagues knocked on my door and asked if I wanted to go to lunch with them. I declined. Instead, I went to Children's World to see Cole. He was asleep when I arrived. I told Lynn I needed to see my son, but I promised not to wake him. She didn't object. So I pulled up a chair to his crib and graded papers while he slept for over an hour.

Del never returned to LSHS. And I never saw him again. It was rumored that he and his wife split up and she moved away to live near her sister in Pittsburg. A few details of Isabelle's suicide were revealed. It was reported in the newspaper by the county's medical examiner's office that the girl died of asphyxiation due to hanging. The brief article used the phrase "apparent suicide."

Some of my colleagues, in hushed tones of belated concern, said Isabelle had been seeing a therapist and was having problems in school for some time. Others said she always appeared to be a typical teenager. It seemed to hardly matter. She was gone. And Del was replaced almost immediately by Kristen McCarthy, a young teacher right out of college.

I couldn't sleep for weeks after this. The truth is that in the middle of the night I would steal Cole out of his room and bring him in bed with me and Joanna. Then I would lie awake, my thoughts uneasy with countless paternal burdens. By the next morning, my mind and body dense under the gloom of exhaustion, I would tell Joanna that Cole cried out in his sleep again and could not be consoled until I comforted him in my embrace.

Thinking about Del's loss made me physically ill. So much so that I left work early a few times over the next month. Without telling Joanna, I would sneak home and sleep in the cool dark of our bedroom. The migraines I had already been having seemed to suddenly worsen. Bright lights and loud noises, I soon learned, only magnified the problem. So being a high school teacher, with those cheap, humming fluorescents hanging overhead everywhere, as well as the droves of wild teenagers competing with one another for center stage, turned me into a caveman.

I became grumpy and solitary. It was easy to convince myself that the migraines were due to anxiety over what had happened to Del Russo's family. This allowed me to evade medical advice for far too long.

Dr. Stewart's secretary calls me during my morning class. One of the ladies in the main office patches the call to my room.

"Dr. Stewart has your test results," the woman said. "He would like to schedule a time to review them with you."

My students are working on a dreadful pronoun exercise I give out each year. They pay no attention to me as I stand by my desk, phone in hand, desperately trying to control my breathing. I watch Maggie, a pretty, dark haired girl in the second to last row, copy answers from Davis, the bright boy she sits beside. In front of Maggie is Jill, a chubby redhead, who has her head down, buried inside her fat folded arms. The voice on the other end of the line continues to talk, but all I can do is watch my students. Nicholas and Zoe and Abigail and Brett. They're all so young and hopeful and unmindful of who I'm speaking to and the delicateness of the matter at hand.

"Just give me the results over the phone. It's easier that way."

"I can't do that."

"Why not?"

"The policy states it has to be in person. You'll need to come in."

"Jesus Christ," I said, causing several of my students to look in my direction.

"Perhaps you'd like me to have Dr. Stewart call you himself."

As I think about her offer, I stare at the top of Jill's head, which rises and falls in a steady, graceful manner. Tomas, a boy in the back row, suddenly sneezes. Half the class offers a *God bless you* in unison. When I look at the clock, I see that there's more than half an hour left in the period. My anxiety is unfounded. I know this. Dr. Stewart's office is operating according to protocol. Still, though, my anxiety is real; I'm becoming more irritable by the second.

"I think I'll just come in now," I said, loud enough for my class to stop working and look up at me.

The woman starts to say something, but I hang up the phone. Then I call extension 180, which is Blanch's number. Someone on his staff answers and I ask them to find Blanch for me. After a minute, he's on the line.

"Can you drop what you're doing and get up here?"

Less than five minutes later he's in my room. He's glad to get away, he tells me. As part of a recent initiative to boost security in the building, surveillance cameras are being installed in various locations. Blanch was in the middle of escorting the installers around campus.

Without offering an explanation, I tell him to cover my class and that I'm leaving the building. The look he gives me, a crooked and bewildered grin, indicates that he thinks I'm joking. He starts to say something, but I'm already out the door and down the hall. My mind is in that space where thoughts come on quickly, too quickly in fact, to be sensible and meaningful. They stack up against one another and their weight is disorienting. Thoughts about Cole and my father and getting high with Blanch. Just as I descend the stairs to the first floor and round the corner in front of the Athletic Director's office, I meet up with Dan Zinser; he is walking directly towards me. Moving slowly and with a cocky sense of ease, he regards the mostly empty hallway with ridiculous satisfaction. I'm walking quickly, my car keys jangling and stabbing at me from within my pocket.

My eyes meet Dan's, and he seems to squint for a bit, as though he's surprised by my presence. Slowing down a little, he points in my direction and calls out that he needs to speak with me. When I hurry past him, he halts before fumbling over his words. Then he turns and begins to follow me, quickly catching up.

"Did you hear me?" he said, his voice hollow and annoyed.

"Now's not a good time."

He snickers. We walk together in silence for a few moments, side by side, Dan's body heat palpable and probably adjusting awkwardly to the sudden change it just went through.

"It's a good time for *me*," he says.

This time *I* snicker. We make our way past the Guidance Department and the main office. When we're just feet from the front entrance, Dan stops in his tracks and demands to know where I'm headed, reminding himself that I teach during this period. I stop in front of the double glass doors that are being cleaned with a squeegee and spray bottle by Mo, a senior member of Blanch's staff. A delivery man with an armful of parcels is approaching the building from outside.

"My kids are in good hands right now," I said.

Mo opens the door for the delivery man, who bids us good morning and walks towards the office.

"We need to have a conversation," Dan said. "Something has come up."

My head suddenly aches. Closing my eyes for a moment, I rub my temples in slow circular motions. Dan is speaking, saying something about how we can use his office for our meeting. I must have had a revelation when he was mid-sentence because I suddenly realize what day it is. At once, I open my eyes and look at Dan, who's watching me with a cool kind of suspicion, as though at any second I might pull an alarm and dash out into the parking lot where my getaway car awaits.

"Today is April 29th," I said. "Isn't it?"

Letting out a deep breath, Dan stuffs his hands in the pockets of his perfectly pleated khaki colored pants and leans against the wall.

"Today's your birthday," I said in a quietly flat voice. "I remembered. I'm not exactly sure why. Anyway, happy birthday. I hope it turns out to be one hell of a day for you."

Tossing his head back, he laughs a little to himself. Then he begins to say something about accountability. And with that, I turn from him and head out the door and to my car.

The receptionist at Dr. Stewart's office, a woman named Beverly, identifies herself to me as the one I had spoken with on the phone. With plain, shoulder-length hair and bright green eyes, she's probably in her early fifties. She tells me she understands my anxiousness when I mention how I was able to free up my schedule to suddenly drop in.

"We'll let the doctor know you're here."

"I'm sorry if I was rude on the phone," I said, half-convincing myself that politeness will stave off potential bad news.

The waiting room, stuffy and sparsely furnished, is long and rectangular with creaky hardwood floors and a bank of windows running its length. A Muzak version of a James Taylor song plays over the surround sound. There's one other patient in the room, a balding man of about seventy; he sits in one of the dark brown chairs, flipping through a Time magazine, his face drawn and bored looking. I begin to sweat. And not just a bit of light perspiration on my forehead, but all over. I feel it under my arms and down my back and on my upper lip. At first I sit absolutely still, trying to breathe easy and bring my body back to a graceful state. Soon I begin fidgeting in my chair, wiping my open hand across my face, pulling at my clothes, and even panting a bit. The man has to notice because he gives up reading his article to study me. His attention somewhat brings me under control; I continue to sweat, but I'm able to temper my movements.

"There's water over there," he said, pointing to a five gallon cooler in the corner by the entrance.

His voice is firm and controlled. He could do commercials with that voice of his. Maybe for Ford or one of those big hardware chains.

After downing half a dozen cups of cold spring water, I swipe a magazine from a beat up end table and sit back down. The man is still watching me. To prevent my thoughts from racing, I begin telling myself I am not an alarmist, that I in fact pride myself on *not* being an alarmist. Images of my own father flash into my mind; his even temperament was impressive to me even at an early age. Memories of conversations he had with my grandfather begin to surface. Heated conversations over politics and music and my father's refusal to move on with his life after my mother died. I always sensed meaning and gravity behind their words—even at a young age—but I never got the impression that they were being histrionic. They weren't. They behaved like men.

Just as the old man begins to strike up a conversation, a nurse appears and asks for me to follow her into Dr. Stewart's office. The place is cool and shadowy; the blinds are drawn, letting in perfect squares of unremarkable light. There's a tiny globe on an oak desk, a large bamboo plant in the corner, a half-dozen hanging diplomas, a candy jar packed to the brim with hearty purple jellybeans.

My eyes go to each of these things, studying them with drowsy intent, waiting, listening, barely able to keep from screaming out loud that I'm ready for my fucking test results. The taste in my mouth is stale and chalky, like I have just sucked on a fistful of aspirin. Eyeing those fat, purple jellybeans, I wonder if I'll have time to lift the cover from the jar, grab a handful, down them quickly, and cover my tracks before Dr. Stewart walks into the room.

Just as I get up the nerve and lean forward, a slight knock

sounds at the door. Dr. Stewart appears; he's wearing black suspenders and a red necktie over a pressed, white dress shirt. In his hand is a manila folder and a soft-cover book with a bright yellow cover. Smiling at me, he shuts the door, closing us in together; those goddamn purple jellybeans never looked better.

My drive home is mechanical. The way I handle the car, my starts and stops, the turns I make—they're all done with mindless ease. It's only when I pull into my driveway that I realize the school day isn't over. There's the matter of my afternoon class. The thought of Blanch covering for me yet again is enough to make me grin. This, of course, will not be the case. Proper coverage will be found, or the class will be cancelled. Sliding the yellow book that Dr. Stewart gave me under the driver's seat, I head inside. Without bothering to so much as call the school, I fix myself a bowl of cereal. Then I make a cup of coffee and take in the silence of my house. It's not often I'm here at this hour during the school year. The place is clean and airtight. It smells of the coconut and vanilla candles Joanna lights some mornings while she tidies the house. The ticking of the mantel clock sounds scratchy and elevated. My head feels clear; it doesn't ache one damn bit.

Before long I find myself sitting at my desk, rereading the pages I had written the day before. My routine has become consistent. I write in the evenings after Cole and Joanna have gone to sleep. If I come away with a thousand words a night, I'm pleased. Joanna has to know that I'm writing again. The legal pads I stole from work are all over the house; on them are random notes and scribbles and cross-outs; chapter outlines, corrections to add, bulleted lists of additions or deletions to make. There are also the fresh pages I'm producing; these are left out in plain view in a neat stack on my desk.

I wonder if she's reading the book behind my back. This is a disheartening thought to have. If she *is* reading it, she can't think too highly of it. There's a strong temptation for me to ask her, to shove the pages under her nose and demand that all else wait, that she read them at that moment, either again or for the first time, and tell me something, anything, about my abilities.

My satisfaction over writing again trumps this disappointment. I'm writing for the first time in years. And it feels purposeful. Like I'm not just filling up time and pages, but that I might actually be getting somewhere. My story of a charlatan who passes himself off as an artistic renaissance man is still intriguing to me after all these years. In fact, I find it completely original.

Without having planned it, I sit at my desk, arrows of late morning sunlight stabbing into the room, and I begin to write. It's slow going at first, but then I achieve some real momentum. I'm at a crucial section of the narrative. Bill Walker, my protagonist, is the object of absolute adulation by Tess Bloomfield, a beautiful and troubled young woman, who drinks too much, falls in love too easily, and is holding on to secrets that may rival those of Bill Walker.

Tess is taken with a particular classical guitar piece called "Recuerdos de la Alhambra." The piece, actually written by Spanish composer, Francisco Tarrega, is the impetus to their meeting. Tess becomes obsessed with the recording of the song, which has been released as a Bill Walker composition. Determined to meet this conman posing as an artist, she tracks Bill down and implants herself in his house, refusing to leave until he plays the song live for her.

An hour passes. By the time it does, I have filled up seven full pages. My hand aches. Slugging back my coffee, which is by now room temperature, I tear the seven freshly written pages at their perforations and head outside and into my car. With no real destination, I drive around town for a while. There are hardly any vehicles on the road. Local businesses are mostly inactive this time of day. I pass by Marty's Auto Repair on Crescent Street; then I turn down Bank Street and drive by Many Flavors, one of the town's retro ice cream parlors; when I approach the corner of White and Eagle, I see a cop car parked in an abandoned lot across from Fine

Styles, the salon that burned down last year, but was recently rebuilt. Pumping the brakes, I pass the cruiser, and before I know it I'm on the interstate heading towards Soundview, home of The Cowgirl Club.

When I pull into the place, it occurs to me that I've never been to a strip club by myself. There are at least a dozen or so cars parked in the lot. Two men stand by the front door; they're smoking and talking with one another. Both are gray-haired and paunchy. They don't look at me when I walk past them inside the establishment, my seven pages folded down the middle and tucked neatly under my arm.

The doorman collects the cover charge from me. He's a wiry, goateed man, probably in his early twenties. The blankness of expression on his face is enough to make me wish I was back at home. He hands me my change and yawns himself into an ugly, demonic scowl.

There are two girls on opposite ends of the stage. Both are topless. They move slowly to the music, which is a strident country tune with some second-rate female singer belting out banal words about smoking cigarettes and sleeping with strangers. I count six other men in the place. Two are playing pool and the rest are scattered around the bar, sitting alone, nursing drinks, swaying to the beat of the song, no doubt waiting their turn to lay out their crumpled, dirty cash. Taking a seat at the same spot where Blanch and I sat, I order a beer. Careful to keep my seven pages from becoming soiled, I hold them close to me on the bar.

After a few beers, I begin to talk to the bartender, who's a petite, pretty young thing with short, straight blonde hair, tight black jeans, and a rose tattooed on her neck.

"Do you like country music?"

The look she gives me makes me feel about twice my age.

"I can't get enough of it," she says with mock enthusiasm.

"You must have nightmares about it."

"Can I get you another beer?"

The bottle in my hand is more than half full; not to mention I'm already buzzed.

"Sure."

When she returns with the beer, I hand her a ten dollar bill and tell her to keep the change. Her expression morphs into a forced little smile. Before she turns away, I ask if she knows whether Callie Starz will be arriving any time soon. Now her smile seems for real. She tells me Callie's shift begins in about thirty minutes.

To keep from feeling as goddamn foolish as I know I am, I pass the time by nursing a few more beers and rereading my seven pages. The light is dim, so I have to lean down close to the bar to see the black inked words against the yellow paper. There's no doubt I must look like an asshole as I sit, alone in a strip club, half drunk in the early afternoon, my nose a few inches from a pile of loose leaf paper.

"Hey, paperboy, your girl's here," the bartender says.

It takes a moment for it to register that she's talking to me. When I look up, I see that she's pointing to the other end of the place where Callie Starz is leaning against the DJ booth talking to a short, stocky man with a shaved head and a black sleeveless shirt and camouflage shorts.

"It's now or never," the bartender says in a tone of tender mockery.

Gathering my papers, I take a long last sip from my beer and head over towards Callie Starz. She and the bald man are having a discussion about boxing. He's telling her about a match he had recently where his nose was broken in an early round. This, he explains, became the catalyst for the beating he ended up delivering to his opponent. I find myself standing on the periphery of their huddle; Callie's back is to me. The man eyes me for a moment and then asks what the hell I want. Callie turns around.

"Back for more?" she says.

"Nice to see you again."

"What's this?" Callie asks, pointing to the pages I'm holding. "Grading papers are we?"

"Can I talk to you for a minute?"

My tone seems far too sober for a place like The Cowgirl Club. Callie excuses herself from her Neanderthal friend and walks with me towards the bar where the light is better and where I can see her more clearly. Her skin has tiny flakes of silver glitter on it and she smells like peaches and brown sugar.

"Can we go back to that little room? There's something I want to show you."

She jokes that there's a policy against this type of behavior.

"There's something I want to *read* to you."

We end up in the same VIP lounge we were in before. After paying her, I tell her to sit next to me on the leather loveseat as I clear my throat and begin to read from my seven new pages, which are now moist from my hands. Blocking out the music, I read with as much reserve as I can muster.

Tess continued to force the guitar into Bill's hands. Each time she did this, he would refuse. The guitar was a nice looking instrument. It was a high-end Taylor he discovered among the cache of artistic artifacts. The instrument was made of Indian rosewood, and it boasted pristine ivory inlays on the fretboard and a tortoise pickguard. It was in immaculate condition. He packed it inside its case and stored it away in his bedroom closet for years, neglecting to ever learn how to play it.

It's a prop. A gimmick. An integral part of the ruse that he is an acclaimed artist. Part of the ruse is the self-directed mystique Bill has manufactured; it prohibits any concert performances. He is nevertheless available to his public. Signing autographs and copies of his recordings are fine. But he absolutely will not perform live. He reasons that his musical graces are so intimate, so temperamental, that they are best experienced alone by the listener.

In private, Bill will pose with the instrument. He practices holding it and fretting it and trying to make it look like a natural extension of his body. He will even look at himself in the mirror as he holds the thing. Occasionally, he will attempt to play it for real. But he doesn't know where to start. It's too awkward and unfamiliar. To him, a guitar is a convoluted box of wood with a gaping hole at its center and taut, unfriendly strings.

As far as Tess Bloomfield, she sure as hell was tenacious that he play for her. Bill's demeanor was most often unruffled, but he now found himself growing irritated by Tess' persistence. Why the hell couldn't she ask him about his newest play, Long Day's Journey into Night, or his highly praised collection of Chicago Poems? He could discuss these at length.

Tess was young and willful. And beautiful to look at. Her reddish-blonde hair was long and wild and would get in her eyes when she would turn suddenly or throw her head back in half-drunk hysterics. Bill had barely known the girl, but already he had fallen in love with how she refused to remove the hair from her face. As he fought off her doggedness over that goddamn guitar, he enjoyed trying to glimpse her eyes through those gorgeous locks.

Tess was just finishing her fourth drink. It was pomegranate vodka. The bottle was now smeared with sticky fingerprints from being touched so often in the last thirty minutes. She had brought it over herself, anticipating that they might have a drink or two together. But Bill did not drink. He had promised himself this when he began his life as a serious artist. No booze, no blunders. This was his mantra. He needed clarity to hoist his scam. Alcohol would only impair his judgment.

She more than likely had a few before showing up at Bill's place. Maybe two or three. Just enough to embolden her to knock on his door so late at night. He had been working, which meant he was applying his own name to the bottom corner of a Cezanne. Bill was not used to visitors and tried to turn her away. But she was not to be deterred. With more dignity than a sycophant, and less mettle than a lunatic, she plied her way into his house with a sort of backwards charm that was both girlish and dangerous.

With the vodka now swimming through her bloodstream, she flitted from room to room, picking up his things and asking about this or that. An old photo of his parents at a seaside villa in the south of France. A pocket-size fishing rod. A handmade walnut keepsake with the key broken off in the lock.

It was unnerving to have her here. There was so much at stake. His cover could be blown. There were piles of manuscripts and recordings; there were dozens of paintings leaning against the walls; most of these were in a transitional period, which is to say that Bill was in the process of *applying his own name to them, readying them for release.*

He had a system worked out. One month he would declare completion on a new literary work—Catch 22 was slotted to be his next novel—and the month after that he would announce his new album; he would be bold on his next one, which was Miles Davis' Bitches Brew. The boldness was in that it would be the first recording to host various instruments. Bill Walker had previously released solo guitar records, but Bitches Brew would be his coming out as a multi-instrumentalist. He was quite sure it would astound his fans. And the trifecta would be completed with a new painting or drawing. Bill's next one would be the Cezanne he had been working on this very evening.

"I'll get my way, you know," Tess said. "There's no doubt."

"You're really something."

"What a boring way to be characterized. Especially by such a genius."

Maybe Bill was paranoid, but he thought he sensed some sarcasm in this last statement of hers. He aimed at redirecting the conversation.

"What is it about that piece? Why 'Recuerdos de la Alhambra?'"

Tess didn't miss a beat before she responded:

"Because it sets my sadness to music. And perfectly, I might add."

"You don't look sad to me."

"You don't know me."

"True. Yet you seemed quite comfortable coming over here tonight with your pomegranate vodka and your vehement requests that I entertain you with song."

"And didn't that take an impressive amount of courage?"

"I suppose it did."

"But not enough to reward with song?"

Bill held his position. It was a matter of principle, he told her. If he relented, his house would soon turn into a tourist attraction. People would flock there to request a tune or an improvised oil painting or who the hell knows what. Tess scoffed at the idea of this before filling her mouth with more vodka.

"Does that seem like egotistical thinking?" Bill asked.

"Do you think it does?"

"I feel like it's practical thinking."

"I thought men like you weren't supposed to be practical."

"Men like me?"

"Yes, men like you."

To celebrate such a man, an abandoned elementary school on the town's front street—four miles from Bill's house—had been refurbished and now housed all of his works. When news of this homage reached Bill, he was astounded. An entire building. A one man museum. After renovations, the clean, sleek brick structure—probably close to twenty-thousand square feet—was a sight to see. Its open, sky-lit rooms were lined with glass display cases and listening stations; crowds gathered to marvel over the work of one man who seemed so suddenly sprung from the brow of Minerva. They paid a small fee to drink wine and fawn over what was as revelatory and confounding to them as any modern day phenomenon.

A docent had even been hired. His name was Franco; he was a young, olive skinned Hispanic boy, probably in his early twenties. Handsome and well spoken, Franco was something of an expert on Bill Walker's body of work. He knew the symbolism in his paintings, the keys of his recordings, and the themes in his poems and books. Which is to say, he knew, and memorized, the information Bill had told him over the few times they had met.

"I think the mark of a sad man is based on how many secrets he shares," Tess said. "The fewer the secrets, the sadder the man."

Bill nodded his head as though he approved of her non sequitur. Tess turned her back to him and studied a family photo on the mantel. It was taken years ago. His father, Bill Sr., who was now long dead, was standing next to his fishing boat, which was named Saint Augustine. Bill's mother, Ruth, a slender woman, with a joyful and naïve disposition, stood beside Bill Sr., her hands clasped and her hip slightly tilted to the side. Ruth had passed away three months before Bill became a phenomenon.

"Ask yourself how many secrets you share with others," said Tess. "I'll bet I know."

As Bill tried to openly dismiss her argument as some callow head game, he thought about what she was saying. And he knew the answer. Then he began to consider her formula for sadness and whether it was credible or just inane.

"What's your point?" he finally asked.

"That we could share a secret. Right here, right now. Just the two of

us. No one would ever have to know."
"What kind of secret?"

When I finish reading, I inhale a deep breath before folding the pages and setting them in front of me on the floor. Callie is looking at me, her eyes and mouth working in concert as they express a sort of mischievous curiosity. Neither of us speaks for a few moments. Callie suddenly rises and moves across the tiny room from me.

"How many great artists named *Bill* do you know?" she said.

I think about it. Bill Evans, the jazz pianist, is the only one who comes to mind.

"*William* for sure," she said, "but definitely not *Bill.* There's Wordsworth and Yeats and Faulkner and Shakespeare and Burroughs. *William* is dignified. *Bill* is blue collar."

"That's the point. He's not a true artist; he's an imposter, a fraud. The contrast between his old life and his new life is pretty vast and even awkward."

Callie barely considers this before she shakes her head, smiles, and says she would absolutely change it if she were me.

"You're a pisser."

"This is *my* classroom. That means I get to call the shots."

We talk for the next half hour. First about language. We bring up words we like; Callie is partial to "squeamish" and "dilapidated" and "transcendent," while some of my favorites are "eviscerate" and "plunder" and "roil." Callie points out that her words are all adjectives while mine are all verbs.

"Interesting."

"What can I say? I'm a man of action," I deadpan.

"Give me a fucking break."

We talk about movies. Callie tells me she's seen nearly every Hitchcock film at least a dozen times. Her favorite is *Notorious.* Her favorite movie of all time, though, is *The Motorcycle Diaries.* After she tells me this, she seems to think carefully about what to say next. She starts and stops a few times. Finally, she reveals that she has a dream to take her own motorcycle trip across the country to the west coast.

"I'd like to do it alone, too," she said before giving me details on her ideal route, bike choice, and stopovers.

When I encourage her to do it, to take that trip, she tells me that she will have to do several hundred more lap dances before she has the money to do so. Looking at my watch, I joke that I better leave before she asks for a loan. As I make my way to the door, Callie tells me she's anxious to find out about what will happen between Ms. Bloomfield and Mr. Walker.

"Me too."

"It's exciting, isn't it? The process."

And with that, not to mention the look she is giving me, which is sort of demure and amused at the same time, I remember what I had previously told her about the novel. Publication was imminent, I had said. I went so far as to discuss my agent, who I had named Gavin Murphy; Gavin was actually an old college roommate of mine who moved back to Virginia after one disastrous semester. Smiling a bit, I look down at the floor and think of something to say. Nothing comes.

"Go, go," she said, her voice light and whimsical, "go be with your family and get out of this creepy place."

"There are no details to give," I tell Joanna over dinner later that night. "I'm fine."

"How long did it take?"

"Not long."

"Did it hurt?"

"No."

"What about the headaches?"

"He gave me a new prescription."

This satisfies her and she drops the matter.

I take the night off from writing. My story is overwhelming my brain, so I decide to give it a rest. Bill Walker, it seems, needs some time and distance from his creator. So I think about him instead, think about what he has done and where he is headed; I think about my conversations with Callie and her reactions to Bill Walker.

Lying in bed, the TV playing some romantic comedy Joanna and I had seen the year before in the theatre, I announce that I'm going to sleep. Joanna watches another ten minutes of the movie before shutting it off and kissing me on the back of the head. We lay there in the cool dark for a while. The room is comfortable. My head feels light and drowsy.

After some time, Joanna turns to me and tells me she's glad I'm okay; that she was worried about my visit to Dr. Stewart. Her voice sounds distant, like she has crawled inside of some portal and is working through a barrier of static. At first I think I'm dreaming. But then she says it again, this time louder and with a hint of urgency. I roll over in bed and face her. In the dark, she looks like a stranger to me, like some other woman whose sleek and shadowy contours I've never before seen. When she lets out a breath, I can smell the mouthwash she used earlier.

"We're all good."

"Thank God."

Then she turns her back to me and says goodnight. I lay awake for some time, listening as Joanna falls asleep. My thoughts become vital and restless. Thoughts of Bill Walker and Dr. Stewart and Callie Starz. For a moment, I considerer getting out of bed and grading papers or watching TV in the family room. But the darkness of the room is pleasing and my bed is warm, so I fold my hands behind my head and try to enjoy the stillness and the silence that seem so hard to come by these days.

Chapter 5: The Graffiti

"Without lies, humanity would perish of despair and boredom."
- Anatole France

It's now evident to me that my father had a sort of preoccupation with what it means to be a man. He would so often talk about the men in our family—never in a dogmatic way, but in a way that indicated he was interested, and even perplexed at times, over what it takes for one to call himself a man. Donato, my grandfather, would frequently come up in conversations.

"The old man was right again," my father would say, rarely elucidating.

He would talk about Donato's modest accomplishments with a sense of earnest pride. Donato was said to have "come through again," or to have "taken care of the family," or to have "honored his word." Because my father was anything but sententious when he said these things, I came to regard what he said as meaningful.

The way he spoke of his brother, my Uncle Alex, was far different. Education, stability, health: These were just some of the topics my father would bring up where his older brother was concerned. Driving home from a family gathering one year when I was sixteen or seventeen, my father called Alex a conman of a son and brother.

As far as my father's own self assessments, these would be mostly revealed in the journal he was keeping for me.

One entry, written while I was a baby, reads as follows:

Dear Marcus,
Having a son is wonderful. No, it's beyond wonderful. My goal is to tell you all about it for the next several years. People always say the feelings

are indescribable. I disagree. All these new thoughts of mine are blessed to have arrived with absolute clarity.

Here's one: We napped together this morning and when I woke an hour later to the sound of your soft cries, I felt I had been filled with something that enabled me for the first time in my life to truly distinguish the difference between love and hate.

My senses are sharper and my emotions seem primitive and beautiful at the same time. God, I sound like a babbling fool.

Love,
Daddy

This next one was written literally the following day:

Dear Marcus,
So much attention new parents receive is thrust upon the mother. I get that. It's fine. They deserve it. What they've endured and accomplished is unimaginable. Shit, if you ask me, they deserve a new car and a cruise to the Virgin Islands.

And as though there wasn't enough fanfare over the mother's body and her hormones and the journey she's been on for nearly a year, there has to be a spectacle made about the mother-and-child bond. The bond is private and the bond is delicate and the bond is real and inspiring and emotional. The bond, the bond, the bond...

Don't mistake this for resentment. It's not. Trust me. All I mean to say is that there's something going on between you and I as well. There's no doubt. No one talks about it – and why should they? But it's there. I can sense it all over. It's in the way we size each other up and in the way you wrap your tiny hand around my finger and it's in the way we breathe in unison as you curl into me and sleep. Nothing I've ever felt in my life has been more acute.

There's so much I now understand – and the understanding has come to me in a violent and immediate rush. There's hardly time to sort it all out. What I know about it, though, is that it's all important stuff. We're blessed.

Love,
Daddy

This next entry was written when I was nine years old:

Dear Marcus,

We had a little tug of war today, you and I. It's not even worth mentioning what it was over. But suffice it to say, you're a willful little shit. For the past few months, I guess I've seen it coming. You look at me from time to time with a sort of sweet defiance – I can tell you're feeling it, but not entirely sure how to express it.

If your mother was here, she'd get one hell of a kick out of it all. She could mediate things, too. God knows we'll especially need her in a few more years. But I suppose we'll have to manage ourselves.

I had a friend stay overnight last week. It was pleasant having a woman in the house again. The energy in the entire place was different. Even the aesthetics changed. She bought a bag of oranges and arranged them in a large white ceramic bowl she placed on the counter. It was nice to look at and eat and smell those oranges. Why couldn't I think to do that?

I'm convinced that men mourn forever while women busy themselves with a constant search for grace and dignity.

Love,
Daddy

There was this one that he wrote when I was fourteen:

Dear Marcus,

I promise not to live vicariously through you – but I can't promise that I won't want to at times. Your youth is your biggest asset right now; it also happens to be your biggest obstacle. What a goddamn racket.

Keeping this journal is good for me. It prevents me from giving an overdose of advice to you. Giving advice is embarrassing. I don't want to be remembered as some intrusive windbag. But I do feel it's fitting for you to recall times when I took you aside and put my hand on your shoulder and said something you can let nest in the shadows for a few years before it takes flight when you most need it, blowing your goddamn mind with its virtuosity, its timelessness, and its sheer gravity.

Being a father, I think, causes one to consider the type of man he is.

111

This is quite inconvenient. Who the hell needs that kind of pressure? But nevertheless, it's there. So I embark upon the daunting task of testing myself, asking those questions that hurt my head to think up, then lying about the answers, then facing the truth, then dismissing the whole endeavor as absurd and wasteful. But I know it's not. How you torture me, my boy. I do love you, though. Very much.

    Love,

    Dad

My father seemed to foster this perception that being a man meant you were bound to obligations that were beyond understanding most of the time, obligations that nevertheless carried with them their fair share of poetic grandeur and haphazard graces. It seems like he was often trying to work out what exactly fatherhood was asking of him. My mother's death must have compromised any possible answers. It had to have. Her being gone must have been a relief on the one hand and a constant heartbreak on the other. He had no one to judge his skills, no one to impress with his seasoned rhetoric, but the loneliness of his mission must have at times been deadly.

His preoccupations, it seems, have been handed down to me. And I'm afraid of them. What the hell do I know about fatherhood and manhood? Whatever I've learned I've learned through osmosis. I might be able to play the parts or look the parts—hell, when I break out Hemingway to my kids, I might even be able to teach the parts—but the truth of it is that I'm wading my way through the dense confusion of expectations. This is as humbling as it is maddening.

One time I spoke about it with Blanch. We were both half drunk and stumbling through the parking lot of Sidewalk Caesars when I braced myself and asked him about his own father.

"Not a good guy," he said. "Used to fuck around behind my mother's back. Even got some woman pregnant when I was about twelve or thirteen. That was the last straw. My mother left him after that. I never saw him again."

Not knowing quite what to say to this, I asked him if, in those thirteen years, he ever learned anything about how to be a man from his father. Blanch scoffed at this and then thought about it for a minute.

"Yeah, I learned that a man's weakness can turn him into a fucking ghost. That he can thrive for a bit on that weakness if he's got something else to go with it: brains or charm or something. But sooner or later it'll make him vanish. And nothing—not even his own kid—can bring him back."

I felt closer to Blanch after learning about his family. I wanted to tell him that it was his father's loss and that the man was a fool for missing out on his son's life. Needless to say, I was shocked when I learned, just two weeks later, that Blanch had a son of his own he hadn't seen in over a decade. The boy, whose name is Dustin, is grown, and as far as Blanch knows, is living somewhere outside of Seattle.

I worry sometimes about my legacy. I understand there's a good chance it will be reduced to the singular feat of having witnessed the murder of my own father. There's no denying the gravity of this event. It seems likely that it will trump anything else I can do in my lifetime. But it's a goddamn shame if I fail to top it. I often wonder if I've already resigned to this legacy and have therefore given up trying to make something of myself.

Thank God for Cole. He will undoubtedly prove to be a fine distraction to those who say, "What a shame about Marcus—the poor bastard saw his old man shot to death right before his eyes. Imagine seeing something like that. There's no recovering from that. I don't care who you are." Then they'll remember Cole. They'll talk about what a good boy he is, how he's handsome and a fine son and all of that. That will be nice. But even Cole can't save me from being remembered as some helpless, dispirited orphan.

Then there's the matter of how Cole will remember me. This is another obsession of mine. I think about it whenever he looks at me and laughs over one of our boyish escapades, or during that quiet time while I'm conjuring a good bedtime story to tell him, or even during those dark, edgy moments of twilight when I find myself nearly etherized by the simple, raw beauty of New England.

It's lately occurred to me that I don't want a second child because I don't want Cole to have a confidant. The thought of both of my children commiserating over me, analyzing my treatment of their mother, scrutinizing my failures, is unbearable. If Cole is an only child, my flaws might fade faster. This narcissism, this self doubt—whatever it's called—is hardly tempered by my coming to terms with it. That's not enough. It's still there. And it's as real as I am.

A therapist might have a field day with such an admission. They would probe into my life and try to solve what they saw as the underlying question: What am I trying to hide? And Joanna would be appalled to learn of my fears. Not that I would ever tell her. Add this to the fucking list of secrets. The all consuming shock and confusion it would cause would make me regret it instantly. She would be justified, though, in her reaction. I'm willing to forgo growing my family so I don't have to envision how I might fuck it up. It's pathetic.

All these thought on my legacy might be premature and even self-destructive, but they sure as hell fuel the creative process. It feels like I've earned the right to be working on a novel. I truly feel qualified. Whenever I touch upon an emotional weak spot in one of my characters, or when I trace its derivation, it feels authentic, like I know what I'm talking about, like even if it's not autobiographical in the strictest sense, it's nevertheless true—true in that I'm fucked up, so I can therefore sympathize with and write about and humanize others who might also be fucked up. It's doubtful that I would have been able to do this with any level of assuredness a few years back.

To think of Cole someday reading my book proves to be nothing but a distraction. This is not to say I haven't considered this as I write it. I have. Time and time again, in fact. And I must fight it. I must instead focus on telling my story, leaving out all the subliminal bullshit where I try to explain to my son who exactly I am and what I've done and what I've stood for my entire life.

As a young man in the army, Donato was a boxer. He was a welterweight and was supposedly pretty good. In the summer of 1940, he was in the 7th Infantry Division and stationed at Fort Ord. He had been with Nana for only a few weeks when she came to see one of his fights. He was up against a veteran fighter named Max Weber, AKA the German Sub., which, given the time period, was a ballsy moniker. Donato was not favored to win the bout. And, true to expectations, he found himself in trouble during the fifth round. Weber had him down twice and was practically toying with him in front of the crowd of around two hundred.

Nana sat alone in the front row, clutching her purse, looking on nervously as Donato took a beating. When the bell sounded, Donato went to his corner where he collapsed onto his stool and had his face worked on by his cut-men. Hurting and exhausted, he could barely focus on the strategies being yelled at him and the warnings to keep away from Weber's deadly jab and body shot. Instead, he found himself looking through the ropes at the opposite end of the ring where he could see Nana intently watching him, the faintest trace of what Donato would refer to over the years as her "oh-my-God grin." It was the first time he had seen her smile this way. He would describe it—when he told this story—as sly and sexy and inspiring. The rest of the story has him pulling himself together, catching his second wind, and fighting like hell to beat Weber in the eighth round by technical knockout.

This is just the kind of sappy story people love to tell. I know Donato got a kick out of it each time he would relive it over a nice meal with the family. And people love to hear such stories. I must have heard it a hundred times growing up, but I never minded. It's true that the facts would change a little: One version had Donato, in what must have been a brief lull in the fight, pointing out Nana to the referee and telling him he would someday marry her; another version had him blow her a kiss after one of the eighth round knockdowns.

These inconsistencies hardly mattered. What mattered was that through this story I was able to get a sense of Donato's strength and charm, of Nana's devotion, and of their love affair and the faith they had in one another. If pressed, I wonder if Joanna could produce a story like this about me. Probably not. She'd most likely opt for the one where I gaze down at my newborn son on his first night home from the hospital and remark how surreal it was to think that he would someday be dead.

My mornings are quiet. Cole has not been to daycare in weeks, so my commute is solitary these days. I don't listen to music or talk to myself or even try to think about the day ahead; with a drowsy focus on the road, I maintain the speed limit and simply get lost in the blankness of my head. My new routine suits me. Not that I don't miss my time with Cole. I do. But I feel like right now, when the morning light is tipsy and drenched in its own precarious swagger, that it's time for me to be strange and withdrawn, and a young boy doesn't need to see his father like that.

My phone begins to ring as I pull in to my parking space in the faculty lot of Louis Sutherland High School. It takes me a moment before I recognize the number. My heartbeat suddenly becomes some discordant chime from deep within my chest. After clearing my throat, I answer, prepared to hear the solemn male voice on the other end.

Before a word is spoken by either of us, I know full well the purpose of the call. It turns out that I'm right. As I listen, barely offering a word, Rebecca Dunham, a heavyset, cheerful member of the Science Department, pulls her silver Lexus into the space next to mine. Her husband is a plastic surgeon and buys her whatever the hell she wants. A few years back, she returned to school with what everyone thought were larger breasts. Being that she's quite overweight, though, it was hard to tell.

Rebecca turns off her engine and works on herself in her rearview mirror. I'm still on the phone, still mostly silent as I watch Rebecca pull at her eyelids and apply lipstick and fix her hair. After a few moments, she turns to me and smiles. I manage to smile back. There's something comforting about having her in the car next to me while I'm on the phone, listening to what I'm forced to listen to. But by the time I write down some vital information given to me over the phone, Rebecca is gone.

Dr. Robertson ends by apologizing for the nature of his call—and for calling so early in the morning. Then we hang up and I sit alone in my car for a few moments before dragging myself into the building and upstairs to my classroom. The thought of teaching now feels exhausting. What I would love to do right now is get high. Cancel each of my fucking classes, smoke an enormous joint, and maybe go back to sleep. A bit impractical, yet I do cancel my first class of the morning by taping up a CLASS CANCELED - GO TO LIBRARY sign to my door. Then I sit at my desk in the dark and mourn and snooze for a bit.

After a while, I dig up my father's old hardbound journal. Without much conscious thought, I turn to the few empty pages at the end of the book and begin to write. What I end up writing flows from me in a steady, natural stream. By the time I'm finished, I'm amazed to see that I've written a poem. And though I'm a lousy poet, what I've written doesn't seem half bad:

Let me write what everyone will understand—
The old and the young and the in between.
I am now the "in between," which I like—
But this is not about me for once.
I say "for once" since I like to write about me.
John Lennon said the same thing, and perhaps

I stole it from him.
Of course I did.
But this is not about John Lennon.
It will be for my Nana, or Min, or Mommy,
depending on who you are and what you called her.
I called her Nana.
But this is not about me for once.
I know what this is about;
Some will claim they do.
And some will, for real.
Others will not, and I cannot help this.
I am the "in between," which means I am not the young;
So I no longer have the time to change anyone.
Nana was "the old" when I knew her.
I liked her this way.
She said her wisdom simply.
I remember most of it—all of it really.
My boy was just born and she told me to love him.
She said to love him everyday.
That was all.
She meant it, too.
The grace and melody of those words are trapped inside
a tune my head is playing right now.
I play it from time to time.
It's slow and melancholy and lovely,
and no one really knows it but me.
This is how I want it.
There's more, too.
There's the coffee and card games.
There're the delicious desserts,
and there's the cooking she did with hands that knew so well the food,
and knew the manual labor, and the soft, perfect skin
of all her babes through the years.
We are grown now, her babes.
This was her plan all along, I suspect.

She must have mused to herself—
Mused when no one was around—
Mused when everyone was around—
Look at these people, she must have thought.
There were more thoughts for sure,
but let's use our imagination.
After all, Nana was a woman who knew how to love.
So we're left to find a tribute.
We must find one, we'll all say.
Soon, we'll turn to one another and wonder who has one,
and what it's all about.
"I have one," I'll say.
It's simple.
It's simple like the memories of Nana will be simple.
Simple like the woman herself—which is to say the good kind of
simple.
Let's all walk into a room and play softly the most beautiful song
we can find.
Then let's leave the room and let the song play on its own.
We don't need to stay and listen.
It will be enough to know that there's something
profound happening,
even if it is separate from all the babes.
This is all right.
We don't need to listen to know it's there,
breathing in and breathing out;
the same sounds we must always imagine
and never forget.

Most of the day goes by in a trancelike blur. I barely speak to my kids. They're fine with this. It's May and they're eager to do nothing. By the time last period of the day arrives, I'm reminded of the presentations that are scheduled to go. The assignment is a short story analysis. Katie Laska presents on Eudora Welty's "A Worn Path." She does a fine job, going well beyond the superficial as she so often does. Up next is Derek Martin, who presents on

Thomas Wolfe's "The Far and the Near." He does an awful job, fumbling his way through his slide show, mispronouncing simple words, bastardizing textual passages, and boring the class senseless with his dry, monotone delivery. Continuing in alphabetical order brings up Owen McAllister. He is presenting on John Steinbeck's "Flight," which happens to be one of my favorite stories.

"Here we go," Owen says, taking his place in front of the class. "Prepare to be wowed. For real. No joke."

He begins by talking about Steinbeck's life and body of work. Steinbeck's writing style, he mentions, is both lyrical and accessible.

"He was quite the cunning linguist," Owen says. "Wouldn't you say so, Mr. DiMatteo? Wouldn't you say Steinbeck was a cunning linguist? There's a tongue twister for you: cunninglinguist, cunninglinguist."

Some of the other students are amused that Owen has involved me in his presentation. But they clearly don't recognize this veiled attempt at vulgarity. I choose to ignore it.

"Let's get on with it," I tell him.

The rest of Owen's presentation is not only didactic, but it's too goddamn long. I begin to fade a bit as he delves into the story's use of foreshadowing. His voice, bombastic and disingenuous, proves easy to block out. My mind drifts back to the notion of getting high. Perhaps I'll hit up Blanch after work. Owen and I make eye contact and I signal for him to wrap it up. He nods and forces a mock expression of studious drive. Suddenly, there's snickering from a cluster of boys in the back. It soon spreads to the girls by the window and then to the rest of the class. They're all whispering and laughing and looking back and forth between me and Owen.

"This is outrageous," Owen says, the same obnoxious mockery in his tone, "and downright rude. This is John Steinbeck for God's sake. Is nothing sacred?"

I try to appear bored as I look around the room for the source of their amusement. It takes a minute before I discover it. At the top of Owen's current slide, which analyzes the story's use of the color black, is the word CUNT in large, bolded letters. All eyes are now on me, no doubt waiting for a reaction. Rising from my chair, I use the remote to shut off the overhead projector before turning the lights back on. Owen, heading back to his seat, is trying to repress a sly grin. A few girls he walks past make comments to him; with his grin now more pronounced, he appears unmoved by the attention.

There are ten minutes left to the period. With no intention of salvaging the time, I straighten my desk and file some papers and squander the remaining moments. When I'm out of futile gestures, I sit back at my desk and wade in the awkward quiet of the room. A few students have put their heads down; some appear disgusted while others look amused. Still, no one speaks. Owen, taking his phone from his backpack, busies himself by staring at the screen, which he mindlessly flips this way and that with his thumb.

When the bell finally rings, the students thank me before pushing their chairs in and heading for the door.

"You," I say, pointing to Owen, and loud enough for everyone to hear, "stick around."

"I know exactly what you're going to say and I completely understand."

"You understand what?"

"I understand how it looks."

That same smug smile he had just moments before is still there.

"Is that so?"

"Absolutely."

"And?"

"And it's not how it looks. It was supposed to say CONT, as in CONTINUED. A little vowel mix-up, if you will."

I don't bother bringing up the "cunning linguist" thing. There are a couple of choices I have at the moment: I can give him a pep talk, telling him how bright he is and how much potential he has and how it would be shameful to waste it. Or I can threaten to write up a discipline referral.

He makes steady eye contact with me. Neither of us speaks for a moment. Owen's phone suddenly starts to ring. He furrows his brow and makes a clownish face as if to ask me if he can answer it. After another couple of rings, I dismiss him.

"Have a wonderful weekend," he says as he bounds into the hallway.

My apathy towards the boy, my utter lack of will to get through to him—or even attempt to—is not so much startling to me as it is intriguing. The feeling of nothing can be quite underrated. I sit in the dark for a while. My door is closed and the only two windows in the room are open. A cool spring breeze enters, smelling of daffodils and dogwoods. It blows some papers around on my desk. As I mindlessly watch this for a few minutes, I'm seized by a sudden impulse.

From my bottom desk drawer, I remove a brand new eight pack of thick, chisel tipped Sharpie markers. Tearing open the package, I select the green one and stuff it into my pants pocket before heading out into the hall, where I linger for a moment near the boys' bathroom. Scanning the area, I check for any signs of the new surveillance cameras that have recently been installed. There are none.

With a deep breath, I enter the bathroom. As usual, it smells of spearmint, the preferred flavor of dipping tobacco the LSHS boys like to use before discarding in an ugly black glob against the chipped mirror or inside the sink bowls. There are brown paper towels strewn about the floor. Both of the plastic soap dispensers have been abused; one is cracked and affixed at an absurd angle from being broken off so frequently, and the other seems to have recently spewed a hot-pink puddle of soap that is now slowly dripping its way down the side of the countertop.

Both stalls, like the rest of the bathroom, are empty. Their doors are littered with graffiti—mostly in black and blue ink—as well any number of half-assed patch jobs in what must be the stock-in-trade beige paint used for public school restrooms. Blanch, I know, likes to do touchups at the end of each month. Taking a minute, I read some of the graffiti written on both sides of the doors. "I literally just pooped here" reads one. Another says "Christine Kennedy sucked me off." "Ain't blowjobs grand!?" reads another. The most creative, though, has to be a short poem written on the inside of a stall door: "My asshole is like a convenience store clerk working round the clock/It opens and it closes and it never seems to stop."

Without giving it much thought, I take the marker from my pocket; with a somewhat trembling hand I write in enormous letters on the wall above the three urinals DAN ZINSER EATS DICK AND BALLS BUFFET. Then I toss the Sharpie into the toilet and watch it get flushed away.

It takes me a while to find Blanch as I'm on my way out of the building. He's unloading cases of desk cleaner in a supply closet by the library.

"Mi amigo," he says, boxes piled high in his arms.

His face is damp with sweat and he's wearing his glasses.

"I need a favor," I tell him.

Dropping the boxes on top of a few others, he wipes his upper lip before lifting his glasses and resting them on his head.

"You look like you need a lap dance, my friend."

"Meet me at my car in five minutes."

This is new. We've never been so bold as to handle the stuff on school grounds. Blanch scoffs a little and looks over my shoulder. Eli, one of his crew, is down the hall wheeling a couple of trashcans.

"You self-medicating these days?"

"Five minutes."

"Fuck. The English teacher is all business today."

Stopping by the main office, I find Dan at his desk, staring into a computer screen, a glazed and somewhat annoyed look on his face. The room is awash in crisp sheets of raw sunlight that pour in through a bank of windows. Diplomas and sports memorabilia adorn the walls. A framed photo of Dan with Mrs. Logan, elusive building principal, rests on a bookcase that is otherwise teeming with texts on classroom management and curriculum and instruction.

"You might want to check out the boy's bathroom across from my classroom. It's not pretty."

Folding his arms across his chest, he tells me we are long overdue for a talk. With as much casualness as I can exude, I take a few steps into the small office.

"We've got a few problems."

The first, he tells me, is that I'm forbidden from ever again having my classes covered by a member of the custodial staff.

"I honestly don't give a shit if Hank Blanchard is the godfather to your child. He's a fucking janitor, not a teacher. You are therefore to follow the proper protocol for getting coverage. And speaking of which, when do you think you'll decide to teach a class around here?"

Up until this point, I've only heard rumors of Dan's verbal tirades. Sure, he's a wiseass with me, pulling rank, flexing his condescension, but this marks the first time he's really let loose like this. Trenton Moore, one of LSHS's gym teachers, was supposedly on the receiving end of such verbal abuse a few years back. It's rumored that Dan questioned Trenton's intelligence and even doubted that he had a valid university degree. Trenton filed a grievance with the union and campaigned against the VP for some time; nothing ever came of it, of course, and the men, from what I hear, now steer clear of one another.

"But let's put professional matters aside for the time being," he said, leaning back in his chair. "Because there *is* something else that happens to trump your repeated negligence in the classroom."

"My 'repeated negligence.'"

"The state police have made an official inquiry on your behalf. You're on their radar, my friend. They've been asking about you— about your background, your reputation, about your *character*."

Then silence. He offers nothing more, no doubt waiting for me to ask questions or begin my frantic explanation. My lips are sealed. We stare at one another the way men do when the bar has been raised and caution discarded. There's no doubt he's thrilled by this. It's unclear who has the advantage. We have each piqued the other's curiosity. After a few moments, Dan swipes a blue stress ball from a corner of his desk and begins tossing it between his hands.

"Is that all?"

What's surely lacking as I say this is the feeling the mind is able to produce when it delivers something that is born out of genuine confidence. What I've said is more of a stubborn impulse, a nervous dismissal of this prick and his pernicious agenda. The truth is that there is a deluge of questions my mind is running over.

Ignoring his obvious displeasure over my reticence, I begin easing my way out of his office. Before turning my back on him, I mention how at the end of the day a student tipped me off that they witnessed Owen McAllister emerge from the boys' bathroom with a green Sharpie marker in his hand.

Blanch is waiting for me at my car when I arrive. He hands me a red box of playing cards and tells me to enjoy myself. Before I'm even over the first speed bump in the parking lot, I'm fishing around inside the box where I discover one perfectly rolled joint. By the time I pull onto the main road, the thing is lit and my lungs are full of smoke. I plan on smoking the entire thing myself, then maybe stopping off at Vic's for some cornbread. After that, I'll go home, avoid eye contact for as long as I can with Joanna, and then begin making funeral arrangements for Nana.

It nearly kills me to be without Cole for a couple of days; my in-laws take him in while Joanna and I go to Jersey for the weekend. My wife is good in situations like this. She is calm and nurturing. The only delicate moment is when I request she take the train home the day following the funeral. The hours of loose ends at Blue Bridge are not a two man job, I tell her. She protests at first, but finally relents when I point out that it will mean less time away from our son.

The funeral is quiet and small. I'm able to keep it a private affair. Nana's death isn't enough to bridge the gulf between me and my aunt and cousins. So I decide to be a petty prick and close off the service to everyone except for me and Joanna, a few friends from Blue Bridge, and some great nephew on Donato's side of the family. It's open casket. The undertaker, a short, soft-spoken man with a heavy Jersey accent and hair dyed black, does a fine job with Nana. He manages to conceal her frailties and present her exactly as I remember. Peaceful and grandmotherly.

I don't cry during the service. Yet Joanna, who doesn't leave my side for a moment, continues to ask if I'm all right. On several occasions, I find myself thinking about how I might react if my wife were not here with me. It seems an absurd focus—and an egocentric one at that—but it nevertheless begins to dominate my thoughts. The funeral marks the first time Joanna and I are faced with something severe. Our marriage has yet to be really tested. And though I know that the death of my 89-year-old nana hardly counts as a true test of any kind, it strikes me that our life together has been pretty easy up to this point.

I therefore can't help but wonder what we're made of, if our vows, our years together, the common love we share for our child, are all enough to stave off something that has the potential to be truly ruinous. It then becomes difficult for me to not think of all the secrets I keep from her. There's the pot and the Cowgirl Club and my visit to Dr. Stewart. And then, naturally, I consider the secrets she might be keeping from me.

"What a place," Joanna keeps saying about the hotel room we've rented. "Good choice."

"I'm glad you're happy with it."

"Did you see that shower?" she said, smiling at me and rubbing my shoulders. "I think we could both fit in there comfortably."

Feigning ignorance, I tell her to go ahead and that I am going to take a nap before dinner; after studying a handful of menus she got from the concierge, she makes reservations at some fancy seafood place.

My sleep is so sound that Joanna has to wake me. It's close to 7:00 p.m. and she's nearly dressed and ready to go. Wearing a backless, low cut dress I've never seen before, she asks me to help fasten a platinum Tiffany's necklace she is struggling with.

"What do you need to do to get ready?" she said.

"Just give me five minutes."

After I use the bathroom and brush my teeth, I'm ready to go. Joanna, staring at my outfit, which consists of the same jeans and Toronto Blue Jays t-shirt I've just slept in, asks if I'm going to change.

"What for?"

Dinner is pleasant enough. Joanna is lively. Though she teases me a few times about my clothes, she tells me how handsome she thinks I am and how she can't wait to go back to the hotel. She orders mussels and the swordfish. I order the seafood stew. We go through two bottles of wine. I imagine we're drinking for entirely different reasons.

The drive back to the hotel is nerve wracking for me. A little drunk, I watch my speed closely. Joanna, who unfastens her seatbelt the minute we're out of the parking lot, is climbing all over me. She is already taking her clothes off by the time we stumble into our room. Pushing me onto the bed, she stands before me in her bra and panties.

"Wait here," she said, before reaching into her suitcase for something and slipping into the bathroom.

The room is dark and quiet. I can hear muffled voices in the hallway and a few doors open and close. Turning on the TV, I flip through the channels and manage to find *The Last Detail* with Jack Nicholson. Just as I start to get into it, Joanna appears from the bathroom wearing a skimpy black negligee. After letting me get a look at her, she asks what I think of it.

"Very nice."

"I thought you'd like it."

Settling on top of me, she lifts up my shirt and starts kissing my stomach. After a few moments of this, I notice a tag attached to the lingerie.

"When did you get this?"

"Get what?"

"This," I said, pointing to the negligee.

Straightening herself up a little, she looks into my face and smiles. The glow from the TV makes her look a bit ominous.

"The other day. I bought this and the dress I wore to dinner. Can we continue?" she said, falling back on top of me.

The alcohol on both our breaths suddenly begins to bother me.

"Turn this off," she said, pulling the remote out of my hand. "We're not here to watch old movies."

Then she pulls my shirt over my head and begins to kiss my neck and chest. I let her do this for some time. Just as she unbuttons my pants, I respond to the last thing she has said:

"You're right. We're here because my grandmother just died."

This stops her cold. Pausing for a moment, she seems to sober up almost instantly. Then she scoffs and tells me I'm a buzz kill. I ask if she made any more purchases besides the dress and negligee. Studying my face for a moment, she says something she has never said to me before:

"You're such a little boy."

With this, she rolls off me and heads towards the bathroom.

"Was this your plan all along?" I said. "Come to Jersey, get liquored up and practice conceiving another child. It does have a beautiful ring to it."

I'm so rarely sarcastic with my wife, that now, given the vulnerability of the moment, it comes across as especially grotesque. With her arm draped across her chest for cover, she walks over to me and looks into my eyes. The glare of the TV casts a pool of light and shadow across half her face. With a sober sounding voice, she trumps the 'little boy' comment she made a moment ago:

"You're afraid of everything."

She's given the word "everything" special treatment, turning it into four syllables.

The following day, Joanna and I sleep until around 9:00 a.m. We barely speak as we move around one another, gathering our clothes and toiletries. There's no doubt we're both hung over. When our suitcase is packed, Joanna sits on the edge of the bed and uses her phone to find directions to the train station. Then she heads to the car while I do a quick room check. It's then that I see, in the bathroom, balled up under a bunch of damp towels on the floor, Joanna's black dress and negligee from the night before. To avoid getting a call from the hotel about them being left behind, I scoop them up and drop them both into the garbage can.

Cleaning out Nana's place is far less laborious than it was to clean out my father's. The staff at Blue Bridge gives me some boxes and tells me to take my time. Most of her things will be donated or thrown away. A few I will take with me. Like her white porcelain dog statue, which will look sweet in Cole's room in a few more years. And a few choice pasta bowls and a fancy cheese grater. Not to mention her collection of romance novels. Most importantly, though, is what's inside the romance novels. There are a total of twenty-three books and each is carefully hollowed out and packed full with cash. The books, which Nana kept in plain view in her living room bookcase, are slightly worn, boasting silly titles like *Stealing Paradise Forever* and *Waterfall Kisses*. Most of them have lurid covers with low budget renderings of horses, mansions, and well endowed women being manhandled by tanned, muscular suitors. *The Beautiful Troublemaker*, the novel I stole from so many years ago, is among the lot. Holding it now brings back the same sick feeling I had when I was just sixteen and was conned out of a thousand dollars by the duplicitous Enid Dahler.

I begin to sweat a little as I load the books into an empty box. They fit perfectly. It's impossible not to consider the sum of cash hidden within them. If each book has a thousand or more, that makes close to twenty-five grand. That's a year of college for Cole. My decision whether to tell Joanna about the money has not yet been reached. She thinks Nana might be worth a few thousand, but nothing resembling her romance novel stash. Nana's stay at Blue Bridge was paid for through not only her social security and Medicare, but through pension funds. The romance novel money has literally been collecting dust for years.

It's likely that Joanna would use the money to her advantage. I know how she thinks. She's convinced I'm uneasy about having another baby due to financial reasons. And even though I've denied such notions, she has made it a point to outline a budget that proves she can be a stay at home mother, raising *two* children. An awareness of Nana's cash would no doubt cause her to revamp her campaign.

As I'm packing up a few items from Nana's kitchen, I notice an envelope leaning against the microwave. The return address is New Jersey State Prison; the postmarking is from five days ago.

Dear Ma,

I can't say I'm surprised you haven't responded to my previous letter. It more than likely came as a shock. If there's one attribute I've developed in this place, it's patience. I am therefore hopeful you'll come around and reach out to me. I know you. There's not a chance you have written me off as being dead to you. That's not who you are. This may sound presumptuous and even foolish of me - especially given that we haven't spoken in so long. But the plain truth of the matter is that I am still your son.

Children:
The Bible says, "Behold, children are a heritage from the LORD, the fruit of the womb a reward. Like arrows in the hand of a warrior are the children of one's youth. Blessed is the man who fills his quiver with them!" As you can imagine, I think often about my own children. Jeannine is the apple of my eye - even though she married a real "culo" as you and Daddy would say. His name is Nathan and he sells exercise equipment. As for my Joey, well, what can I say? He's been a bit aimless at times and gotten into some trouble here and there. He's approaching his third divorce. If I weren't in this place, I'd set him on the straight and narrow. He and his sister visit me when they get a chance. It's a lot easier for me to look them in the eyes these days. I went through a lot to get to that point and I'm proud to be able to hold my head high during our time together. Being a parent, I believe, means you have made a constant commitment to everlasting heartache, that you are choosing to endure emotional tragedies - however big or small - for the rest of your days.

The Past:
As you can imagine, I have a lot of time to think. My spiritual advisor, Cal, calls this place the ultimate think tank. He's right. The kind of thinking a man is able to do in here is especially unique. Your senses sharpen and your focus becomes nearly animalistic. I can recall moments

throughout the years when I've been able to stare at a single spot of cracked cement in my cell for several uninterrupted hours, or listen so intently to water pipes inside the walls that I was able to block out all other sounds. Initially, I felt I might be going mad. I soon discovered, though, that my mind was retraining itself. It had been lost in a sort of wasteland and was working towards hacking away at the thicket of the old, dead world. It needed to make room for my new world – my more insular world. To say there was a process to this would be absurd. It has merely been a survival instinct. Cal thinks those of us who have this instinct are the chosen ones. I'm proud to say I have it. And it has served me well, allowing me to revisit the past with a much keener sense. And it is often that I think about the past. I think about you and Daddy and Tony. I think about our trips to Cape May and about your terrific home cooking and about the time Daddy built a makeshift bowling alley in our basement. I think about the time Tony and I started that lawn service business and you and Daddy ended up doing most of the work. I have divided my past into two very simple categories: the real and the unreal. The "real" constitutes those life moments that have a pure and transforming energy. There is a modesty to them, a wild-eyed fit of longing, an almost laughable sense of innocence. The "unreal" moments are all the others; they are so often blurry and boring and without purpose. The harm they cause is subtle and eventual. Much of my childhood and adolescence were, to put it bluntly, filled with unreal moments. I blamed Tony for this. Probably because his own life seemed teeming with realness. The Bible says, "Why do you see the speck that is in your brother's eye, but do not notice the log that is in your own eye? Or how can you say to your brother, 'Let me take the speck out of your eye,' when there is the log in your own eye? You hypocrite, first take the log out of your own eye, and then you will see clearly to take the speck out of your brother's eye." I must have read this passage a thousand times before it made any sense to me. Regardless of the past – regardless of what happened and who's to blame – I have opted to experience only what is real. I have eschewed all else.

I miss Anthony sometimes. But the truth is that I now have new brothers. I hope you do not find this upsetting. It's honestly what has allowed me to endure in this place for as long as I have. Please reach out to

me and know that you are in my prayers.
    Your son,
    Alex

Upon finishing the letter, I vomit into the kitchen sink. It's hard to tell if it's due to the previous night's alcohol or if my body is reacting to the vile absurdity of my uncle ranting and preaching and philosophizing. Another sanctimonious letter from the man who thinks redemption is earned through self aggrandizement. His timing could not have been worse. Nana, who was in her final days, must have weakly thrown up her arms in surrender after reading his bullshit letter, which I fold into fours and stuff inside of my back pocket.

It's close to 3:00 p.m. by the time I pull on to the interstate. Traffic seems especially sparse. Despite this, I take my time. The day is sunny and warm and I put the windows down to allow the spring air into my lungs.

After driving for close to half an hour, I give in to what I've been thinking about for a good part of the afternoon. So I pull the car into the breakdown lane and climb into the backseat. Then I begin emptying the contents of each of the twenty-three romance novels into my lap. There are more fifties and hundreds than I expected. It takes me a while to count the cash. When I am finished I cannot believe the total. So I count again. And then a third time. I get the same amount each time. There's no doubt that I look ridiculous. Here I am, on a main interstate, sitting in the backseat of my car in broad daylight, still hung over from the night before, with ninety-three thousand dollars in cash strewn all over me. What else can I do but laugh about it? So that's exactly what I do.

Chapter 6: The Baby

"Don't cry. I'm sorry to have deceived you so much,
but that's how life is."
- Vladimir Nabokov

The first story I ever wrote is called "A Missing Dog Story." Nothing in the way of early sophomoric drafts or half-assed sketches led up to my writing it. It simply appeared out of nowhere one day, taking a single evening to write. That was the summer after I turned twenty-five. It occurred to me then, and still does now, that twenty-five seems too old to begin writing. But there I was, your average young man, bored, horny, without even a trace of artistic inclination, and endeavoring to make something out of nothing. As an adolescent, I never played an instrument or composed romantic poetry for girls. No one, I'm sure, would have labeled me the creative type.

The motivation to write was neither impulse nor contrivance. It was not born out of some belated need for catharsis or because I had something remarkable to say. It came about, quite simply, when I discovered my own ignorance where my family life was concerned. How my parents met; what my father was like as a teenager: There were countless unanswered questions.

There was the Ohio trip my father and I took when I was in high school. That was meant to fill in some of the many blank spaces of my past. But that was an aberration—a dramatic journey to help a bewildered teenager reconcile with the impossible loss of his mother at such a young age. And God love my father for thinking of it and carrying it out. But it was a one-off. An isolated rogue sojourn of bonding and modest storytelling. When it was over, I was once again subject to the dense wilds of my own imagination to construct—or in fact concoct—the many other missing pieces.

133

Writing allowed me to compensate for this. For every untold or unknown story about my family, I could simply make up my own in order to strike a better balance. Not that I was being particularly autobiographical in these stories. I wasn't. But there are definitely moments as well as characters that owe their existence to the gray matter that makes up my past.

"A Missing Dog Story"
Ted Mallows lay awake in bed studying the twilight that shot across the ceiling. His heart broke for poor Liza whom he heard outside his window. It was day four since the disappearance of Bailey, and the third morning his daughter had woken an hour before school and searched for the dog. They owned six acres—counting the pond—and Liza was granted permission to tramp through most of it, given that she wore her snow suit, took the heavy-duty flashlight, and steered clear of the frozen pond.

"Bailey...c'mere...Bailey-boy...c'mon boy," was her luckless, yet spirited plea.

What a racket, Ted thought to himself: We buy her the most passive animal God gave a sweet face to, and he runs away after only a week. His sorrow was not only for his daughter's loss; it was for the poor, clumsy animal that had probably been hunted by a savvier species, or caught in a barbed wire fence and had frozen to death. Ted dialed the heat to seventy and threw on his bathrobe. Then he made his way downstairs. Liza was just coming inside, and the two met with the same pursed, dolorous look.

"We'll search again tonight, Peanut, okay?" he said, touching her cheek.

She told him she'd continue the search after school as well.

"Good idea."

He made them both some oatmeal as she gathered her things for school.

"Where's Mommy?"

"You know she's still sleeping; c'mon and eat before the bus comes. Bear is gonna pick you up from school today, okay?"

She nodded as she drove a spoonful of the steaming cereal into her mouth. The gear grinding of the school bus sounded in the distance.

"Don't forget, Bear's gonna pick you up today."

"And don't you forget, we're going to look for Bailey some more tonight," she said, nearly shattering her bowl in the sink.

Ted smiled as he watched his daughter pull her tiny hands into her mittens. He kissed her on the nose and pinched her cold cheek.

"We'll find him, Peanut. Have a good day."

Ted watched as she ran down the snow-covered driveway before disappearing behind the winding curve where Mrs. Loomis always waited for exactly two minutes. He eyed the grounds outside as though they were guilty of something. The packed coat of snow was thinning, and footprints of earth began to show through.

Ted looked across the frozen slab of pond into the woods. He secretly blamed Bear for the whole mess. Bear was the one who'd bought the beagle in the first place. Ted shook his head, remembering his father's ironic rationale: "Every kid's gotta have a dog, for God's sake." Funny how he turned away from Ted in favor of the more appreciative Liza the second these words were uttered. Even funnier how after a day or two, Ted began to regard Bailey as the dog he'd always wanted as a boy. Ted even came up with the name.

Liza fell for the animal immediately. The timing of course concerned Ted. It wasn't like the girl's mother to get in a tangle over a little thing like a dog, but it was near impossible to ignore the coincidence of timing. Bear was too insensitive to ever put this puzzle together, even after Liza proclaimed Bailey to be "My own little baby brother."

The shotgun sound of the pickup's muffler jarred Ted. Bear was flying down the driveway like the road behind him was on fire. Ted moved away from the window and began working on the pile of dirty dishes.

"Anyone home?" Bear called, slamming the truck's door.

His heavy footsteps ceased every few seconds as if he were stopping to pick up fallen change. Ted didn't answer, knowing he'd walk into the house whether he heard a voice or not.

"Anyone home?" he called again, opening the side door.

Ted ran the water harder instead of answering.

"Teddy, where are you?"

"Dad, I'm in here," he answered, shutting off the sink.

"Well, I'll be," Bear said, entering the kitchen.

Bear was a massive man with no great supply of breath. He had the kind of round face that excited children and reassured adults. A graying, reddish beard hung from his mug with no regard for a mouth or chin. His gleaming white teeth shocked nearly everyone he met.

"You think you can pick up Peanut today? I already told her you would."

"We can do that," he answered, recouping his breath.

"You want some water, Dad?"

"That'd be good. But don't let me forget what I came for—that auger of yours."

"What for?"

"That sonofabitch Charlie Renshaw."

"I thought you and Charlie were friends."

"We are, but he's always hot on our heels with every goddamn idea we come up with."

"Well, ice-fishing is hardly our idea," Ted said, handing him the water.

Bear seemed disappointed, and looked to be considering whether they actually did invent the sport.

"I guess it's just as well. We cut those holes damn near two months ago, and haven't used 'em but once."

He finished the water in one loud gulp and handed back the glass. Ted looked at him, searching for that corner of his eye that evokes pathos.

"Yeah, well I've got other things to worry about these days," Ted said, motioning to the ceiling.

Bear looked up and thought about it for a moment.

"I suppose you do."

"And who knows how many more personal days Wes'll allow me—and now with the dog missing," Ted added. "Anyway, the auger's in the shed."

It was a curious thing to Ted as to whether his father understood such familial matters. Every talk they shared brushed on the subject, and it was always Ted who threw the aim elsewhere. Bear was comfortable in his present role as grandpa, father-in-law, and even father; a minimal amount of responsibility had always appealed to him.

When Ted was five, Bear "went away" for two years, leaving him alone with his mother, Peg. When he returned, the family abandoned their ranch house and moved across the state into a rented duplex with the Andersons, a loud, truculent family with bad skin. Peg, the only person who could *explain what had happened, died of a brain aneurysm a year later. Ted had never confronted Bear with any of it.*

"Why don't you let me buy her a new dog?" Bear asked.

Ted shot him a look of derision, and turned back to the dishes.

"The auger is in the shed."

Just as the water heated up, Bear's footsteps began.

"I'll pick Liza up at three o'clock."

"She gets out at three-fifteen," Ted called over his shoulder.

"Then I'll be early."

Dr. Perez had said to check on Dorri every few hours. She kept to the master bedroom, sleeping for much of the week she'd been home. He tiptoed around, bringing her soup and magazines, careful never to touch her or stay in the room too long. They barely spoke—or rather, she barely spoke. And she was still refusing calls from her folks, who had phoned nearly twice a day. The only progress he saw was her recent willingness to take vitamins and drink some juice. Ted's pep talk on trying again in the future was dissolving with every passing minute.

On a breakfast tray, Ted placed a hardboiled egg, a glass of juice, and a one-a-day Centrum on a doily. He gingerly climbed the stairs and set the tray on the folding chair in the hallway. He rapped lightly on the door before entering. The room was blackened, except for sporadic thrusts of a sharp blue beam from a muted television. The glares framed Dorri's face, etching thick bars of sick looking light into her complexion. She neither adjusted herself nor looked in Ted's direction when he entered. He watched the TV for a moment, pretending to be interested.

"You must be getting your appetite back," he said, retrieving the tray from the hallway.

The screen went blank, as if to answer, and in seconds, threw a darker pool across his wife.

"You're looking better," he lied. "How do you feel?"

The tray seemed heavier in his hands than before; his forehead began to perspire.

"I'm going to set it down here."

Ted placed the tray on the bed; he looked back at the TV.

He knew he wouldn't get a word from her today. So he collected the

Time and People magazines he'd been bringing her, and stacked them on the bureau. A black screen was followed by the most brilliant glare yet, and when he turned to his wife, she looked like a searchlight had finally caught up to her. On the TV, a beefy man in overalls and a tool belt stood in the middle of an empty house, cupping his hands while he spoke to the camera.

"Bear's going to pick up Peanut this afternoon. So I'll be around all day if you need anything."

He inspected the bulge and angle of her limbs under the sheet, trying to capture a pattern in his mind. He would compare it to what she looked like when he checked on her later in the day.

Bear's phone call was hardly a surprise; he rarely stuck to the plan, and often "just had an idea."

"Well, what is Liza gonna do at Charlie Renshaw's place?" Ted asked.

"I'll show her how to scale a blue gill. God knows her Pop's not showing her any Goddamn thing about it," Bear said.

"We were gonna look for the dog together."

"Why don't you let me buy her a new Goddamn dog?"

"We've been through this. And good luck, by the way, getting Liza to go fishing."

Knowing Bear meant knowing that a fast-food meal would follow any unpleasantness he subjected his granddaughter to. Going to Charlie Renshaw's, Ted knew, would hardly be fun-filled for the child. They'd come back during suppertime, and Bear would have that rutted look of guilt and insane pleasure slapped on his face.

The full sense of the thing got a hold of him once he hung up the phone: He and Dorri would be alone at nighttime. It was the heart of winter and the darkness moved in silent waves, and was upon them with a startling suddenness. Ted knew his thoughts were foolish, but this brought no comfort. They hadn't been alone during the evening since Liza slept over Emily's house. That was in the third grade, before Emily's family moved upstate.

He wanted to sleep. He wanted to feel his breath and blood run lazily throughout his body, lulling it to a warm blackness. The past week had worn him to a shelled version of himself. The leather bound recliner cracked underneath him, heating him like he'd hoped. It faced the eastern side of the house, and as Ted closed his eyes, the tremendous sunlight heaved itself on him, performing a painless, joyful operation on his body. A thick, liquid sleep found him in minutes.

The house had grown cold, and a light snow was falling through the darkness outside. Ted shook himself free from rest and refocused his eyes as he stood up. It was a few minutes past six o'clock by the time he lit up the house and turned up the heat. To save time, he warmed up the raviolis he and Liza had the night before. Not wanting to make a second trip, he contorted his upper body to a shelving unit and carried the meal up to Dorri.

She was still covered in bed, and though he couldn't remember the shapes she'd made before with her body, he knew this time it was larger and had more points to it. A greater portion of the bed space also seemed to be used.

"I didn't forget you; I just figured I'd let you rest awhile," he said, knowing the lie wouldn't be challenged. "It's snowing out."

He looked around the room for the breakfast tray, spotting it atop the still muted television.

"Why don't you put a light on and eat something," he said, noticing the untouched egg from earlier. "Your body needs nourishment."

The word "body" made him uneasy. It evoked intimacy and made him feel guilty. He removed the breakfast from the tray and loaded on the new meal. Then he moved to look out the window by the bed.

"That poor dog," he said. "Bear, of course, wants to buy her a new one."

A missing beagle wouldn't move a tear of hers, he knew, but what about for her daughter's sake? Did she think how it must have affected Liza? Ted found himself, suddenly, for the first time, wondering what occurred in the bedroom these past few nights during the minute or two it took for Liza to say goodnight to her mother. Did they speak? Was it haunting for the child to see her mother in a near catatonic state?

"You're not the only one who's hurting," he said gently. "You've got a husband and a little girl."

The heat suddenly stopped humming through the wall. Ted took a long drag of air and began fingering the cooled ball of egg he held in his hand.

"I'll send Peanut up before she goes to bed," he said, walking towards the door.

As his hand touched the knob, Dorri spoke in a sullen, hoarse voice:

"Tell your father to stay out of it."

"What?"

"Your father doesn't understand what's happened. He needs to mind himself."

"I think he just wants to help."

"Does your father know what it's like to be a woman? Do you think you know what it's like to be a woman?"

With this, she slid inside the covers and turned away from him. He stood in the near dark with his mouth slightly agape. The barreling of Bear's truck down the driveway slowly filled the room with a strange release.

Bits of falling snow stung at Ted's hot flesh as he walked towards the truck. Liza came running at him; he scooped her in his arms and held her close.

"Hey, Peanut. What do you have there? A Happy Meal toy?"

She flashed a bright green dinosaur wearing a suave smile and dark sunglasses.

"She's a beauty," her father said.

"It's not a girl, Dad, it's a little boy."

Bear secured some gear in the truck's cab by banging things around before waddling over to them.

"Boy, you sure did teach that little one to hate fishing," he said wide-eyed.

"I told you," Ted said, putting Liza down.

"Wouldn't even go near the Goddamn pond," said Bear.

"Dad, she's a nine-year-old girl."

"I know what she is, but she's a Mallows first and foremost—should be in her blood."

They both stared at the girl who worked on flipping the dinosaur's sunglasses up and down.

"So what'd she do the whole time?"

"Ah, Charlie had a couple of cats she took to."

Ted propped up Liza's chin, massaging the smooth skin with his fingers.

"Peanut, what do you say we go looking for Bailey?"

She was still focused on her toy, which gave Ted enough time to stifle Bear's upcoming offer with a staunch expression.

"Liza, you want to go look for your dog?" he asked again.

When she rolled her eyes upward, they paused at her father's tilted expression of love and concern, and found something beyond him. Ted turned around to where the girl was looking, and was taken aback to see his wife's silhouette in a barely lighted bedroom window. She was peering out from the angle of the curtains, watching the three of them under the snowfall.

"Peanut, do you want to look for your dog," he asked a third time, looking back at the child.

"Well, someone's feeling better," said Bear, looking at the motionless figure in the window.

"Liza," Ted said, trying to shake the girl loose from her daze.

"She'll be up and at 'em in no time," Bear went on.

Ted called his daughter again. And when he shook her a second time, she broke free, throwing the dinosaur into the snow. Before he caught his voice, she darted past the both of them, and ran towards the fishing pond.

"Liza!" Ted called after her, turning back to the house.

"Little firecracker," Bear said.

The light in the bedroom window had vanished; the curtains were closed. And through the dizzying snowfall, Ted knew he needed to warn his daughter about the holes in the pond, but he didn't. For some reason, he couldn't keep his eyes from staring up at the second story of the house, which was all pitched in blackness. And even though he squinted through the storm and the dark, it was impossible for him to determine—as though it were somehow important—where exactly that light had come from just moments before.

My goal back then was to write a cryptic story about a quietly divided family. And there had to be a specter-like female figure, and a male protagonist who has an impossible time understanding her. The character of Dorri is drawn in a very elusive way, probably to reflect what little I knew about my own mother. Ted seems an amalgam of both me and my father; reserved and content on the one hand, blasted in the face by ever confusing fate on the other.

I like the title of the story. It's simple, yet effective. And obviously metaphorical. The story is all about missing pieces. There's the miscarriage and the lost dog and the inability to reconcile with any of it. All the characters have experienced a loss of sorts, but no one has the wherewithal to open up in any meaningful way. I have no idea what happened to that dog; it seems as mysterious and impalpable as parts of my past do. It's hardly a wonderful story. But it's not a complete disaster, either.

If "A Missing Dog Story" was my initiation, then the next seven or eight stories I would write served as basic training. Some are better than others. All were conceived on the spot and finished in a matter of a few days. They have titles like "A Burnt Lawn Story," "A Cheap Diamond Story," and "A Reckless Child Story." My simplicity in titling became an absurd source of pride. I saw some luck when "A Burnt Lawn Story" was accepted by an unknown literary magazine called Pigskin Press. The story focuses on two feuding neighbors, Pete and Gil. Gil is an amputee, having lost a leg as a child; yet his maltreatment of everybody in his life, including his neighbor, Pete, prevents him from evoking sympathy. The story ends when Gil sets fire to Pete's lawn and ends up burning his house down.

Most of my male protagonists are extremists; often searching for some lost, inscrutable piece of themselves, they are brazen and uncompromising. Nothing about them can be easily defined; not their pasts or their relationships or even what they're after. They were all created in bursts of stubborn contemplation over my own father and grandfather and how I might resemble them.

Besides the staff at Pigskin Press—as well as their meager fan base—no one has ever read any of these stories. Except for Nana. She read them all. When she would be just a few pages into one of them, she would turn to me with dire concern in her eyes.

"Questro ragazzo e una cattiva notizia, Marcus," she would say.

I would agree with her that my main character *was* in fact bad news. Then I would let her finish the story, studying her reactions, which often ranged from amused to stupefied.

"Come pensate di questa roba?"

"It comes from up here," I would say, pointing to my head. "Imagination."

I never had the energy to tell her the origin of my male characters. Yet she was no dummy, so it's likely that she knew.

It didn't take long for me to get cocky and think I could write something longer. Something with greater scope than a short story, which I foolishly believed I outgrew. So I decided to write a novel. The idea for my Bill Walker story seemed fresh and vital and worth exploring. After crudely outlining a few chapters, I plunged into the thing with full force. I was inspired by the newness of my task, the interplay between myself and the blank page, the constant, turbulent hopefulness that comes from contemplating the pristine, wide open spaces of a brand new world.

I was all alone with my pride and enthusiasm. It's the kind of loneliness you can get used to; and you can use it to foster your own ego or to make excuses for bad behavior. The writer, I believe, must convince himself that he is doing something remarkable, that he is spending his time wisely, that the new friends he is creating will never desert him and will always be thankful for their immortality.

My Bill Walker story is about a conman. I thought nothing of this when I first began the book. The premise, as well as Bill Walker himself, interested me enough to preclude any type of deep analysis. Whatever research was required was done in my own head. This seemed both thrilling and dangerous. But in a controlled way. After all, it was only a story.

My thoughts now on the book have evolved; I can't help but wonder how much of me is in Bill and how much of Bill is in me. The thought is both disturbing and intriguing. And though it's not clear as to how or when I will find out the answers, I'm certain I'm well on my way.

* * *

The Jersey incident has forced Joanna and me into a strange new world. A quieter world. A world with forced sentimentality and overarching gloom. It's as though we're now actors reading scripts written for some foreign species. Though we're still on speaking terms, Joanna's voice has softened to the point of absurdity. I can barely hear her when she asks me to start the barbeque or put the clothes in the dryer. She'll often look away from me when she speaks, pretending, unconvincingly, that she's misplaced something.

It's always on the tip of my tongue to apologize and denounce my edict of not wanting to have a second child. The speech is somewhat worked out in my mind; it's short and humbling. We'll be doing the dishes together or tucking Cole into bed, and I'll open my mouth and summon the words, but nothing happens. My brain must sense the danger in such a proposition. It must know, probably in the way every other part of me knows, that especially after my last visit with Dr. Stewart, it's simply never going to happen.

After work one night, Blanch and I head to the bar. It's Wednesday, the third day of Owen McAllister's suspension for the bathroom graffiti incident, and Blanch tells me we have to celebrate the occasion.

"You fucking married guys are all the same," he says as we get high in his truck. "Selfish, selfish, selfish. You got the weight of the fucking world on your shoulders, and you're pissy that no one's there to help you lift some of it. Why should we? It's forever yours to bump and grind with, baby."

All this because of an offhanded comment I made about Joanna's disdain for marijuana. Blanch is perceptive; I'll give him that. My response is to shrug off his comment and ask him to get me more weed. I find that it does wonders for my migraines, so I decide to self-medicate.

"How expensive is it?"

"Don't worry about the money."

The following day, Blanch enters my room during my planning period and tosses me one of those small cylindrical film containers filled to the top with misshapen clumps of dull olive green weed that is spiked with streaks of brown. I insist on paying for it, but he tells me to forget about it.

"The fact that I'm able to corrupt you is payment enough."

"You have no idea," I tell him.

Once school ends, I stick the weed in my glove compartment before driving to the police station. The grayish brick building, located just a few exits north of East Stonyfield, appears cold and gothic-like. After being buzzed in, I state my business through an intercom. I'm then told to wait in a small vestibule that has a handful of red plastic chairs and disorderly bulletin boards. No one else is waiting. I take a seat and close my eyes and put my head into my hands. The lights in the place are bright and loud.

After about fifteen minutes, an officer appears and asks me again how I may be helped. His name is Jarvis and he is clean shaven and broad shouldered.

"I'm looking for Officer Walsh."

"What's this in reference to?"

"Please tell him that Marcus DiMatteo is here."

He leaves the vestibule and I end up waiting another fifteen minutes. When the door finally swings open again, Officer Walsh appears. He's talking on his phone in a hushed voice. When he sees me, his expression changes a little. It goes from a sort of casual grace to a more masculine one. When I smile, he doesn't smile back.

Rising from my seat, I stand motionless, tugging at my clothes, pretending to smooth wrinkles. Walsh continues to talk on the phone. He eventually turns his back on me to continue his conversation. It's impossible to hear what he's saying. When he quietly finishes, he hangs up and greets me with a handshake. Then he ushers me past a series of cubicles where cops sit at computers and drink coffee and do idle paperwork.

Walsh leads me into a small office with his name on the door. There's a computer desk covered with water bottles and manuals and stacks of papers. Against the wall is a rickety metal shelf that barely clears the ceiling. It's stocked with books and piles of loose manila folders and a handful of athletic trophies. Clearing a chair, Walsh invites me to sit. He then walks behind his desk and picks up a nearly empty water bottle.

"How's the teaching business?"

"Wonderful," I said, taking a seat.

"Can I get you anything?"

"I'm okay."

"Pardon the mess."

He's still standing. Looking at me with forced friendliness for a moment, he takes a slow sip from the water bottle before placing it on his desk next to a picture of a little girl.

"Your daughter?" I said, motioning to the photo.

"Chloe. She's five."

I nod.

"I hear you've withdrawn your little boy from daycare."

"Yeah."

"We had some routine follow-up questions there," he said, "about a week ago. We were informed by the owner that your son is no longer an attendee."

"That's right."

"What a shame. It seems like a nice place."

"For peace of mind, really."

This makes him nod his head.

"How's that weather outside? I've been cooped up in here all day."

"Sunny. Pretty mild."

"I was thinking about doing some fishing later."

I don't bother responding to this.

After a few moments of quiet, Walsh asks what brought me to his office.

"Why are you speaking to my employer?"

Walking over to the door, he gently closes it.

"I'm not at liberty to discuss that with you?"

"I think a line has been crossed."

"I assure you that it has not."

He laughs to himself when he says this.

"What do you hope to accomplish?"

"A clearer picture. That's all. It's very simple."

"A clearer picture of *what*?"

Walsh leans against the wall behind his desk. Cocking his head some, he bites his bottom lip.

"Police work has a lot of blurry spots. We're simply trying to isolate them and give them clarity."

"But you must admit that some spots will remain blurry despite the best efforts to make them otherwise."

"Absolutely. But I like to think that most of us know when there's potential."

"Potential for what?"

"Potential to clarify something."

He looks at me with a slowly widening grin.

"Maybe I romanticize my profession a bit too much," he says. "My wife will attest to that. And maybe I've seen *Serpico* one too many times. But the best that I can tell you, Mr. DiMatteo, is that I am doing my job."

Opening the door to his office, Walsh tells me he will see me out. I follow him to the vestibule where I waited moments earlier. There is a heavyset woman sitting in one of the red chairs. At her feet is a carseat with a sleeping infant. Officer Walsh smiles at them both. Then he shakes my hand and ushers me outside.

"Thanks for stopping by."

"Please don't contact my employer again."

Walsh tosses his head back at my comment. Then he braces himself for what he says next:

"You want all of this to go away. And I understand that. But it's not going to. It's not. You should realize that right now. And think about it on the drive home. Think about what that really means. It's disturbing me: this thing we've been talking about. And perhaps I've made it more personal than it needs to be, but I'm okay with that. Because the bottom line is this: I don't believe you. And I'm going to pursue this. Now, even I don't fully know what that means yet. And though the stakes may not be very high, and we're not talking about jail time, we are talking about some type of disruption to your life as you know it. And even though you seem like a normal guy—family, good job—I have no misgivings about taking things to another level. Because I can see beyond the normal guy thing, which, really, must be a façade to some degree. I'm not saying you're batshit crazy—though you could be for all I know—but to do something like what I think you did, well, there's something going on. So as I said earlier, there's potential to clarify some things. And I'll stop once they're clarified."

When he's through talking, he looks up to admire the sky. It's clear and sunny.

"Hell, I'll be fishing later for sure," he said, turning to head back into the building.

"Officer Walsh," I said, seized by an impulse to say something, anything. "Would you rather be good or lucky?"

He answers without missing a beat:

"I'd rather be *right*. But like I told you, I might have seen *Serpico* one too many times."

The five days without Owen McAllister are blissful. My anxiety level is markedly lower. Even the other students in my class appear happier, less inhibited. The rumor of his suspension spreads quickly. There are many versions to the story. They're all amusing. It's difficult to not grin when I hear the details distorted. One version has him spray painting anti-Semitic slurs in the boys' bathroom; another has him vandalizing Dan Zinser's car. It would be false to say I feel bad about what's happened.

On the last day of the suspension, I'm visited by two women who introduce themselves as Owen's parents. With visitor passes draped around their necks, they find me at the end of the day in my classroom grading quizzes. Their names are Trish and Danielle. Trish is tall and sinewy; her auburn colored hair is pulled tight into a ponytail, revealing a pleasant face spangled with brown freckles. Danielle is short and fit. With dark framed glasses resting atop a pierced and peaked nose, she has the appearance of a bohemian college professor. She's holding a brown paper bag, which she places on one of the student desks.

"Are you available to talk?" Trish asks.

"Sure."

"We've heard a lot about you from Owen. He enjoys your class."

"I'm speechless."

"It's true."

Danielle glances around the room while Trish and I talk. She studies the posters of James Baldwin and Eugene O'Neil hanging behind my desk; and the quotes from Kafka and Emerson and Dickinson that adorn the upper part of the dry-erase board; and the student projects on *The Crucible* that have been hanging since the fall on the bulletin board by the door.

"I'm embarrassed that the school year is nearly over and we're just now meeting," said Trish.

"Don't apologize," said Danielle.

She says this barely above a whisper. Trish, turning to her spouse, says she is not apologizing; she is simply concerned about her son.

"We're *both* concerned about him," said Danielle.

Trish takes a deep breath and looks at me and smiles.

"We know Owen can be a handful," said Trish.

"We're not what you might call a couple of clueless dykes," said Danielle. "That's what she's trying to say."

Trish cups her face into her hands and takes another deep breath. I let out a little laugh. Trish seems at ease when I show that I'm not offended. Danielle seems emboldened. She continues:

"That being said, Owen did not deserve to be suspended. He can certainly be a little asshole, but he's an honest asshole."

"You'll have to take that up with our vice principal," I said.

"We did," said Danielle.

Trish explains. Dan summoned them to his office to discuss a graffiti incident that occurred exactly one week ago on the previous Friday in one of the boys' bathrooms. It was reported that Owen's English teacher was tipped off by another student who claimed he saw Owen leaving the bathroom with a Sharpie marker in his hand. Dan, therefore, had no choice but to suspend Owen for the standard five days. Their son, when confronted with the charge, vehemently denied it.

"It's his word against some nameless, faceless student," Danielle said.

"I suppose it is."

"That's it?" said Danielle. "That's the best you can do to placate a couple of lesbians?"

"I'm not sure what else you'd like me to say."

Trish chimes in; perhaps, she reasons, I was upset with Owen last Friday; upset over the contents of his Steinbeck presentation, as well as his flippancy when we spoke of it.

"Revenge?" I said, surprising myself with the use of this word. "You're suggesting I sought revenge against your son?"

"Is it possible?" Trish asks.

I find myself suddenly staring at the brown paper bag, considering its contents.

"Anything is possible, Mrs. McAllister," I said. "But the truth is I was only reporting information I was given."

"By this nameless, faceless student."

"Yes, by this nameless, faceless student."

The two women look at one another. Then Danielle picks up the paper bag and offers it to me. Trish says it's a gift from their greenhouse. Peeling open the bag reveals a generous bunch of deep red tomatoes still connected to their vines.

"These are beautiful. Thank you."

"Do you have children?"

"A son. He'll be three this summer."

Trish looks to Danielle who seems to balk for a moment. She adjusts her glasses before inviting me and my family to their home for supper tomorrow evening.

"We've already spoken to Owen about it," Trish said. "He's all for it."

"Really?"

"We all agree it would be a nice way towards a fresh start."

Trish asks me not to answer, but to think about it. She tears off part of the paper bag and swipes a pen from my desk. Writing down their address and phone number, she apologizes for the short notice and says there will be no hard feelings if I'm a no-show. Owen, she adds, is a bit timid about coming back to school.

"We think this will help."

Trish shakes my hand. Danielle does not. When they leave my classroom, I sit at my desk for a few moments, rubbing my temples and breathing in the musky, athletic smell the two women have left behind.

I am regretful the moment I tell Joanna about the McAllister's and their dinner invite. I must have been desperate for conversation with her. She perks up and remarks how it's a noble offer and asks where they live and what we should bring.

"I think it's a conflict of interest. I teach their son."

"So what."

"So, I don't really want to break bread with him."

"It might be interesting."

"How so?"

"You're a writer. A gay couple with a troubled teenage son. That sounds like something."

It might have been that she called me a writer, something I would have sworn was lost on her, or that she was attempting to be good-natured. Either way, I agree to go. I even offer to whip up my hot crab dip for the occasion.

The McAllister's house is a modest, yellow clapboard Cape set far back from Brickyard Drive, a woodsy and rural part of town. An immaculate standalone greenhouse sits on the eastern part of the property. It's filled with stacked tiers of brightly colored potted plants. In a makeshift carport made out of poles and green

151

tarpaulins is a primer gray Mercedes station wagon up on blocks. The vehicle looks like it might be from the early 1960s. Engine parts and tires are strewn about. Cole likes the look of the car and asks if we can take it for a drive.

Trish answers the door; she is wearing coveralls over a black concert t-shirt. Smiling at us, she takes the crab dip from me and invites us inside. The house smells of cooking. A Johnny Cash tune is coming from surround sound speakers. Sleeping on an overstuffed leather chair is an obese calico cat with mottled brown and white fur. Joanna remarks how lovely their home is. Trish thanks her and then apologizes for her own appearance.

"I was gardening earlier and lost track of time," she said. "Owen's napping. He always sleeps around this time. He'll be up any minute."

We follow her into a spacious and sunny kitchen where Danielle is drinking a beer and stirring a pot on the stove. Looking past me, she welcomes Cole and Joanna.

"Smells wonderful," said Joanna.

"It's seafood bisque," said Danielle.

Trish gets Joanna and me a beer, and Cole a juice box. We stand around in the kitchen for a while and discuss their home and greenhouse and the 1960 Mercedes Danielle tells us she has been restoring for close to three years. Trish asks Joanna if Cole might like to see Sundance, their lazy cat. The three of them head into the other room, leaving me and Danielle alone. She checks on some bread in the oven and takes a sip of her beer.

"You do most of the cooking?" I said.

"What do you mean?"

"You seem like you know what you're doing."

"We don't have roles around here. We're versatile dykes. True, I can bake bread. But I can also overhaul the drivetrain on a 1960 Mercedes. And take Trish. She can frolic in the garden with as much femininity as she can muster. But she can also execute more moves than I can count that will put an absolute end to someone."

My speechlessness causes her to explain. Trish served in the Army for more than a decade. For close to three years, she was

152

stationed in Belgium. And besides learning a little Dutch and French, she became involved in martial arts. Her instructor was an American ex-patriot named R.W. Standard. R.W. had been overseas for years and made his living by teaching Shotokan Karate to interested military personnel. Trish signed up and became a natural. Not to mention one of Standard's prized pupils.

It didn't take long for Standard to offer Trish a new opportunity. So one evening, after a bout of particularly brutal sparring, he showed her a controversial video called *Black Medicine*. Featuring Peyton Quinn and Mike Haynack, two renowned black belts, the film is essentially a tutorial on how to kill someone with nothing more than bare hands. Trish was riveted. The grace of the two men. The simplicity of their moves. The sheer violence of the art form. This was dangerous stuff. And though perhaps not terribly practical, Trish wanted to learn. Aware of the difficulty women faced in distinguishing themselves in the military, she regarded the new discipline as something by which to make a name.

Just then, Owen walks into the room. I'd nearly forgotten I was in his house, talking to one of his mothers, the bitter, sarcastic one, who is telling me one hell of a story. Owen's hair is messy and he rubs his eyes as he looks at the floor in front of him. The outfit he is wearing, black basketball shorts and a maroon University of Southern California t-shirt, is wrinkled and baggy. Fumbling with my beer for a second, I manage to put it on the counter and shake his hand. Yawning, he asks Danielle about dinner.

"I was just telling Mr. DiMatteo how your mom is a real badass."

"You're obsessed with that story," he said.

"It's a good story," she said.

"I agree," I said.

This makes Danielle smirk a little at Owen. Then she turns to me and picks up where she left off, telling me how it would be an understatement to say that Trish excelled at the deadly combat, which she mastered in a matter of months.

"Impressive," I said.

"Fucking unprecedented is what it is," Danielle said.

Just then, Trish walks into the kitchen, Joanna and Cole following close behind.

"I don't like that word," said Trish, motioning to Cole, who's oblivious to the expletive.

Danielle tells Trish she was bragging about her.

"It's true," I said, picking up Cole who runs into my arms.

"Wonderful," said Trish, "but the language."

"What kind of moves can you execute?" I said.

Danielle, not missing a beat, tells me that Trish can break nearly any bone in her opponent's body, drop them unconscious to the ground, or even shut off the blood to the brain. This makes the room go quiet for a moment. The only sound is the slight hissing from the pot on the stove. I turn to Joanna; her nervous grin straddles the line between politeness and horror. Another moment of silence goes by before Cole, in his sweetest little boy voice, full of harmonious reserve and recklessness, announces that he's hungry.

The seafood bisque is exceptional. I have a second helping—as well as a few more beers. Joanna kicks me under the table, probably fearful that I'll become intoxicated in front of my own student. But I want the evening to continue. For some reason, I find myself fascinated with Trish and her time in Belgium. More specifically, I suppose, I'm interested in hearing about her martial arts training. So I ply her with questions. At first she's modest, but she ends up relenting. She seems to like the attention. Joanna, meanwhile, looks on with disinterest as she argues with Cole about eating the hotdog barbequed for him. It pleases me that she's annoyed. Probably because she's the one who wanted to come to the McAllister's, and also because I don't have to fake my enthusiasm over my conversation with our host. As for Owen, he's busy hitting up Danielle for money she's reluctant to give.

Trish tells me about the difference between mass and velocity when delivering a blow. She talks about breaking the clavicle and tearing tendons. Chopping at the carotid artery, she tells me, can lower blood pressure to the brain and cause an eventual blackout.

"Maybe this isn't the best dinner conversation," she says sheepishly, looking in Joanna's direction.

"She doesn't care," I said.

Forcing a weak smile, Joanna turns to Owen and asks if he enjoys high school. He says he does. Then she asks if he plays sports. He says he does not.

"He used to play soccer when he was little," said Danielle. "I keep telling him to get back into it."

"I hated it," he said.

"You did not hate it," Trish said.

When there's a lull in the conversation, I ask Trish if she could show me some of her moves. Joanna lightly scoffs. Not loud enough for everyone to hear. But loud enough for me to hear. My interpretation of this is that she doesn't regard me as much of an athlete. Which I'm not. With the exception of Little League for a few years when I was a young boy, I've never played an organized sport in my life. Picking up Cole's fork, she begins to bargain with him once again over his hotdog.

"Absolutely," said Trish.

"Great."

"I have a dojo in the basement."

"Great."

Danielle, with perhaps too much ebullience in her tone, suggests we go right now.

"Great," I said, standing up.

Joanna puts her hand on my arm and tells me to first let my food digest. I tell her I'm fine. Danielle tells Joanna not to worry, that Trish will go easy on me. Then she looks at Cole and asks if he wants to see the Mercedes she's got up on blocks in the yard.

Trish's dojo is a cold, bright, windowed space with interlocking blue mats on the floor, and large, clean mirrors affixed to the surrounding walls. There's a black punching bag hanging in a corner and a large rack of dumbbells against a far wall. Adhered with tiny suction cups to one of the mirrors are four framed certificates embossed with gold stamps. They indicate that Trish is a third degree black-belt.

We take our shoes off and get to work. Trish asks me to steady the punching bag while she demonstrates some techniques. With

155

deft power and precision, she simulates an open hand strike to the throat. Then a heel of palm blow under the chin. Then a vertical fist to the nose and a back fist to the temple and a hammer-fist to the clavicle. This last move, she says, is her favorite. I make a joke that I would like to use these moves on a few of my students. Her demeanor has transformed since dinner. Terse and straight-faced, she's as focused as some hunter stalking its prey. My attempt at humor is therefore ignored.

We abandon the bag and Trish uses me as a fight dummy, demonstrating the same techniques. Her hands are warm and calloused. There are traces of dirt running through the lines in her fingertips. I can smell the raw, clean earth in her sweat, which begins to bead up at her temple.

"Your turn," she says.

A bit self-consciously, I do what she tells me. Without being too didactic, she corrects me a few times. When I perform well, she lets me know. Her praise is modest. Still laconic and austere, she is clearly in her haven.

"I can see why you like this," I said. "It's very empowering."

"That's exactly what it is."

She suggests we do one last technique before heading upstairs to meet the others.

"Punch me," she says, positioning me a few feet from her.

"For real?"

"Don't get all macho on me."

"You want me to punch you?"

"I do."

I know she wants my best, so I don't bother with some limp, half-assed attempt; I practically wind up before coming at her with a fist aimed just between her eyes. Barely blinking, she sweeps my arm away from her, counters with a controlled chop to my neck, and takes me down hard. Looming above me, she grins a little, breaking for the first time the intensity she has shown since entering this place. My hand is in her grip as she applies a pressure point that makes me wince.

"This is the opportune time to bargain with your opponent,"

she said. "Because you know they aren't going anywhere."

"I guess so."

Taking a deep breath, she continues to look at me. Neither of us says a word. She suddenly eases the pressure, but continues to hold my hand in hers.

"So let's bargain," she says.

"What do you mean?"

"We're okay with a little revenge in this family. I know how that sounds, but it's true. Call us old fashioned. The only caveat is that you get one shot at it and then it's over with. You took your shot. Now get back to the business of teaching my son."

For dessert, Danielle has made organic banana bread. Cole has a piece while Joanna and I each have a cup of decaf.

"You made it out alive," Danielle says to me as we all take a seat.

"I did."

"How was it?"

"Humbling."

"I'll bet."

Trish says nothing. It suddenly dawns on me that this entire evening might have been a ruse. A ploy to put me in my place and let me know I have been warned. Danielle leans towards me and clears her throat a little. Then she whispers low enough for just me to hear:

"She doesn't fuck around."

The drive home is as I figured it would be. Joanna fires off a litany of complaints about the evening, but is careful to not address me directly. She wishes to vent, but only while keeping her distance. Danielle, she says, is foul-mouthed and arrogant; Trish is a neglectful parent and a man hater; as for Owen, well, he is quite obviously the product of two obnoxious, destructive parents. As I listen to her rant, all I can think about is how she was right to convince me to go. She said it would be an interesting evening, and it was certainly that.

The sun is starting to set. Cole announces to us that he's tired. With one hand on the wheel, I turn around and grab hold of his little foot, which I shake in my hand. He simply stares at me, which means he's too weary to even smile.

"Please watch the road," Joanna said, finally breaking down to talk to me.

As she says this, something catches the corner of my eye. It's bright yellow and has slid out from underneath my seat, now resting in plain view on the floor behind me. It takes a few seconds for me to realize that it's the book Dr. Stewart gave me. Turning back to face the road, I wrap my arm behind my seat and try to conceal the damn thing. Joanna admonishes me once more for being distracted. She's right to do so as I'm veering into the oncoming lane. I don't relent, though, until I manage to slide the book out of view.

Calmness suddenly washes over me. My wife takes a deep breath. The gorgeous sun is mountainous against the horizon; its inspiration is splayed out in streaks of red ribbon over the vast, clean, crystal sky. When I look in the rearview mirror, Cole is asleep. The delicious fat in his face gives way to gravity and he looks chubbier than he really is. Nudging Joanna, I motion for her to look at our son, which she does. This causes her to smile a little. Without thinking, I put my hand on her leg, where it stays for the rest of the drive back home.

By the time I get Cole into his bed, Joanna has already washed up and is turning in for the night.

"Some dinner party, huh?" I said.

"If you could call it that?"

"I'm glad we went."

Scoffing, she puts her hair up in a ponytail. Then she removes a bottle of hand cream from her nightstand drawer and squeezes some into her palm.

"I'm glad you enjoyed yourself."

Her voice contains that typical end of the week exhaustion, though perhaps with an additional trace of irony. It sounds artificial to me. And alien as well. I search her face for some familiar sign and notice that she suddenly looks twice her age. Still, I manage a smile, which she doesn't even see, as she is pretending to read the label of the hand cream. Then, because I need a way to send her off to bed in a puzzled state, I announce that I'm interested in studying martial arts. When she looks up at me, a dour, unblinking expression plastered across her face, I smile again. This time she sees it.

With the house now to myself, I set up at the kitchen table to do a little writing. A development in my Bill Walker novel is that I've heeded Callie's advice by renaming my protagonist William. And as homage to my teenage past, I've changed Tess' name to Enid. As for plot development, Enid was able to entice William to drink some of her pomegranate vodka the night she visited him with importunities to play "Recuerdos de la Alhambra." Always vowing he would abstain from any vice that might impair judgment—especially alcohol—William broke down after Enid struck a deal with him: She would leave him be, deferring her request that he serenade her, if he would have a drink or two with her. A drink or two turned into the rest of the bottle; William woke the following morning with cotton mouth and an unreal hangover. Enid, of course, was nowhere in sight. It was only when William pulled himself together that he realized some of his future works were missing from his place. An epic poem called *Paradise Lost*; another called *Howl*; two oil paintings, "Nighthawks" and "The Drinker"; and a novel called *To the Lighthouse*. The original artists' names had already been removed from these. This was the only saving grace.

A frantic search proved fruitless. What William did find, adhered to the empty vodka bottle that was a centerpiece in the middle of his kitchen table, was a handwritten note from Enid. It read, *"I enjoyed our night together. I'll be in touch, but you probably figured as much. PS: Your talents are undeniable. I'd like to think that mine are as well."*

This is where I'm stalled. It's not clear to me what happens next to William. Does he search for Enid and demand she return to him what she clearly stole? Does he put it out of mind and dismiss the girl as some benign fanatic? One thing is clear to me: William Walker's conscience must begin to burden him. His imagination must be rampant, conjuring thoughts about getting caught and being exposed and humiliated and destroyed. So I start with this:

The twilight was devastating in its coarse and surreal beauty. It loomed above the earth, crouched, majestic, in prayer, waiting with might and fierce glowing fury to electrify the brand new day. William watched it from his bedroom window, where he stood, clad in only his underwear, gazing out with more apprehension than he was used to. He gave himself an exercise: describe the twilight in a few words, something unique and lyrical. Something befitting an artist. Running his hand across his bare chest, he smiled over the inane challenge. Soon he cleared his head and he focused. Barely blinking, he became fixated on the horizon, his eyes piercing through a few bruise colored clouds that hovered in a slow pulsing monotony above distant roofs and treetops. After a minute, he opened his mouth and produced three words:

"Ghost faced twilight."

His immediate response was that he was pleased with himself. This seemed like a unique turn of phrase. Though an inaccuracy—the twilight on this morning was not at all ashen or haunting like a ghost—it nevertheless struck him as a good little bit of imagery. Then, as quickly as the words fell from his tongue, he began to doubt their merit. By the time he said them over and over in his head, he grew to hate them. They seemed generic and possibly cliché. Even overly dramatic.

He tried again. This time he didn't think so hard. Maybe his instincts were well honed. Maybe there was not such a vast chasm between him and someone like Anton Chekhov. Maybe he would surprise himself. It was just possible that he too could produce original thoughts that were awe-inspiring. Groping at the sides of his head as if to shake the words loose, William braced himself before uttering the only thing that came to him:

"Open faced twilight."

This had a nearly blank effect on him at first. He had no opinion on it. Other than it sounded very similar to "ghost faced twilight." Reality soon set in. This was even worse than "ghost faced twilight." It was not only derivative of that, but it was entirely meaningless. Hell, it sounded like something off a deli menu.

William was no artist. This was plain to see. He laughed in spite of himself. Laughed in embarrassment, secretly wishing this wonderfully humbling gesture would free him of the tremendous burden he had imposed upon himself. But it wasn't that simple. He didn't just impose it upon himself; he smothered himself in it, defining his very existence with impossibly high standards, becoming alien to his community, untouchable and idolized, solitarily stuffed into a warm one-man chrysalis.

There hadn't previously been time for such thoughts. The demands put on any man who has a stranglehold on an entire industry or proposition are vast. William was busy living the life of an artist. This meant traveling and late nights and acts of philanthropy and dedications of his works to wealthy patrons. It meant he barely had the time to consider the prospects of his fate. So these thoughts he was now having were new; thoughts on his reputation and his safety and of where he might be in a year or three or five. And the sensation of such new thoughts came over William Walker in a dizzying assault.

"How long, how long, how long? How long can this go on?"

He sang these words in disgust, pulling with both hands at his flattened, thinning hair. After throwing on a pair of grey pants and a black v-neck t-shirt, William splashed cold water on his face, brushed his teeth, and went for a drive. It was a mostly overcast October morning with a warm breeze whipping up and down the desolate back roads. The sky, pale and powerless, looked like the unfurled flag of some foreign nation that had recently surrendered.

"Fucking twilight," William said aloud. "There it is! That's the phrasing I was looking for: fucking twilight!"

A man was jogging too close to the middle of the road. William slowed and crept around him. Without looking, the man put a limp hand in the air as a thank you. A young couple was pushing a baby stroller on the sidewalk. Neither of them was smiling. The town looked washed out to William. Its blue collar people lacked any kind of ambition that went beyond simple survival or getting the most out of their modest paychecks. The houses, medium sized clapboard Colonials with mossy shutters and crumbling walkways, were mostly hand-me-downs; they were bestowed from parents and grandparents, who holed up in one of the remote bedrooms until they died and the place was willed to the next in line.

When he broke through as a success, he thought about moving. But there was no such thing as an artistic hub. It was wherever he was. So he remained in New Jersey, in this beleaguered industrial town, and hated it.

The slate gray marble sign for the W.B.W. Institute of Sound and Vision was still on backorder; it was being customized by a sculptor in Brussels who had a reputation for not only being truculent, but for being an absolute perfectionist. The proprietors of the Institute, a Mr. Guest and a Mr. Larson, two young entrepreneurs from New York City, claimed the sign would finally be shipped by the end of the week.

The Institute would not open its doors for another few hours. This was a good time for William to visit. It had become something of a routine for him. With his own key, presented to him by the town with enough fanfare and champagne to overwhelm royalty, he would enter the building and roam the place by himself, awestruck by the gravity of this elaborate thing he had manufactured. Listening to recordings by Thelonious Monk and John McLaughlin, reading excerpts of works by Hawthorne and Kerouac, studying paintings by Monet and Dali, William would end up laughing to himself. But it was forced laughter. The obligatory kind that attempts to distract the mind and prevent the conscience from flaring up.

When he reached the front entrance, he found that the door was unlocked. Walking into the vestibule, William came face to face with his oversized portrait, an ostensibly candid photo of him sitting at a large oak desk and looking slightly off in one direction. It was taken by a local photographer named Lillian Knight. Underneath the frame was a short bio engraved on a glossy sterling strip that was adhered to the wall. The photo had been a source of contention between William and his backers, Guest and Larson; they felt it was more fitting for the Institute to boast a self-portrait of the artist, painted in any one of his celebrated styles. Walker, for obvious reasons, refused; yet he made sure to denounce the proposition as tasteless and self-involved. So it was he who found and hired Knight, arranged a fee and location, and even hung the picture himself.

"Anyone here?" he said, stepping into the common area, which was lined with red leather sofas and polished glass cubes that were coffee tables.

The air conditioning was on and the place was cold and dark.

"Hello," he called, his voice echoing off the acoustic tiles.

Walking into the Poems room, William flipped on the lights and strode around. There were mazes of thick glass display cases with original handwritten manuscripts he had painstakingly copied; there were autographed collections of verse; and there was even a kiosk of commercially available copies for sale to the public. On a far wall, in enormous black decals, were the words "Poetry is the supreme fiction..." This was copped from Wallace Stevens' "A High-Toned Old Christian Woman."

As he now summoned the energy to find amusement in this dark comedy, he suddenly heard footsteps. They were quite a ways away, but they were fast approaching. William decided they were the footsteps of a man. They were just heavy and steady enough to suggest this. William stayed put. And as he listened to this person close in the distance between them, he mindlessly read a short Emily Dickinson poem that had garnered him some mixed attention from religious pundits:

Faith is a fine invention
For gentlemen who see;
But microscopes are prudent
In an emergency!

It was one of those poems whose straightforwardness was evident. Nothing too complicated. About faith. Clever and sardonic. Then, as though the words could immediately morph into some dense, blackened matter, the poem would become a foreign object, a figment born out of some wild and grotesque confusion. It was this latter reaction that now struck William; he honestly had no idea what to make of the poem he had referred to in its only public reading as "A studied exercise in the controlled miracle of brevity." Even this was nebulous to him. He began to perspire.

Just as the absurdity of this thing began its awful chant in his eardrums, a man walked into the Poems room and stared dumbly at William. He was over six feet tall and had dark, moon shaped eyes. Slender and handsome, he looked like an early twentieth-century matador.

"Franco," William said, "how are you?"

"Mr. Walker, is everything okay?"

Franco was wearing a pair of khaki colored pants and a white t-shirt. Both were speckled with yellow and red and blue paint. He was shoeless;

therefore, his eyes, probably in embarrassment, stared down at the floor every few seconds.

"I have a key," said William, pulling it from his pocket and holding it in the air.

"I understand, sir."

"I didn't think anyone would be here."

"We open in a few hours," Franco said, regarding his watch.

The two men looked at each other. William was focused on the speckles of paint on the docent's clothing.

"Be assured, sir, that I will change my clothes before opening the doors."

"I'm sure you will."

Franco revealed a slight boyish smile.

"We finally found appropriate places to hang 'American Gothic' and 'The Singing Butler.' I think you will be pleased."

"Wonderful."

Franco started to say something, but suddenly stopped himself. Then he took a step closer to one of the display cases. Noticing a smudge on the glass, he used his shirt to clean it.

"This is one of my favorites," he said.

Then he read an e.e. cummings poem:

i like my body when it is with your
body. It is so quite new a thing.
Muscles better and nerves more.
i like your body. i like what it does,
i like its hows. i like to feel the spine
of your body and its bones, and the trembling
-firm-smooth ness and which i will
again and again and again
kiss, i like kissing this and that of you,
i like, slowly stroking the, shocking fuzz
of your electric fur, and what-it-is comes
over parting flesh...And eyes big love-crumbs,
and possibly i like the thrill
of under me you so quite new

"Very erotic," Franco said.

"I suppose."

"Is there a muse behind this one?"

Almost immediately, Franco looked to his bare feet.

"I hope you'll beg my pardon for asking, sir," he said. "I didn't mean to pry."

"It's fine. All part of your job, I suppose. It was written for a young lady I used to know many years ago when I was a younger man."

"She was beautiful?"

"Very much so."

Franco opened his mouth and tried to speak. No words came initially. But after some time, he found them:

"May I show you something, sir? If you have a moment."

He led William out of the Poems room, through the common area, down the hall past the Fiction and Paintings rooms, to a door that was adjacent to Franco's small office. It was a supply closet, probably 10x8, lined with shelves stocked with bottles of blue cleaner, paper towels, and neatly stacked cardboard boxes. In the middle of the closet, a white bed sheet was splayed out on the floor. An easel holding a linen canvas stood upright on its center. Paintbrushes, razorblades, and a palate of paints were strewn across a beat up barrel the young man was using as a work station. Empty cups of coffee were overturned and scattered on the floor and around a tiny black mesh garbage can in the corner of the room.

But the centerpiece of the tiny, windowless closet was the image painted upon that linen canvas. It was an explosion of yellows and reds and blues that made up a striking portrait of a rain slicked street at night; there was a two-story building in the foreground of the painting, and a man was atop, his back turned, smoking a cigarette and looking off into the horizon. The details were exceptional. From the illumination of the streetlamp to the beads of rainwater on the ground to the wisps of cigarette smoke circling the man's head.

"It's a work in progress," Franco said.

William walked towards the easel. He didn't know what to say. He *suddenly noticed a blanket in the corner of the room.*

"Have you been sleeping here?" William asked.

The young man looked again towards his feet. He muttered something about working late nights and being too tired to drive to his apartment, which was over forty-five minutes away.

"It's fine," William said, picking up one of the razorblades and studying the crusts of dried red paint at its tip.

He complimented Franco on his painting. This made the young man beam. A dam suddenly burst. Franco began to talk excitedly. He told William how he loved being a docent in the museum. William's work, he said, was a tremendous source of inspiration. He was also quite lonely, he confided, since leaving his family, who were in Cadaques, which was on the outskirts of Barcelona. So he tried his hand at painting. And writing. And he was even interested in playing the guitar.

William was only half listening. He heard some of what the young man was saying. A few choice words stuck out. Words like "fiancée" and "opportunity" and "America." The truth was that he couldn't get over that painting. It was quite a thing to see. And he had some questions to ask the young man. Questions that were banging around his head that he couldn't quite get a hold of at the moment. And one of them, though perhaps not terribly important, was what exactly was that razorblade used for?

By the time I stop writing, it's close to 1:00 a.m. I fix myself a bowl of cereal and read over what I've written. It's surprising to me to see how much I've developed the character of Franco. His initial purpose was simple and almost secondary: to show how a museum has been dedicated to displaying all of William's work. Someone, naturally, had to work at this museum. It was my intention to give him only a few scenes, showing the awe he felt over William's work. Something ended up taking me in a different direction. An instinct must have told me that Enid, in all her mystifying beauty, is not enough of an obstacle for William. So now there's Franco, the humble and handsome docent who knows William's work and seeks to emulate it, perhaps giving him a little competition.

As thrilling as this new direction is to me, what's even more thrilling is to see how William will handle it. Will he immediately succumb to jealously and insecurity? Will he initially embrace the young man and then sabotage him? Will he begrudgingly pass the torch to the ambitious upstart and then fade away into obscurity? As these thoughts pass through my head, I find myself musing over the same notion over which my main character mused. The razorblade.

It seems to have come out of nowhere. Why did I choose to mention it on three separate occasions, even ending the scene with it? It's true that I've witnessed my own wife use a razorblade not only to clean paint from a brush or pencil or canvas, but to paint with as well. This is a method called sgraffito; it's an ancient European technique that multi-layers paint before scratching out a design. This stuck with me for some reason or another. And its appearance in my book now appears portentous—and its purpose obvious. It will be used as a murder weapon.

Smoothing over my brand new pages, I put them with the others before turning in for the night. Joanna is asleep on her side. Climbing into bed, I curl my arms around her before pulling myself towards her. After a slight stir, she awakens, opening her eyes and greeting me in a dreamy haze. I kiss the tip of her nose. This makes her smile. Just then, something seizes me, some profound need to celebrate, to boast, to be generous and affectionate. I have no misgivings about the cause for all of this. It's the writing I've done. It's made me feel the way I envision all men should feel when they're full and satisfied.

"You were right," I whisper to Joanna, who's on the verge of sleep once again.

She shushes me; then she shifts her body a bit to one side.

"It's true," I said, this time louder. "You were right. I can admit it."

She suddenly opens her eyes.

"About having a second child," I said. "You were right."

This makes her sit up in bed. In the dark, she looks bewitched. Beautiful, but bewitched. Her hair and her skin and her eyes all look shades darker. Her lips tremble a bit, but she says nothing. After a moment she throws her arms around me and begins to sob. I don't feel guilty for what I've said. I feel so goddamn good right now that the least I can do for my wife is to make her feel this good, too.

Chapter 7: The Letter

"His lies were so exquisite I almost wept."
- Dave Eggers

One of the saddest things about my father being gone is that we'll never have the chance to commiserate over something I know must have been dear to him. Guilt. Just the guilt he felt over my mother's death had to have been a lifetime supply. Add to that the guilt he felt over having to raise me alone. And for never giving me a sibling. For his drinking binges. For sending me to Jersey all those summers.

It seems fitting that he was an attorney. I always pictured him feeling at home in a courtroom. Being in a place where guilt was discussed and denied and revealed must have made him seem like an avatar to whatever sin and secrets he worked to expose. And in that way, he could somehow come to terms with it all and learn to live with it.

This all came to a head at a holiday parade during my sophomore year of high school. It was mid-December and the town had gathered on the green for its annual lightshow and caroling. Though I had attended the parade in the past, sometimes with friends, sometimes alone, this marked the first time my father and I had come together. Since he had recently cleaned up his act—his drinking was mostly under control and his spirits had improved—he was making a conscious effort to be the father he thought he ought to be. This meant he was adamant about having dinner together every night; and instituting a strict curfew; and teaching me how to drive on the weekends.

It was a bitter evening. Snow had fallen during the day and the air was still heavy with its chill. Downtown shop windows were illuminated with strings of clear and colored bulbs; people lined both sides of the street, huddling against the cold, sipping coffee and hot chocolate, watching as Santa and Mrs. Claus waved from a makeshift float atop a gleaming red fire truck. Cheerleaders from my high school, clad in their spirited yellow and black leggings and sweaters, marched in procession, chanting fight songs that promised to defeat the basketball team's rival they would face the following night.

Just then, the slurred ramblings of a stranger grew louder and closer. The man they were coming from—we learned later that his name was Russ Frey—had sidled up alongside a woman standing behind us. What began as boisterous, drunken comments, aimed at no one in particular, grew into racy overtures directed at the cheerleaders, the woman next to him, and any other female within earshot. My father and I turned around on a number of occasions to get a look at the offender. Probably in his late twenties, he was over six feet tall with sunken cheekbones and a broad, flat nose.

Aware that we were irritated over his antics, he moved next to us and began clearing his throat very loudly. Before long, he took to widening his eyes and snapping his head forward like a chicken. My father saluted the man before escorting me across the street. Without hesitation, the man followed us, announcing his presence by singing some out of tune nonsense in a strident, nasally voice.

We set ourselves up in front of Heaven on Earth, the frozen yogurt store, and the man did the same, leaning towards us, smiling his gnarled smile, and occasionally spiting globs of phlegm inches from our boots. My father sighed. Probably he was inured to the boredom and bullshit of such a character after years of lawyerly dealings.

With his hand on my back, my father began to usher me down the sidewalk. Sure enough, the man followed, this time calling out to us:

"What's the matter?" he said. "Where you goin'?"

We continued to walk, my father chuckling in disbelief over the man's perseverance. The elementary school choir, lined up in neat tiers in front of the firehouse, began to sing "Holy Night."

"It's rude to walk away when someone's talking to you," the

man said. "Where's your Christmas spirit?"

My father began musing about what a prick this guy was; he was dignified enough, though, to keep it to himself.

"Did you hear me? I said where's your fucking Christmas spirit?"

This stopped my father in his tracks. Since his hand was guiding me as we walked, my momentum ended at once as I jerked backwards in a clumsy involuntary motion. He wheeled to face this Neanderthal. With as convivial a tone as he could muster, he told the man that he was here with his son, trying to enjoy the parade and he didn't want any trouble. Unmoved, the man said something about parades being for pussies. My father, not bothering to comment on the absurd irony of such a statement, agreed. This made me laugh.

"You think your old man's a fucking comedian?"

"Okay," my father said, stepping towards the man, his curt tone gathering the attention of a few passersby. "I think that's enough. Why don't you go home and sleep it off."

With slow deliberation, the man cocked his head upwards as though he were surveying some rare eclipse; then he said something that took the entire exchange, from absurd beginning to absurd climax, to a new height:

"Why don't *you* go home and suck off your son, fuck face."

This pulled the switch, turning my father into an automaton. I witnessed nothing on his part that resembled thought. His brain must have foregone all it knew while his body picked up the slack. Rushing towards the man at a breakneck speed, his right arm swung with the reckless force of a wild bird. He connected, hitting him in the ugly bull's-eye that was his broad, flat nose. The sound it made was like one of those clapboards film directors sometimes use when they are calling for action. The blow immediately sent the man off his feet and onto the ground. Blood spurted from his nose and covered his face in a matter of seconds.

An older couple who had been standing a few feet away hurried over to the melee. The woman fished for some Kleenex in her purse while her husband checked on my father, who was pacing the sidewalk, muttering to himself and holding his fist inside his hand. I heard the husband say that he knew the man had been asking for it. When I looked over at the man lying on the ground, I saw the wife remove a blue scarf from her neck and use it as a tourniquet. Within a few moments, two police officers were on the scene; they arrived on foot from down the way where they had been directing traffic and acting as sentinels to the blocked off front street. After clearing the area, they went to work taking statements, radioing other officers, and applying first aid.

A crowd had gathered, including some of my friends; they were impressed when they learned what had happened. We watched together as my father was questioned by the officers; he was calm and apologetic, all the while still holding that clenched fist of his like it was some precious, fragile artifact. With a distracted smile and slightly puffy eyes, he looked over at me a few times. Because I didn't know what else to do, I gave him a thumbs-up.

The man whose nose he had shattered turned out to be a New Hampshire resident. His name was Russ Frey; he was visiting his brother for the holidays. When the inevitable question of pressing charges arose, the man, who was now on his feet, holding the mass of gauze and cotton to his face, didn't hesitate in saying yes, he would absolutely like to press charges. With his head elevated, and through bared teeth, he taunted my father, assuring him he would take him for all he was worth.

A few onlookers chimed in on my father's behalf; they said the man was intoxicated and looking for trouble. My father, who didn't bother mentioning to the police that he was an attorney, accepted the consequences. The arresting officer, to his credit, did attempt to dissuade Mr. Frey from pressing charges. To no avail. So in front of his own son, he was handcuffed and led down the street towards a squad car. I was given permission to accompany him to the station. As we walked together through processions of our own townspeople, my father turned to me, his hands chained behind his back, a slight and bewildered grin on his face.

"What do you think of the parade so far?" he asked.

My father's arrest made the paper. Not the headlines by any

means, but the local patch. This did not cause a blight on the DiMatteo name. We were not made into pariahs; nor were we scorned by the community. If anything, I believe it elevated us. My father, known for being fair and mild mannered, developed a cult following once his story spread. Not that people came out of the woodwork—they certainly did not—but more than a few neighbors and local businessmen, as well as my own peers, made comments about his gravitas, likening him to a pseudo vigilante.

His colleagues teased him about the episode, which ended up being resolved out of court. I remember answering the phone once to the blaring hollers of Elvis singing "Jailhouse Rock." When I asked who was calling, a man's voice, one I had heard before, laughed and asked to speak with my father. It turned out to be his partner and friend, Myles Dickinson, a bawdy man who my father assured me was anything but malevolent.

Home life was something else altogether. I wouldn't say it was strained, but it did become more of a fragile enterprise. A stone-like smile could often be seen on my father's face for months after his arrest. It was a carefully affixed expression, precarious even, always appearing as though it might at any moment morph into something sinister. There's no doubt he was learning to cope with a new type of anxiety and humiliation. And in typical fashion to the men of his generation, he did this by himself.

"We're not going to tell your grandparents about what happened," he said to me a day or two after the incident. "Promise me."

Of course I promised him. And we dealt with it together, which meant we either joked or brooded about it on occasion, and always with a healthy dose of incredulity. And the matter, like so many others that stop you dead in your tracks and incite a moderate existential crisis, eventually receded into the past.

Because my father never presented himself as being infallible to me, I never experienced that moment of shock every child has when they learn their parent is mortal and imperfect. Not that this dawned on me as a fifteen year old boy. But I can distinctly remember appreciating back then that his arrest didn't cause an earthquake in our lives.

"I fucked up," he told me one night over pancakes at a diner in town. "What else is there to say?"

His journals, however, reveal that he did in fact have a bit more to say on the matter.

This is one he wrote a couple days into the new year that winter —just a few weeks after his arrest:

Dear Marcus,

I've been cleaning a lot lately. Very strange. And I'm not talking about a little Windex and some light vacuuming, either. I'm talking about deep down to the bone and marrow kind of cleaning. Today I polished all the door stops in the house. Then I counted them to see how many there are. There are fourteen. I also wiped down the cover to every book on the shelves in the family room. Then I counted the goddamn books. There are two-hundred-and-twenty-three in case you're interested. I swept out the basement and set ant traps; I consolidated the linen closets after scrubbing them down and replacing the shelf liner.

There are worse ways I suppose I could spend my time. The truth is that cleaning, for some reason, has proven a nice little catharsis for me. I like the immediacy of the before and after. I like knowing that I was a catalyst for some type of progress. This sounds like the babbling nonsense of a mental patient, doesn't it? Someday, my son, when you are faced with the insurmountable burden of having to always consider what you look like in your child's eyes, you will also be a proponent of manufactured progress.

And I'm not talking about physical appearance. I'm talking about actions and reactions; I'm talking about priorities and responsibilities. There should be mirrors and cameras installed in the home of every parent. They should be fixed to the ceilings and walls of every room in the house. This way we might get some feedback on the job we're doing. Because we sure can't count on the feedback we get from you. You're

either too hard on us or too goddamn easy.
    Love,
    Dad

This next one was written in the middle of January, days after the previous entry:

Dear Marcus,
    As absurd as it sounds, I've been eavesdropping on your phone calls lately. You might be in your room or in the study, talking to someone—usually it's a girl—and I'm crouched against the door, cupping my ear, holding my breath, listening intently while you talk about those same things I talked about when I was your age.
    It's pathetic. I can't even tell you what I expect to hear. There's a part of me, I suppose, that thinks you'll be discussing the arrest. Then I'll learn your true thoughts about what happened. Clearly I'm flattering myself. We both know you have matters of greater importance in your life than my middle-age fuckups. But still, I keep telling myself you're harboring some complicated feelings about what happened. Sure, we've acknowledged the incident a few times, remarking on the injustice and the absurdity; hell, we've even joked about it. But those are all polite substitutes, aren't they?
    I can't imagine a guiltier enterprise than fatherhood. It's full of more self-doubt and self-loathing than anything I know. I even vacillate on how fathering should be done. It should be improvised—done on the spot, by instinct alone; no, it should be carefully orchestrated, followed according to a meticulously laid out plan. No, it should be improvised...
    In my darkest hours I thank God your mother isn't around to see me in such a perplexed state. My confidence, believe it or not, is what attracted her to me. In my lightest hours I am grateful for being able to write these journals to you; they have, in a way, been my community service.
    Love,
    Dad

* * *

Avoiding real grownup guilt is about as likely as avoiding bad dreams. It can be repressed for a time, but I imagine its potency is too strong to be truly subverted. So I don't fight it when it comes. I simply let it take hold and bully me around until I can talk myself out of having any kind of memory. This often takes a long time. And memory, goddamn it, always returns.

Joanna's mood over my late night revelation about wanting a second child is inspiring. It turns out to be a perfect companion to the breathy, sunlit spring. There's an air of renewal in our lives. She suddenly starts wearing pretty cotton dresses each day, and putting her hair up in simple ponytails tied with clips adorned with decorative pink roses. Dragging her easel onto the front lawn, she begins painting outside, something she hasn't done in years.

"Your daddy is looking so handsome today," she will often say to Cole.

To my astonishment, all logistics about this up-and-coming pregnancy are negated. Timetables and finances and baby names. She will have none of it. The order of every day is joyful spontaneity. All this means is good food, good talk, good sex, and unlimited optimism for our future together.

Joanna, in an act of earnest naiveté, tells me we have to ride out the remaining five weeks of her Depo-Provera, the quarterly injected birth control she's been taking since Cole was born.

"That's fine," I assure her. "We're in no rush."

"Speak for yourself," she said, wide-eyed and giddy.

"Let's not tell Cole about this," I said. "Not yet. It might be premature for him to know."

Without so much as a pause, Joanna agrees. The boy's questions on the matter, she adds, might be enough to drive us mad.

Getting my wife's hopes up, I reason, is good for all of us. In the wake of Nana's passing, there's a need to topple the gloom that has begun to tower above my family. Something had to be done. An act of resuscitation. A way to restore harmony. This is what I keep telling myself. But because such pep talks are hardly enough, I find I need to keep especially busy. So I call Trish one Monday morning from school and ask if I may stop by after work.

"I don't meditate or do yoga," I said, "and since my son was born, I'm not reading as much as I used to."

"You're looking for something to ground you," Trish said.

"Yes."

"Something both spiritual and empowering."

"Yes."

"Something that offers maybe a little excitement."

"Exactly."

I insist upon paying her. She doesn't argue. After settling on a price and time, I ask what I consider an important question:

"Will Danielle be there?"

"No."

It turns out that a question I forgot to ask is whether or not Owen will be. This occurs to me when he walks into my last period class, reminding me of his existence. Since returning after his suspension, he keeps a low profile, which includes staying the hell away from me.

He is of course at his house when I arrive an hour later. Answering the door in his dirty bare feet, clutching a handful of potato chips, Owen seems primed for my appearance. With an expression of epic boredom somehow turning his face into something more handsome than I remember it, he invites me inside. Barely speaking, he motions to the basement door before resuming his position at the kitchen table where an open bag of Lay's and an iPad await him. I mutter something about how funny it is that we saw one another just a short while ago. Nodding with a mouthful of chips, he agrees. As I descend the basement stairs, I hear Owen in his well-honed insincerity tell me not to hurt myself.

During the hour workout, there's nothing initiated in the way of small talk between Trish and me. We work the entire time, me listening and asking a few questions, her demonstrating techniques by using my body as her dummy. With a confident and booming voice, she proves to be a fine teacher. Explanations are given on what Trish calls the two elements of power: mass and velocity. We do a candle drill, which consists of snapping a crisp punch at a candle in attempt to extinguish it. She goes over the delicacy of the human hand. She shows me the body's pressure points and vulnerable areas, as well as how to relax my mind and muscles with breathing exercises. With the exception of a short water break, we never stop.

"When can I come back?"

Trish says she's available most weekdays. Wiping my forehead with my tie as I put it on again, I ask about the following afternoon. Then I remove some of Nana's cash from my pocket and offer it to her. Taking the money from me, she says the following day will be fine.

"Bring a change of clothes this time—and a towel. That looks like a nice Father's Day tie."

When she walks me upstairs, Owen is gone, replaced by Danielle, who's watching a small TV on the counter and cutting red and yellow peppers into thin strips.

"Survive all right?" she asks.

"I think so," I said.

Trish comments that I did just fine.

"We'll see if he comes back a second time," Danielle said, deftly removing the stem from a new yellow pepper.

"I will only if you promise to be here," I said.

My comment is met with silence at first. Then Danielle lays the knife next to the cutting board and turns to Trish:

"Owen never told us about his sarcastic side," she said. "What do you think?"

"I like it," Trish said.

On my drive home, a thought occurs to me: What would Nana think about me spending part of my inheritance money towards learning how to disable a man by kicking the inside of his knee and tearing at his ligaments?

My muscles ache from the workout, but that doesn't stop me from going the following day. As well as the next and the next. There's a brief department meeting on Thursday, so I take that day off, but I go on Friday. Blanch is disappointed when I tell him I can't go drinking with him.

"You're turning into a real candyass these days," he tells me. "It's Friday night."

"What can I say?"

"And don't think I don't see your ass sneaking out of here early everyday. Ballsy move."

"So am I ballsy or am I a candyass? I can't be both."

Thinking on this for a moment, he rolls his eyes and walks away. He's right about me leaving work early. All teachers are required to stay forty-five minutes beyond their last class—I've been staying about ten to fifteen. This is just enough time to let the procession of school busses exit the campus. Since there are no assigned parking spots, I've changed mine to the rear lot. Sneaking down the back staircase near the greenhouse, I end up outside where I walk across a courtyard to my car. It's true that I have to circle the building, which means driving past the line of windows to the main office, but my sudden surge of adrenaline precludes me from considering whatever ridiculous consequences there might be.

When I return home that Friday, Joanna has cleaned out the entire house. Six overstuffed black trash bags sit in a neat row on the driveway. Cole is across the street being looked after by the Sandstrom girl.

"You wouldn't believe the junk this family accumulates," she said, greeting me with a kiss on the lips.

Every window in the house is open; a gentle breeze from outside pushes the curtains around in a slow, circular motion. A new bunch of bright wildflowers stand tall in a vase on the kitchen island; Bonnie Raitt is pouring through the surround sound speakers.

"You're really getting into this whole spring thing, aren't you?" I said.

Joanna tells me about her day. She cleaned all morning and organized all afternoon. Thank God for Cole's marathon nap, she said; this is what allowed her to be so productive. Closets and drawers and bookcases in every room were subject to being purged. Floors were mopped; windows washed. What began as a simple list soon turned into a story:

"I had just begun making my yard sale pile when all of a sudden a police car pulls into the driveway."

If I was a casual listener before, she now has my full attention.

"I thought maybe the neighbors had complained about the music."

She goes on, her expression animated with wide, bright eyes. Watching from the living room window, she saw an officer sit in his vehicle for some time before climbing out and heading to the front door where she greeted him.

""You must be Mrs. DiMatteo,' he says. This is the first thing out of his mouth. And he looks a bit intense. So the panic really sets in at that moment. Guess what comes to mind right away? School shooting. There's been a school shooting and Marcus has been killed."

"Jesus."

"I know."

She's not talking fast enough. So I motion with my hands for her to continue.

"Then he introduces himself."

She suddenly pauses and her expression changes to a sly sexiness as though she was just complimented on her looks.

"And?"

"And it was your friend, Officer Walsh."

"My friend Officer Walsh."

I repeat the words with a soft and robotic finesse like they are some brand new mantra whose effectiveness I am testing.

"He was looking for *you*, naturally."

Teasing follows. Joanna says she thinks it's cute that I have a new friend. And that summer is coming, which is the perfect time for a sleepover. She asks if I was ever able to play with Walsh's firearm.

"Did he say what he wanted?"

"I think just to say hello."

"How long did he stay?"

"I didn't know when you'd be home," she said, "but I invited him inside and told him he could wait awhile."

"And?"

"And so he waited inside."

"For how long?"

"Twenty minutes or so."

As casual as I'm being, the questions I'm asking have to seem suspicious. Walsh, however, must have done one hell of a job selling the idea of this friendship because Joanna doesn't skip a beat. Walsh came into the house, she said, and they drank some iced tea. And they talked.

"What did you talk about?"

"You."

"Me?"

"He has a lot of respect for teachers," she said. "He said you two hit it off when you first met—that you've been out for coffee, and that you even met up at his precinct."

What she says next is inevitable:

"How come you never told me about your new friend?"

My struggle to respond must seem endearing because Joanna smiles as she fixes her hair a little. Cole and the Sandstrom girl suddenly enter the house. Cole begins calling out for his mother. Answering that we are in the kitchen, she begins making her way towards him. As she brushes by me, she touches my face.

"Don't worry," she said, "I'll be able to see the two of you in action together next weekend, you and your new cop buddy."

"How so?"

With a triumphant ring in her voice, she tells me that Walsh, in all his thoughtfulness, has invited our family out on his new boat next Saturday.

"He's a boat guy," she said. "So you better foster this friendship."

Taking a seat at the kitchen table, I am again without a response. One week. I have one week to think about this get together with Officer Walsh. Then, in a voice of tender mockery, Joanna kills me with what she says next:

"No pressure."

* * *

It's during cafeteria duty in the middle of the following Tuesday that Dan tracks me down. Rich Gilson, the AP Calculus teacher, is convincing me to take up golf when Dan interrupts us.

"Mr. DiMatteo, we need to talk."

"Sure."

As I motion to follow him out of the cafeteria, he remarks that we will speak at the end of the day. Smoothing his crisp white shirt and yellow tie, he tells me to find him in his office after last period.

"So I guess you'll need to cancel whatever you had planned after school today," he said.

The rest of the day drags. Naturally. Dan's bullshit threat hangs over me like a lazy, useless fog. After calling Trish to let her know I'll be late, I find Dan in his office. Standing at a large dry erase board, he's at work on next year's faculty schedule.

"Close the door," he said.

Taking a seat, I watch him for a few moments as he stands, his back towards me, and works out a conflict in the Tech. Ed. department. The room is quiet and stuffy. As I wait for him to finish, I gaze out the window onto the track where the girls' team is stretching in orderly rows.

"You're going for broke this year," he said. "Do you know that? You got the police looking into you; you got your custodian friend covering your classes; you got more absences than some of our kids; and now this business of leaving early everyday."

Laughing a little to himself, he remarks how he and I are really getting to know one another lately.

"And yet I feel like you're the most mysterious guy in the building," he said, taking a seat across from me. "But we'll get to that part in a bit. First, I want to make myself clear about this leaving early business. It's not to happen again."

I nod my head.

"You are by no means entitled to any type of special treatment around here. The sooner you get that in your head, the sooner these...*behaviors*...might change."

On the spot, without any preconceived plan, my decision is to remain silent throughout the meeting. Dan, who loves to pontificate, will be all too pleased to hold court the entire time.

"I've always been suspicious of people who are generally well liked," he said. "I'm not sure why. It might be my general sense of paranoia; I don't know. Like their smile and their charm is a ruse for something else—something darker that lurks beneath the façade. Gwen calls me a cynic, but I'm unfazed by it. Gwen's my wife."

My attention shifts for a moment to the girls outside Dan's window. They have begun to run laps around the track.

"And you, I suppose, are pretty well liked. Your peers like you; your students like you; your students' parents like you. This may be convenient. It helps make the days go by with a sense of ease and purpose. But we both know it's bullshit. It's not real. It's based on perception, not reality. I'm learning the reality."

A blonde girl I recognize from a study hall I had last year has a wide lead over the others. Alicia or Andrea is her name. Her strides are graceful and she's exciting to watch.

"I, on the other hand, am not terribly well liked. I know that. And I'm okay with it. It goes with the job. But I'm all here. What you see is what you get."

The Alicia or Andrea girl has a sizeable lead. Her closest teammate is a good hundred meters behind. The rest of the girls, with their limbs pumping and their ponytails swaying to their own rhythms, run in a unified cluster.

"But by all means, enjoy being well liked. I mean that. Enjoy it. I'm sure as hell not going to blow your cover. This thing will be between you and me. Whatever *this thing* is—this mystery you carry around in your back pocket. But just know that every time I look at you, even though I don't have all the details, I'm still aware. I'm aware that you have some ridiculous secret. You, Mr. Nice-guy. Right? Whoever you are."

Some girls are now walking their warm-up laps. Others appear to be slowing down and on the verge of walking. The Alicia or

Andrea girl has lapped a few and continues to go strong. When Dan stands, I do the same. He walks me to the door.

"This secret of yours...don't flatter yourself that I give a shit. Because I don't. But I *have* thought about it. I went through all the usual fare: drinking and gambling and what have you. And the biggie, too. An affair. I imagined you cheating on that poor wife of yours with some slutty barfly you met one night with your pathetic janitor friend. And the more I thought about it, the less I found that I cared. A general lack of curiosity when it comes to certain matters: Maybe that's a character flaw on my part. Who knows?"

As I step out of Dan's office, I move past the secretaries to a window that looks out onto the track. And I continue watching that Alicia or Andrea girl run circles around her peers. It's not so much the effortless way she defeats them that reassures me, but rather the independence she seems to exude in every stroke of her body's engine. I wonder if she inspires or disgusts her teammates. It's no matter. For now I'll just stand there in my school's main office and admire this young, naïve thing from afar.

Walsh greets us at the Sea Star Marina at 10:00 a.m. It's a place I've driven by for years and never thought twice about. Chloe, Walsh's blonde haired little girl, is aboard their boat playing with a collection of Barbie dolls. She announces to my family in a sweet Disney voice that she is five years old. Juliet, Walsh's wife, is just returning with bagels, juice, and coffee. She is slim and pleasant and has the same big green eyes as her daughter. Introductions are made before boarding *Go West*, Walsh's new 30' Sea Ray, and setting out into the waters.

The sky is a clean blue canvas with a flawless blazing sun perched high in its corner. The ocean air is cool and tastes like early morning rain. After thirty minutes of heading due south, Walsh anchors the boat in still water, talking his way through the process.

"Let me give you the tour," he said, chewing on a bagel.

With boyish enthusiasm, he ushers us around, pointing out what has recently been updated or replaced on the nine year old boat. All new stainless appliances in the kitchen. A new toilet and shower in the head. Refurbished seat cushions on the messdeck. The list goes on. Juliet, who has been making a pitcher of Bloody Marys, teases her husband, calling him a kid in a candy store. Walsh smiles and agrees. Joanna seizes the moment by thanking our hosts for inviting us. They tell her it's their pleasure. When I say nothing, Joanna nudges me in the arm.

"Yeah, this is great," I said. "Thank you."

Walsh, nodding ever so slightly, seems pleased over the influence my wife has over me.

"Let's drink up," says Juliet, passing each of us a tall stemmed plastic goblet filled to the brim with Bloody Mary. "It's Saturday. And it's gorgeous out here. To my man-child and his big expensive toy."

"I'll drink to that," Walsh says.

We all raise our drinks. Joanna adds a brief coda to the toast:

"To new friends."

Walsh and I lock eyes as the four of us tip our glasses back and fill our mouths with what ends up being the first of many drinks.

Cole plays nicely with Walsh's daughter. She's a sweet and nurturing little girl who enjoys directing her new companion in a series of adventures. Dolls. Hide and seek. Coloring. While the children occupy themselves, the adults eat and drink. Juliet has moved from Bloody Marys to sangria. With fresh raspberries, orange slices, and wedges of granny smith apple floating in the glass, the concoction is irresistible. And Walsh, donning an apron and chef's hat, cooks up spare ribs and teriyaki chicken and lamb burgers all on a small charcoal grill.

"Never too early for some barbeque," he said.

Joanna, who I can tell is starting to become a little drunk, tells Walsh that her father told her throughout her life to befriend a priest and a cop if possible.

"I'm happy to check one of those off the list," she said.

Besides the fawning nature of her remark, I doubt its sincerity;

never once have I heard my wife or father-in-law utter anything resembling this nonsense. What she says seems almost flirtatious.

"My father-in-law is very old fashioned," I said, not knowing at all if this is really true.

When the wives take their drinks below deck to escape from the sun for a bit, Walsh asks how I'm doing. His face has changed expressions. Gone is the blithe charm of my convivial host; it's replaced with something inscrutable and even menacing.

"This is ridiculous," I said, looking over my shoulder at Cole and Chloe, who are taking turns with a handheld videogame. "What am I doing here?"

"You tell me."

"I haven't the slightest idea."

"I can take you back if you'd like."

"You crossed the line—bringing my wife and son into this."

"Into what exactly?"

"Into this petty fucking game you're playing."

"Is that what I'm doing? Playing a game?"

"You know what I mean."

"Lower your voice."

I sip my sangria. Walsh turns over some of the meat on the barbeque. Juliet calls up to her husband, asking when the food will be ready. He tells her in a few minutes.

"What does your wife know about all this?" I said. "Have you shared your absurd suspicions with her? Is she in on this little subterfuge of yours?"

"Subterfuge?"

"Subterfuge."

"Always the English teacher."

"Is she?"

"Lower your voice."

"Is she?"

"Is she what?"

"Is she putting on a pretense the way you are?"

"She's doing her best, as am I, to entertain our guests."

"You crossed the line. Again."

"You accepted the invitation. Didn't you? I mean, you're here."

"My wife," I said. "She was curious."

"Curious about what?"

My drink is empty. So I begin eating the fruit in the glass. The raspberries are slushy and sour tasting.

"About you and me. About this *friendship* we've cultivated behind her back. She was curious."

"I can understand that."

"This is ridiculous."

"Do you want me to bring you back?"

Joanna suddenly laughs at something Juliet has said. Soon, both women are laughing. Juliet calls up again, asking about the food. Walsh says it will be ready shortly.

"Is my wife down there being judged by a total stranger?" I said. "I need to know if she is."

"I told Juliet I wanted to invite my new friend and his family out on my new boat. Being as social as she is, she welcomed the get-together with open arms. And here we are. But if you'd like me to turn this sloop around and bring you back, say the word."

More talk and laughter from the wives below. Then Cole appears and puts his arms around my waist.

"We'll stay. We'll stay and eat your food and drink your alcohol. We might as well make the best of it, Officer Walsh, because this is the last time you and I are going to see one another."

With this, the women emerge and ask again when we will be eating. Walsh, whose face is once again aglow with the bright embers of hospitality, stammers a bit before announcing that the food is ready and for everyone to grab a plate and fork.

The day wears on in a languid, sun-filled haze. More food. More drink. More pretending. The women sober up enough to take the kids tubing. Walsh breaks out his fishing gear and promises me we will catch some souvenirs for me to take home. Every now and again I find myself lapsing into a state of revelry where I begin to enjoy myself. We would catch a few stripers or bluefish, drink a few beers, and the charade between us would fall to the wayside. Then I would look into the sharp sunlight before rubbing my eyes and suddenly remembering. No sooner would I reassert my polite indifference.

"How's work? The students and your lessons and all that?"

On the verge of answering, I am struck with the image of him and Dan Zinser discussing my character. They might have bonded, I realize, over such a discussion. It might have been had in Dan's office, where Dan would be eager to make Walsh comfortable while he indulged whatever questions were put to him. Walsh would maintain an air of professionalism throughout their meeting; he would let Dan know that he might be in touch in the near future. Dan would repress a grin over such a statement.

"You must be looking forward to summer," he said. "It's right around the corner."

Reeling in my line a bit, I nod my head. Walsh opens a fresh beer.

"Your wife mentioned that the two of you will soon be expanding your family. Congratulations. That's terrific. A playmate for your boy. He'll be thrilled. We had one hell of a time having Chloe, so we are *one and done*, as they say. Neither me or Juliet come from big families, so it's all good."

It's astonishing to me that Walsh has no misgivings about delving into the details of my life. Both personal and professional. Behind my back is one matter, but to discuss them openly with me is another. He knows no boundaries. I find it impossible to believe that the Connecticut State Police has the time to invest in the likes of me. There has to be unsolved crimes of far greater magnitude. Rapes and murders and muggings. For Christ's sake, we aren't living in some rural backwoods county with a population you can fit it in your back pocket and an annual crime rate that barely registers.

"I'll strike a deal with you," Walsh said. "Because I'm feeling inspired. It's a beautiful day. And we're fishing on my new boat. We've got the sunshine and nice cold beer and our children. Tell me what I want to hear. Tell me and I'll put this entire thing to rest right now. I can do that. That will be my part. But I need you to do your part. Tell me what I want to hear."

"Do you have any paper?" I said, struck with a sudden urge to write.

"Paper?"

"And a pen or pencil."

Leaning in to whisper, even though the wives are not within earshot, he tells me he does not need a written confession.

"Do you have the paper?"

After rummaging around the boat, all Walsh can produce is a chewed up blue pen and the brown paper bag the bagels came in.

"This will do."

Excusing myself, I head below deck where the cool, dim light relieves the ache that has begun in my temple. Sitting on the edge of his bed, I begin to write.

Dear Superintendent Freeman,

This is not going to be an easy letter to write. It is, however, imperative that I finally unburden myself and relay to you my gravest concerns regarding a pressing matter of which you need to be apprised. The events I wish to elucidate on pertain to goings on at Louis Sutherland High School during this current academic school year.

If I may, I would first like to express the unwavering devotion I have to my profession as well as to our beloved school district. I entered the teaching profession because I not only enjoy influencing young minds, but I also happen to love my chosen discipline. Put simply, I cannot see myself doing any other line of work. My job suits me and I believe I do it quite well. Being a married man with a family, I cannot imagine any other way of life.

As with any profession, obstacles arise that sometimes prevent one from doing their very best. This is to be expected. A true professional, however, will circumvent those obstacles and prevail with doing their job. I am a firm believer that challenges and hardships are building blocks to a sturdier character. Yet there are obvious limitations as to what a teacher —or anyone for that matter—is expected to endure. Unruly students, yes. Complaining parents, certainly. Fickle changes in educational trends, absolutely. But we can all agree for sure that harassment, bullying, abuse, and threatening of any kind are as intolerable as giving up on our students.

I have reached an impasse this year at LSHS. Though I am a professional, I can no longer cope with the obstacles that have found me. Though I value my job, I can no longer perform it effectively due to the unreasonable circumstances that have become part and parcel of my existence at LSHS. The harassment and bullying, the abuse and threatening I speak of are the impetuses for this letter. Not a day goes by that I am unscathed by what has essentially become a living nightmare.

Before I divulge anything further, I wish to impart to you that I have nothing but respect for the relationship between the superior and subordinate. It's a symbiotic relationship. We largely exist for the purpose of the other. And if the relationship functions the way it should, there's no reason why both parties shouldn't benefit. Conversely, when the superior decides to compromise this paradigm by misusing their power, the bond becomes distorted and fractured.

I am insistent upon imparting to you, as emphatically as I may, that my only intention now is to clear the air and finally bring to light these bothersome events that have plagued me for too long. My aim is not to cause harm upon anyone or make trouble unnecessarily. In writing this letter, Dr. Freeman, I place myself entirely in your hands. That said, I would like to go on record as stating that Dan Zinser, LSHS's Assistant Principal, is the individual about whom I am writing.

I am not quite certain what your relationship is like with Mr. Zinser. As far as my own, it is, in a word, deplorable. During my first few years at LSHS, Mr. Zinser and I had few interactions with one another. There was no need for any. Yet we were cordial when discussing a student and courteous when passing in the halls. Both personally and professionally, we were neither friend nor foe. This dynamic has changed drastically this current school year. It began one day back in February when Mr. Zinser visited me in my classroom during my prep period. He informed me that we needed to discuss a student of mine; I listened as Mr. Zinser voiced what I thought were not terribly pressing concerns. When he finished, he remained in my room, pacing the floor as I tried to get back to work. When I asked him if there was anything else, he said, and I quote, "What did you have in mind?" When I struggled to respond, he moved in closer to me and asked the question again. With as much decorum as I could muster, I told

Mr. Zinser that I only wished to do my work, alone. This immediately angered him; saying nothing, he stormed off in a huff.

A few days passed until the next visit. Mr. Zinser, who was affable and professional, at first, said nothing of our previous meeting. Ostensibly, he wanted to discuss another student. Yet it became clear to me that this was a ruse. Mr. Zinser asked how I usually spent my prep periods. When I told him I spent them working, he informed me that he could suggest better ways to pass the time. I rebuffed his offer and he once again became angry before exiting my room.

This cycle continued for weeks. Gratuitous meetings. Coy innuendos. Hostile departures. At another one of these visits, I suggested to Mr. Zinser that I believed he had no true agenda and was behaving inappropriately. He lost his temper and threatened me with violence. The next day, Mr. Zinser called me to his office at the end of the school day. He said he wished to apologize for his behavior and that he had only been fooling with me. He said I should put the entire matter out of mind. Time went on, and other than faculty meetings and occasionally in the hallways, we saw very little of one another.

This all changed about two weeks ago when he called me to his office once again. It was a Friday, and school had just gotten out. Skipping the façade this time, Mr. Zinser closed and locked his door before drawing the blinds and exposing himself to me. He made a lewd proposition and told me if I didn't appease him that he would, and I quote, "Fuck up my life beyond repair."

There is more to this humiliating saga. But I feel I have exhausted myself with more than enough details for now. I know you will want to meet with me to examine this matter in person. Suffice it to say, I am not ready for this step. This letter took more deliberation than you will ever know. Though I am no martyr, I will nevertheless suffer in silence for a bit longer until I feel ready to seek you out in person. Please be patient with me.

Kind regards.

The letter takes up both sides of the paper from the bagel bag. When I finish, I fold it and rejoin Walsh, who is reeling in a small bluefish.

"Well?" he said.

"Well what?"

"Is that for me?"

The ladies are helping the kids as well as each other out of the water. Walsh looks back and forth between them and me.

"Don't flatter yourself, Officer," I said, stuffing the paper inside my back pocket.

The women and children wrap themselves in towels before joining us. Juliet tells her husband how Joanna is curious about the name of his boat. Walsh, who I'd like to think is recovering from our exchange, takes a while to respond. The name *Go West*, he finally says, is a reminder to himself. His dream is to someday sail to California. Juliet chimes in, telling us that her husband is obsessed with California. Its history and deserts and culture. All of it. He has been, she said, since he lived there for two years after college.

"Is that possible?" Joanna asked. "To sail from coast to coast?"

"Not unless his boat has wings," I said, "to fly over the Rocky Mountains."

"He's right. But there are ways through the Northwest Passage. Canada, basically. So it *can* be done."

I suddenly remember Callie Starz and her own western fantasy. Only she wants to travel by motorcycle, roughing it a bit more than Walsh. For a fleeting moment, I think about announcing to everyone that a scholarly stripper I recently befriended has similar ambitions.

"Well, I think that's a wonderful goal," Joanna said. "And a terrific name for a boat."

"Guess what *she* wanted to name it," Walsh said, pointing to his wife. "Aquaholic."

Juliet slaps his arm and defends herself against the charge, claiming she had been joking. Then she tells us about some of the absurd boat names they've come across over the years. Seas the Day. Miss Behavin.' Wet Dream.

"What did you do out west?" Joanna said, turning to Walsh.

Juliet answers, telling us that her husband worked at California

Correctional Institution, which is a maximum security facility. He was living in Tehachapi, she said, only minutes from the prison.

"Not exactly the romance capital of the west coast," he said. "But I loved it. I was a few hours from Yosemite and Santa Cruz and San Jose."

"And Death Valley," his wife said.

"And Death Valley," Walsh said.

He asks if we can guess the annual average rainfall in Death Valley. I shake my head. Joanna guesses ten inches.

"Two," said Walsh. "Two inches. It's pretty well bone dry there all year round. Barely any rain. And the only recorded snow accumulation goes back to the early 1920s."

"The name of the place is fitting," said Juliet.

"Most of the time it is," Walsh said.

Years ago, he explains, starting in 2004 and ending in 2005, three times the normal amount of rain fell. This caused not only ephemeral lakes, but unprecedented wildflower blooms.

"I think I remember reading something about that," I said.

"I guess it goes to show," Walsh said, "that anything can thrive under different circumstances. Right? Remove something from its usual environs, tend to it with kid gloves, and see if it produces something fruitful. It's almost like being out here, isn't it? All this calm and natural beauty. It's got to change the way we normally behave. Right? Otherwise, well, I don't know—I suppose some are open to it while others just march to their own drummer, as the saying goes."

No one says anything for a moment. Juliet catches me looking at my watch. It's getting late. Our day together is coming to a close. Time to head back to shore. The last thing I say to Walsh is when we're back at the marina. We're alone for a short time as we divvy up the fish we caught.

"I'm not Colonel fucking Kurtz," I said. "And you're not Willard for that matter."

He just stares at me. I don't bother to reveal to him the *Apocalypse Now* reference.

"I have no idea what you're after, and to what end you'll be satisfied, but you are misguided to say the least. I meant what I said before: This is the *last time* you and I are going to see one another."

Before he can respond, I take my share of the fish and walk away. Thanking his wife and little girl for their hospitality, I collect my family and drive home. I overcook the fish on purpose that night. Joanna is upset, but I manage to placate her by ordering a large clam pizza, which is her favorite.

I spend a little time the following day cleaning up the letter I had written to Superintendent Freeman. No major revisions are made. Just a punctuation mark here and there; maybe an occasional change in diction. When I'm happy with it, I type it up, print a copy, and stuff it inside an envelope I make out to Dr. Freeman at Central Office. The letter contains no return address or even a signature.

The next morning I put it in the mailbox and hoist the little red flag. Then I drive to work, trying to picture Dr. Freeman's reaction to what I've written. He's a lanky man with beady eyes and a thin, graying beard. We have few interactions between us. Probably in his late forties, Freeman has only been in district for three years. He keeps a low profile and is tolerated with mild acceptance. I once heard a fellow teacher accuse him of being "cautious to a fault."

Not at all certain on the protocol for such a volatile matter, I can only assume what Freeman's recourse will be. Contact the union lawyer. Maybe its president. Meet with the Board of Ed. Either way, the letter will sure as hell shuffle around his priorities. There's also the matter of the letter's anonymity. Freeman will no doubt run through a list of LSHS's male faculty members, surmising who the poor bastard actually is.

Then there's the possibility that Freeman will cross paths with Dan a day or so after receiving the letter. A visit to the high school. An administrators' meeting at central office. Getting a good look at Dan, Freeman will endure a private battle with himself. The disgust and doubt alone will be enough to distract him to the point where his sleep might even be invaded.

My head begins to throb in the new morning light. It vacillates between feeling like a sieve and a cinderblock. I'm unsure whether it's my health or the chaos I'm about to start with my letter. Either way, I'm seized with an impulse to make a u-turn and head back home.

When I pull up to my house, I can see through the living room window into the kitchen. Joanna is sitting at the table drinking coffee and reading from her iPad. Watching her for a few moments is peaceful. Every so often she will pull her hair behind her ear or take a slow sip from her drink. Other than this, she hardly moves.

My car idles quietly in the street. None of the neighbors are out of their houses yet. Other than Jim Coyle's sprinklers next door and a few hummingbirds overhead, the neighborhood is restful and still. Pulling the car to my mailbox, I retrieve the letter to Dr. Freeman. Then I open it, careful not to tear the envelope, and read it from beginning to end. When I finish, I watch Joanna for another few moments. Her position has shifted a little in her seat, but she's as motionless as she was earlier.

Forcing any type of deliberate thought process out of my mind, I open the glove compartment and find a blue ballpoint pen. Then I sign the letter in my neatest possible print. Sealing it once again, I return it to the mailbox before heading off to work.

Chapter 8: The Forgiveness

"Any fool can tell the truth, but it requires
a man of some sense to know how to lie well."
- Samuel Butler

The truth about my family history is out there somewhere. It's been hiding out for decades, lurking in the shadows of plain sight. It's far too late for me to track it down now. In this age of information, I know I could research it on my own—or pay someone to do it for me. There might be a few worthwhile discoveries. A renegade maiden who helped the slaves escape to the north. A crooked politician who crossed the mob and was never heard from again. The reality is that I've actually lost interest at this point. So I don't know shit about my family history. There are worse things, I suppose.

I didn't grow up with storytellers. My father dealt more in fleeting bursts of nostalgia; this seemed a necessary balm to the many lacerations that accompany raising a child alone. As for my grandparents, who seemed to belie the notion that seniors like to pontificate about the romance and simplicity of some bygone era, they were too busy being proud of me to bother with tales of the past.

So stories went unheard. Not that there weren't countless opportunities for me to have asked for them. There were. But what child or adolescent thinks to take time away from the present, when he is the focus, when he is being assailed with all kinds of positive attention, to ask about the nebulous past? By the time I reached my twenties, it suddenly seemed too late to learn anything useful about my family; I would have been too embarrassed to ask.

My own ignorance, I was convinced, was a sort of punishment for my years of indifference. I used to imagine that everyone I came across had a complete family tree tucked neatly into their back pocket. One replete with interesting and endearing characters. One that obliterated any murky misgivings about identity, and one that offered up a sense of blissful permanence.

As for me, I knew I could always make something up. That is if I chose to do so. Something detailed and believable. Something memorable. I would insist, however, that the story first have a seed of truth in it. This would appease some innate, unexplored sensibility having to do more with ego than conscience.

Take the story of my mother's great-grandfather. All I know about him is that his name was Bartholomew Paxton and he was in the business of devising intricate robbery plans for crime syndicates. In the early 1900s, he devised a scheme to rob a Boston bound train carrying a million dollars worth of pharmaceuticals. The real story goes that he was taken hostage and made to commit the crime himself. Unaccustomed to being on the front line, things went afoul and Bartholomew was gunned down by authorities just outside the Massachusetts state line.

My father learned of this story from my mother who supposedly produced an authentic newspaper clipping from the era. I've never researched it myself or asked for any further details. And though my memory of this man is hardly some well worn charm from my childhood, I've thought of him often through the years. His face has changed very little in my mind's eye. It's narrow and handsome and a bit pale; he wears wire-rimmed glasses and has smooth skin and a slight build.

During the get-to-know-you phase, when conversation is new and sometimes sparse, the story of Bartholomew was brought up to Joanna. Her reaction was mild. More amused than put off, she even tried to match my tale with one about a great uncle of hers who once stole a car and drove it to Canada.

But save that one time, the story of my mother's train robbing great-grandfather was never mentioned. There was no need for such a story. He was a ghost from my distant past, his transgressions and shameful death a receding blemish that held no significance over the present. Yet his very existence, and my knowledge of it, was somehow salient to me. I knew of him not just in name; instead I felt I had some insight into his very lifestyle. Though tragic, and even sort of pathetic, this man, my ancestor, has a story etched firmly in my family's past. That story, however succinct, permits a landslide of rosy-colored daydreams. Not to mention, it begs for embellishments. I like to think that the Boston job was in fact a double-crossing gone terribly wrong. My re-imagined version of the story calls for an entire cast of characters who add dimension to the original tale by humanizing Barth.

So there's Charles Willoughby, the head of the crime family who hired Bartholomew. Willoughby would have fronted an organization that ran their operations throughout the northeast. Gambling, prostitution, racketeering: the usual fare. Willoughby's associate, a man named Frank Buckman, AKA "The Dairy Farmer," was hired to keep tabs on Bartholomew while he devised his plan. Buckman's nickname stemmed from owning a sprawling dairy farm in the Windsor County area of Vermont. The farm, which had been in Buckman's family for over a century, was a suspected gravesite for more than a few law enforcement agents, as well as colleagues, who had been uncooperative through the years.

Sylvia, The Dairy Farmer's younger sister, had a falling out with her brother when her husband, who was rumored to have crossed Buckman, disappeared one New Year's Eve. Though Buckman denied ever having harmed his brother-in-law, Sylvia knew he was responsible. So when she discovered her brother's ties to Barth through an ex-cop she used for recon work, she tracked down and befriended the unsuspecting man, who was just finishing his plans for the train heist.

It was no surprise that Sylvia quickly gained Barth's trust, aided by liberal use of her wit and sex appeal. He had fallen for her in no time. And it was then that the young woman suggested to him a plan of her own: rob the train and keep the merchandise for themselves. Through her dead husband's contacts, she promised, she could easily line up buyers to take the goods off their hands for a fair price.

Bartholomew agreed. Yet on the day of the robbery, things

unraveled. The men who would be doing the actual deed, a man named Huey Pinover and his cousin Rudy, were two of Willoughby's best. The plan Bartholomew had engineered involved a brush fire as subterfuge, a disconnection of the cargo car from the rest of the train, a waiting fleet of rowboats to make off with the goods, and no live firearms. None of this came to fruition.

Instead, things ended in bloodshed and mass confusion. Huey and Rudy were greeted by a sinister crew who threw the two from the moving train just outside of Dorchester; the perpetrators were a degenerate crew Sylvia's ex-cop had hired to usurp the heist. The conductor and two passengers also ended up being killed, all by a barrage of gunfire from the masked, trigger-happy men. The train was then hijacked and the cargo was removed and put into hiding.

Barth, who was waiting at his home for Sylvia to return to him, was seized by Buckman, who beat a confession of the double-crossing out of him. Not to mention Sylvia's whereabouts, which ended up being falsified. It seemed that she had duped Barth, using him for his expertise, and then disappeared. Buckman and Willoughby soon tracked down the young woman, as well as her ex-cop and the rest of their crew. They were holed up in Atlantic City, blowing through stacks of cash they had made from unloading their stolen merchandise. They did not go quietly. A shootout ensued. Two more causalities. A concierge and a nine year old girl. Before the gang's capture, fifteen thousand in cash and buckets of codeine were confiscated.

Rumor has it that Sylvia and her minions were held prisoner and eventually buried alive in a mass grave somewhere on her brother's dairy farm. As for Barth, he was also taken to the farm, where he was made to work like an indentured servant for the better part of a year, all the while being forced to imbibe large amounts of codeine, to which he became addicted. One night, during a half-crazed escape attempt, he was nearly decapitated on a razor sharp barbed-wire fence; he was supposedly buried where he fell.

The details of this story came to me over the years during bouts of make believe. And though I've never shared it with anyone, I know it would kill at a party. I've actually thought on a few separate occasions that I might test it out on my students. Their reaction is tough to gauge. It's a wild tale for sure, but it lacks any link to their beloved modern world. It's a horse and buggy tale, filled with enough prehistoric archetypes to cause a maelstrom of teenage apathy. It's an old western, really. Set in the northeast.

It's a story that seems intended for a mature audience. Maybe even a sophisticated one. It might make one hell of a novel. Or screenplay. Or both. What I have so far seems to be a sort of blueprint. Writing it would be a self-indulgent miracle. It would be a way, however circuitous or fraudulent, to put my family on the map, to resuscitate their legacy in some artful fashion.

But it will never get written. This I know. Not a single word. Nor will anything else for that matter. Not by me. It will be a wonder if I can even finish the story of William Walker. As I approach the end, I find my concentration waning. It seems as though my subconscious has fully accepted William into this life, *my* life, for better or for worse; like there is an awareness that he will be my one and only creation, making his permanence all the more vital.

A gift falls into my lap when I happen upon what could be one of Walker's final works. It's both dramatic and elegiac. And it's as much of an ironic plea as it is a bold mission statement. It's a sonnet by English poet, John Keats:

When I have fears that I may cease to be
Before my pen has glean'd my teeming brain,
Before high-piled books, in charact'ry,
Hold like rich garners the full-ripen'd grain;
When I behold, upon the night's starr'd face,
Huge cloudy symbols of a high romance,
And think that I may never live to trace
Their shadows, with the magic hand of chance;
And when I feel, fair creature of an hour!

That I shall never look upon thee more,
Never have relish in the faery power
Of unreflecting love!—then on the shore
Of the wide world I stand alone, and think
Till Love and Fame to nothingness do sink.

The poem will not necessarily serve as a deliberate eulogy to his career as an artist; its publication will merely indicate a man contemplating the drab reality of endings. It will be a good primer for another work to follow, a longer work, something with a narrative, something that can proudly close out his service and duty as champion poet to the people.

The reason for this departure will be the guilt he feels over his deception. The wellspring of inspiration has been evaporated by his conscience. This might allow for a little redemption on William's part. It seems appropriate that my protagonist have a fall from grace by his own hand. He was responsible for his rise; thus, it seems fitting that he destroy himself as well. As far as his actual fate, I haven't decided if he should die or be killed or just fade away into obscurity.

There's also the matter of Enid and Franco. I have unwittingly created *two* major obstacles for my main character. Franco, the artistic young docent, is envied by William; this alone could put murderous thoughts in his mind. The vileness of carrying out such an act will further punctuate William's downfall. Yet part of me wants Franco to prevail and for William to be killed off. I'm not certain whose death would make the story more tragic.

Enid's fate is just as perplexing. The last role she had in the narrative was when she absconded with some of William's work after a night of heavy drinking. Maybe she inscribes her own name on the pieces she stole and claims them as her own. Or maybe she has discovered William as a fraud and somehow blackmails him. Either way, her return needs to be bold and purposeful.

The Keats poem is one hell of a personal reminder that I'm on borrowed time to think, to write, to live, but I still want natural results each time I put pen to paper. So I won't force it. Life will go on and I will trust that something spectacular will happen to me—something will purr and then roar and I will translate it and it will be mine to capture, until I decide to write it down and hand it over forever.

Jim McArthur always spends his free period in the teacher parking lot, chain smoking in his big red Dodge pickup. The other members of the English department tease him about this as often as we remember to. Smoky. Marlboro Man. These are just a few of the nicknames we call him. Jim, who has a mild temperament, shrugs it off and asks only that we keep his gravesite clean. So it's surprising when he interrupts my class during his free period by asking to speak with me in the hallway.

"Did you hear about what happened?"

Practically out of breath and perspiring a little, Jim is talking in a low voice. A package of cigarettes and a green butane lighter jut out of his breast pocket.

"To your buddy," he says when I respond in confused silence. "You'll never fucking believe it."

All I know about Jim is that he graduated from LSHS himself, probably close to thirty years ago. He has two daughters, one of whom did an internship at the White House last summer. And his wife, Molly or Maggie, had a mastectomy two or three years ago.

"He got arrested," Jim said. "Taken away in cuffs. It happened early this morning. Right here in the building."

"Dan Zinser?" I said.

Just then, Samantha, a pretty but boring girl in my class, pops her head out the door and asks if she can use the restroom. I nod.

"Hank Blanchard," Jim says, his voice loud enough for the girl to hear. "He was hauled away this morning."

"What the hell for?"

"I thought *you* might know."

"Why me?"

Jim shrugs. Then he takes his cigarettes and lighter from his pocket and remarks how we'll find out the cause of the arrest soon enough.

"Sorry to be the bearer of bad news," he says as he fishes a cigarette from the pack before turning and walking down the hall.

I'm on the verge of calling after him that the actual bad news is that it *wasn't* Dan Zinser who was arrested and escorted from the building. It's a good thing I keep quiet since Samantha emerges from the restroom just as I'm about to say this.

By noon, the news of Blanch has spread and it's all everyone is talking about. Even the kids have picked up on the salacious story; this must mark the first time that a custodian has made it onto their radar. But I suppose that's what rigging cameras in the girls' bathrooms will get you. I make a point of asking every colleague I come into contact with whether or not this vile rumor is true. Rene Simonson from World Language. Caleb Snyder from Math. Wyatt something or other from Tech Ed. They have all heard the news of Blanch. And the charges, from what they've each learned, did in fact have to do with hidden surveillance cameras in the girls' bathrooms. Caleb remarks to me how he witnessed Blanch being taken away by the police.

"He didn't seem too bothered by it," he said. "He was cooperative and pleasant. He was even smiling."

There's no one to call or alarm bell to sound. Blanch is gone and he won't be back. For the rest of the day I keep a low profile, confining myself to my room. I can't teach. It's too depressing to look at these teenage girls before me. It's likely, after all, that Blanch taped them as they used the bathroom and did God knows what to himself in the process. With less than two weeks of the school year, the kids are pretty much checked out anyway. They are satisfied to use the time I give them to catch up on their reading.

My last class of the day ends up being a different story. With this Blanch situation, Owen has found the perfect fodder for his crudeness. With a devious grin and snakelike agility, he makes his way up and down the rows of desks, sniffing at the girls in the class.

"Who could blame him?" he says. "Right, Mr. D? Teenage girls are delicious. They smell like cream soda and candles."

The girl he is hovering over swats him away and tells him he's disgusting.

"Sit down, Owen," I said.

He makes a circuitous zigzag back to his chair, commenting the entire time how teenage girls are appetizers, entrees, and desserts all at the same time.

"Even when they're taking a dump, I suppose," he said.

The class erupts in laughter over this. Even some of the girls.

"Get out."

"I hit a nerve, I see," he said. "Listen, a fetish is a fetish is a fetish. No one's judging."

Rising from my chair, I make my way towards him. The class looks on in wonder. Owen is fighting back that goddamn arrogant smirk of his. I am at once struck by something he has said.

"What did you just say?"

"I said no one's judging."

"Before that."

"I don't know."

"You said, 'A fetish is a fetish is a fetish.'"

"Okay," he said, looking to his peers for their reaction. "Did I hit a nerve?"

"You were mimicking Gertrude Stein," I said.

A puzzled look suddenly seizes his face. Reminding him of my brief lesson on the Modernist Renaissance woman and her poem, "Sacred Emily," does little to jog his memory. I remind him of her famous line, "A rose is a rose is a rose" that derives from the poem. His brain seems to be processing this.

"Interesting that you decide to quote Stein. In all my years of teaching, I've had kids quote back to me a fair share of Shakespeare, some Tennessee Williams, a little Thoreau here and there, definitely some Fitzgerald, but never any Gertrude Stein. Interesting. Something must have struck you about her."

His eyes are unblinking as he ponders this. He seems caught between dismissing it as dead-end nonsense and waiting to see what follows.

"Let's review what we know about Ms. Stein," I said, walking to the front of the room. "Who wants to go first?"

After a few moments, answers are forthcoming. Her role as an expatriate in Paris. Her penchant for boxing and art. Her influence on Hemingway.

"Anything else?" I said, looking towards Owen, who by now has surrendered to intrigue.

Nothing else is offered. So I come out with it:

"She was a lesbian."

A few chuckles. Owen's expression is now fixed and placid.

"Remember? We talked about how uncommon it was for a woman to be openly gay during that era. And how Hemingway himself was disgusted with her homosexuality."

This is all directed at the entire class, who must be anticipating some kind of punchline from me. Then I shift my focus to Owen; he is pursing his lips a little and doing his best to stare me down.

"There's something to this, Owen, don't you think? There's a reason for everything. And as sure as I'm standing here, I'm positive you chose to quote Stein for one reason or another. And let's be honest: I doubt it had to do with her impressive collection of Picasso's. Most teenage boys might have had Hemingway stuck in their heads; all of his ruminations on bravado and stoicism. But not you. You're hung up on a different trip altogether: the middle-aged behemoth lesbian trip, I might add. So maybe *you're* actually the one with the fetish. Is that possible? I think it is, Owen. And I just can't help but wonder what that fetish might be."

Juvenile monologue aside, I suddenly feel wasted. The blood in my head is heavy, like one enormous clot. The class is mostly quiet; they watch Owen who tries to pass the time by looking at his phone. Nothing happens for a few moments. Then Owen rises from his seat and walks out of the room. As I follow after him, I feel the eyes of my students upon me. Abruptly stopping myself, I flip off the lights and head over to my desk, all in one fluid motion.

Indifferent to any possible spectators, I unlock the bottom drawer and remove ten thousand dollars of Nana's money, which I slide into my pants pocket. Then I sit in dark silence with my students for the remainder of the period.

On my way out of the building that afternoon, I run into Andrew, a member of Blanch's staff. He's cleaning the glass of an athletic trophy case. A young kid, probably in his mid twenties, Andrew is handsome, yet awkward. With a tall, sinewy build and a shaved head, he avoids eye contact, and has a strange habit of fattening his bottom lip by pushing his tongue into it in a slow, deliberate back-and-forth motion.

When I greet him, he stops what he's doing nearly at once. Looking just past me, he starts the lip business right away.

"What the hell happened?" I said.

"We don't know."

"Are the rumors true?"

"We don't know."

"It's unbelievable."

"Yeah."

"We'll see what happens."

"I guess so."

We stand there in silence. After some time, I ask about Blanch's son, Dustin.

"I don't know much about Mr. Blanchard's personal affairs," he said.

"Do you know who might? About his son in particular."

"Some of the other fellows might know that sort of business."

"Could you find out for me?"

"Sure thing," he said, resuming his lip trick almost immediately.

It seems likely that Blanch's misdeeds will make the newspaper. This prevents me from using him as an excuse to Joanna for an after-work get-together. So I call her and say the English department has planned a happy-hour, a sort of end of the year celebration. Fine, she says, forgetting the unlikelihood of this ever happening. There's been a luncheon here and there, or even a

Christmas party or two through the years, but we mostly keep it professional.

With her blessing still ringing in my head, I hang up and make the short drive to the Cowgirl Club. Callie Starz is sitting at the bar, bullshitting with a male bartender. It takes me a moment before I recognize her. She's wearing a purple lace body stocking and her hair is pulled back and streaked with pink highlights. With the sleazy confidence of a regular, I approach her and offer to buy her a drink.

"How about a shot, Professor?"

"If you think just one will do."

Turning around in her seat, she studies me for a moment before telling me I look like shit. Then she asks the bartender to leave an entire bottle.

"What's with this?" I said, pointing to her hair.

"An experiment."

"Pretty bold."

"What's the point otherwise?"

The bartender pours two shots of scotch before leaving the bottle. Callie and I toast and drink to her new bold experiment.

"Wanna rendezvous?" she asks, swiping the scotch and two glasses.

Scowling from the taste of the liquor, I nod and follow her to our usual spot. Callie curls up beside me and pours some more shots. We drink a little and talk about the pleasant spring weather and how the end of the school year is approaching.

"The summers must be nice for you," she said.

"They are."

"I bet your boy loves having you home for those months."

I can feel something rise in my chest when she says this. My breathing becomes a little louder; the music that's playing, some slick power pop shit, isn't loud enough to drown it out.

"What happened? Did I say something?"

All I can do is shake my head, which is now teeming with the purest images of my beautiful son. Cole riding on top of my foot up and down the hallway in our house. Cole pushing his bubble mower in wild zigzags across the lawn. Cole eating his very first cupcake while sitting on his mother's lap. What a place to have these thoughts.

"I bet you're a wonderful dad," she said.

My eyes are closed and I discover that I'm crying. Callie pulls me into her. My tears are absorbed by her body stocking.

"I don't think so."

"Why? Because you're here? Because you're not home tossing him a ball?"

"For starters, yeah."

My voice is low and quavering. Callie wipes my cheeks and kisses me on the forehead. After a few deep breaths, I straighten up and scoff at myself.

"I cried in a strip club. And in one of the VIP rooms, to boot."

"Listen," she said, "stranger things have happened in this place. Trust me."

She tells a story of a man she was dancing for who began to choke himself. At first, it was with moderation, so she paid it little mind. But he soon began gagging and writhing until she had to pry his hands from his throat.

She pours some more shots and makes a toast to the strangler, wherever he may be. We drink and then sit for a while without saying much. It crosses my mind to tell her about Blanch, but I don't. Callie asks if I want a dance from her. After a moment, I nod my head. When she climbs on top of me, I close my eyes. The music is a remix version of a country power ballad I've heard before. Callie is not moving to the song's rhythm; she's on a different trip altogether, swaying back and forth, running her hands down the sides of her breasts, crinkling her nose and smiling at me like we're college sweethearts and this is my birthday present. A minute or so into it, she collapses on top of me and throws her arms around my neck. I slowly lift my hands from my sides and put them on her back. We stay like this for a little while.

When she sits up and looks me in the face, I tell her I have something for her. Then I take the stack of neatly wrapped one-hundred dollar bills from my pocket.

"This is not a rescue mission," I said. "Because I know you don't need rescuing. I'm not that fucking arrogant. But you do have a motorcycle trip you're planning and maybe more books to write. So for Christ's sake, sleep late and be safe and all that shit."

I hand her the money, which she takes with reservation.

"Is this a joke?"

"This is a lousy thing to say, but the truth is that I can't find an ounce of humor in much of anything these days. But then I suppose I vacillate and think it's all just beyond hysterical. All of it. That it's just so tragically funny and pointless—and then there's nothing left to do but say *fuck it*."

This has not really shed much light on the matter. Callie flips through the cash and then shoots me a bewildered look.

"Besides," I said, "it's too sad for me to picture you having to endure countless more men who might very well strangle themselves or bawl like goddamn babies just so you can say you earned it the hard way. There's no more virtue in that than in you taking it from me, right here right now."

"That sounds like a rescue mission to me."

"It's not. I'm positive. There's so much uncertainty right now. In everything. And it's pretty goddamn consuming, this uncertainty. It's about where I come from and it's about today and tomorrow and next month and whether I'm even going to see a year from now. I'm in a sort of doubting phase at the moment, I guess you could say. I feel like I don't know shit. Like my thoughts and my instincts have been stolen right out from inside of me. But a few of those thoughts were left behind. They must have hidden in those dark creases in the brain where ghosts come and go at all hours and they never introduce themselves. And one of those thoughts was to give you this money with full disclosure that it's *not* a rescue mission. I say all of this knowing full well that we barely know each other. That, to me, seems exactly the way it should be."

With this, I move Callie off of me and stand up.

"This has become my confession booth," I said.

Callie sits there looking at the money, asking about my family and what they would think of such a foolish act on my part. There's no way to respond to this. As I make my way towards the door, Callie says she has a question:

"What did you mean when you said you're uncertain about whether you'll see a year from now?"

The staid look on my face either says it all or causes more confusion. She's about to say something when I cut her off by telling her I have a question of my own:

"What's your real name?"

She thinks on this for a second, possibly considering the sanctity of this character she's created, the one with the purple lace body stocking and pink-streaked hair and the cool, contented smile that's strong enough to hold back whatever demons might desire to break through. Then she tells me her real name. After thinking about it for a moment, I nod and tell her I like it very much. She scoffs at this.

"Just be glad you have choices," I said. "I'd kill for choices right now."

And even though that seems a bit dramatic, yet hardly more so than anything else that's been said in the last hour, I leave her with those words, knowing full well they're cryptic and maddening, but still altogether true.

There's no way to avoid telling Joanna about Blanch's arrest. It will either come from me or one of her online news sources. So I tell her that night over dinner. And I can't help but be suspicious over her reaction. Her disgust is sincere, and easy enough to identify; those wide-eyed scowls and face scrunches are often reserved for such lascivious offenders, both on TV and in real life. But lurking beneath these expressions is something else, something that reveals a small personal triumph. It's all in the way she nods her head. And how her mouth becomes elastic as it tries to settle on a position. And how her voice is controlled and monotone. It's as if she's fighting back the notion that something positive will come of this awful story. But it's no use; she recognizes not only that there *is* something positive, but that it will benefit her. And then out it comes:

"You're better off. Obviously. And now with baby number two."

She must be repressing the urge to jump for joy; my social calendar has just been cleared. It crosses my mind to inform her of something: that she's not actually pregnant. I don't, though. This may be an obvious fact, but it will come off as cruel.

She's whispered the *baby number two* comment. This is due to Cole, who's busy sawing a green bean in half with his fork. Reaching across the table, I pinch his chin a little; he doesn't look up. Joanna continues to talk about Blanch as well as baby number two, whispering or spelling most of what she says. I try to listen, but find that I'm transfixed with Cole. It occurs to me that I'm on the verge of bursting with wild haymaker love for my son when just moments earlier I was receiving a lap dance from a stripper. I have no intention of reconciling this; there's no way to. So when my musing is interrupted by the ringing of the telephone, I welcome the distraction.

It's Superintendent Freeman calling. He asks if I can come to his office the following morning. Holding a finger up to Joanna, I excuse myself from the table and make my way to her studio.

"What's on the agenda?"

"I'd like to meet with you about your letter. I received it this afternoon. Needless to say, I'm taken aback."

His voice is steady. There's a pause after every couple of words.

"I can imagine."

"This is a delicate matter."

"I agree."

"And needs to be handled accordingly."

"I understand."

He lets out a long exhale into the phone.

"Can you shed a little light as to what I'm up against with this thing?"

"How do you mean?"

"Well, this thing requires due diligence," he said. "There's no doubt there. But in order to best handle the matter, we're going to require some discretion."

"You're wondering how many people I've told."

"It won't do anyone a whit of good if this thing becomes a smear campaign before it can be fully investigated."

It suddenly dawns on me that he must be dealing with the Blanch situation as well. The poor bastard. That's some dinnertime conversation he must have had with his wife. I picture him in his home office, some A-framed room over his garage, outfitted with dark stained wood floors and custom built bookcases filled with hardbound texts crammed with boring administrative jargon, psyching himself up to deal with these disasters. Today must have seen him up to his eyeballs in the case of the perverted high school janitor. And now it's on to the case of the perverted high school assistant principal. Both are mind-blowers. And both have headline news potential.

"You're the only one I've spoken to about Dan Zinser. No one else knows."

"Okay."

One simple word. Yet its cadence is brighter than anything he's said previously. His relief over my discretion brings about a little spasm of guilt. So I say the only thing I can think of, hoping it will cleanse my conscience:

"I was friends with Hank Blanchard."

My hope is that he might be struck by the randomness of such a comment—that he'll see it as a sort of apology for involving him in the ugliness that is sure to unfold as a result of my letter.

We plan to meet at his office at 9:00 a.m. the next day. My morning classes, he tells me, will be taken care of. I can't help but wonder if Dan will cover them.

When Freeman and I hang up, I sit down in the swivel bar chair Joanna picked up at a yard sale last spring. She likes to sit in it and paint sometimes. As I slowly spin around, I think about what the hell I'm going to say tomorrow in my meeting with Freeman. And what he's going to ask. And where this thing is headed. I try to remember the specifics in the letter I wrote to him.

Joanna has turned on the TV for Cole in the next room. Cookie

Monster's muffled rant suddenly rises in its volume. Then the clatter of dishes being cleared from the table. Then Cole laughing. Swiveling some more in the chair, I scan the room and all its clutter. Boxes of old magazines on the floor. Sagging bookcases filled with pewter knickknacks and dusty picture frames and how-to art texts. An old secretary desk that belonged to Joanna's parents. A small flat screen TV on top of this. But it's a rectangular glint of silver on a small corner table that catches my eye. Walking over to it, I pick it up and turn it over in my fingers. It's clean and new and unused. I mindlessly run the blade across the palm of my hand as my mind drifts to the meeting I will have in the morning with Superintendent Freeman.

"Everything okay?" Joanna asks when I return to the kitchen.

She's opened the windows to let the clean evening air topple the smells of dinner. Her hair is now pushed away from her face with a dark gray headband. Her big, clear eyes appear full of health and ambition.

"What was that all about?"

Looking in on Cole as he watches TV in the family room, I see that he's shirtless. This is a recent fad of his. Just as I'm about to comment on this, Joanna asks about the razor blade, which I've continued to brush back and forth against my hand. I shrug. Then I tell her I found it in her studio.

"I was researching more about sgraffito," she said. "There are some great videos about it online."

After a slight pause, she apologizes for the dangerous blade being out in plain sight. Just then, Cole laughs at something on his show. Then he turns to us and waves. We join him in front of the TV. He asks his mom to scratch his back. Joanna has now forgotten about the phone call from Freeman. Or at least she doesn't ask about it. This is a relief. It means I don't have to lie by telling her that he's asked me to attend some last minute curriculum workshop the following morning.

I massage Cole's neck a little as his mom continues to scratch his back. His skin is warm. After a moment, he scrunches his body a little and turns to me with a silly face. So I quit massaging. It's pleasant enough to just sit here with him as he watches his show and has his back scratched.

On the TV, Bert and Ernie are fishing in a little rowboat. Ernie is hollering out to the fish, which are jumping into the boat. Each time a fish enters the boat, Cole turns to me and smiles. By the time the segment ends, I notice that all the while I have been grasping the razorblade inside a clenched fist that is now hot and red and sweaty.

Vic's is nearly empty. Aside from me, there are only two others in the place. A man and a woman. Both elderly. They are not together, but they each sit at the counter, nursing mugs of hot coffee and picking at hunks of cornbread. I order the same and sit down at a booth by a window and look out at the early morning sky. A sepia toned battery acid explosion has hurled itself across the horizon; it's dark and oily, yet beautiful.

Time passes slowly. The waitress, a middle-aged, bleach-blonde woman with heavy make-up and oversized glasses, refills my coffee twice. A few more customers appear. Some stay and order eggs and bacon and French toast; others grab a muffin or coffee or cornbread to go. After finishing my third cup, I call Freeman's office and speak to Denise, his secretary. She is polite and understanding and tells me to reschedule another time with Freeman. Maybe tomorrow morning, she suggests, or maybe the day after that. I'll have to get back to her, I say. After we hang up, I call in sick to work. It's last minute, so chances of getting a sub are sparse. It dawns on me that this might possibly push Dan over the edge. After shaking off some silent, wicked laughter, I throw a few bills on the table and head out to the parking lot where I call Trish. She answers on the first ring.

"Got time to fit in a workout this morning? I'm playing hooky today."

"I'm around."

"I can be there in fifteen minutes."

"I'm here."

I'd like to believe that her invitation suggests she's in the dark about my last interaction with her son.

A note is taped to her front door inviting me inside and down to the basement. There are no signs of Danielle anywhere. The house smells of coffee and maple syrup. Trish is stretching and adjusting her gi when I find her in the basement.

"Our first a.m. session."

"Thanks for doing this last minute."

Before we begin, she gently mocks my choice of clothing; this is something she's done a few times before. With a black Polo t-shirt and khaki colored shorts, I must look more suited to getting sushi than to learning how to incapacitate another man.

She pushes me hard. Knee blows and throat chops and pressure points. We hardly talk during the workout. The hour goes by quickly. When it's over, we make our way upstairs to the kitchen and drink ice water and eat two clementines apiece.

"Why are you doing this?"

"I'm headed to Jersey this morning," I said. "To see some family. I'm anticipating a bit of stress. I figured I'd put a little Zen in the bank to draw on later when I'm all pent up."

"I mean in general. It always seems like there's a sense of urgency to you being here."

"Well, we never know how much time we've got left, right?"

"How's my son doing in your class?"

I'm mid-chew when she throws this non sequitur at me. But I nod my head and manage to utter that all's well and that Owen's doing fine. There's a long pause. Too long. So I fill it by telling her I wouldn't be surprised if Owen finished the year with a solid A in my class. This causes her to smile. Throwing another clementine at me, she says it's for the road. Then she walks me to my car and wishes me luck with my family.

Bruno Hauptmann, the man who kidnapped the Lindbergh baby in the 1930s, was housed here when the place was known as Trenton State Prison and when it still employed the death penalty. It was home to Rubin "Hurricane" Carter as well as the Kuklinski brothers, one of whom was connected to the Gambino crime family. One of the oldest prisons in the country, it was built in the late 1700s and today holds close to two-thousand inmates. I discovered this some years back when on a whim I did a little research. It was during one of those unproductive mornings at work when my mind conjured up Uncle Alex, presenting him to me in any number of ways. The clean cut model prisoner who spends his time writing letters and learning Chinese. The muscle-bound recluse who meditates and fights the powers-that-be for a vegan diet. The well-respected veteran who's embraced his fate and sees to taking troubled lifers under his wing. Inevitable musings, I suppose.

Traffic is light and I arrive at the prison in just under three hours. The burning sunshine mixed with clouds has turned the sky into a vast field of fiery wildflowers.

The corrections officer who greets me in the lobby asks if I'm on Alex's visitor list.

"I don't know how this works."

"I'm telling you how it works. There's a visitor list. Are you on it?"

He's looking at me through a clean window with a circular cutout at the bottom. His eyes are red and his dirty blonde hair needs to be cut.

"I've just driven all the way from Connecticut. I'll sign whatever I need to sign or do whatever it is you need me to do."

He rubs his eyes with his knuckle before taking a deep breath. Then he tells me to produce some ID and he'll see what he can do. Handing over my driver's license, I thank him and take a seat. I'm alone in the lobby. There are no magazines to read, so I watch the man make a few calls while he works on his computer. Every now and again he looks in my direction before swiveling in his chair to open a drawer, remove a file folder, flip through some papers.

After some time, he calls me to the window where I fill out some paperwork. Then he returns my ID and tells me to wait a bit longer.

"My first time inside a prison," I said, taking my seat again.

He barely looks up.

"It's pretty much what I imagined."

He punches a few keys on his computer.

"This part anyway. I'm sure it's unimaginable past this point."

He stops what he's doing and looks at me for a moment. But he doesn't speak.

"Unimaginable," I repeat.

After about thirty minutes, a corrections officer enters the waiting room and introduces himself. His name is Rudy and he's a broad shouldered redhead with dark green eyes and the beginnings of a beard. After some additional paperwork, I follow Rudy through the door and into the prison. As we walk through a corridor, he explains the rules to me. The preferred time for a visit is one hour. Visits are held in the auditorium. Alex is entitled to contact visits, which means he will not be manacled. This also means we will not be separated by a wall of glass. Corrections officers will be present during the visit.

Rudy walks me to the metal detection area where there are more officers. I'm patted down and asked to remove my belt as well all items from my pockets. I put my phone and car keys and wallet into a tray and watch it pass through a machine. Then I'm scanned with a wand before being made to walk through the detector. The men are all cordial to me. One of them, a tall and toothy behemoth with a lip full of snuff, even asks me about the weather and my drive from Connecticut. No alarms sound. No glitches. So far it has been a smooth operation.

With Rudy leading, I'm brought to the auditorium.

"You're doing good," he tells me, resting his open hand on the door. "This is not an easy thing, but you're doing good."

"I appreciate that," I said, looping my belt back into my pants.

"I know you haven't seen your uncle in a lot of years," Rudy said. "He okayed your visit, though. That's good."

I nod. Rudy says he knows why Alex is serving a life sentence. Then he gives me some tips. Talk slow and soft. Smile if possible. Don't agitate the prisoner.

"That's the most important one," he said. "That last one."

I nod. He asks if I'm ready. I nod again. Rudy opens the door to a large all-purpose room with brown rubber flooring and rows of tables and chairs. A corrections officer is supervising three other inmates and their visitors. One inmate, a pot-bellied Latino man, slouches in his seat and reaches over the table to hold the hands of a pregnant woman across from him. Another inmate plays checkers with his two young boys while their mother looks on with pleasure. And the oldest prisoner, a white-haired facsimile to Gregory Peck, is having what appears to be a solemn conversation with a man half his age.

No one looks up upon my entrance. This is no doubt precious time and they don't want to waste it. Rudy ushers me to a chair a few rows away from the Latino man. Alex, Rudy tells me, will be out shortly. Then he wishes me luck before leaving. With my hands folded in my lap, I sit with my head down and wait. I try to block out the conversations around me and consider what my own visit is going to be like.

Alex has agreed to see me, even adding me to his visitor list. This might have been out of curiosity. Or maybe desperation. Either way, hearing that I have showed up like this, on the spot, and have requested a meeting after all these years, must be a mind fuck for him. At this very moment, he might be summoning up strength and nerve and any ancient, long-forgotten rhetoric that vacillates between explanation and apology for murdering my father. What a process this must be. It has to overwhelm the brain to the point where either humility or apathy takes over.

It suddenly strikes me that there's a process of my own that I should be working on. Too late. The double doors at the far end of the auditorium have opened and Alex is heading towards me. He's alone. I stand. Then I sit again. Alex moves towards me with the slow, deliberate steps of some proud, preening zoo animal. His hands are open and pressed together underneath his chin. Though he's looking in my direction, he appears to see right through me. The fixed expression on his face is at once grave and pensive.

It's been ten years since we've seen one another. He looks good. Better actually. He's lean and fit and healthy with a full head of short grayish-brown hair and mid-length sideburns. Clear, lucid

Robert M. Marchese

eyes illuminate like brand new rainwater on a glassy surface.

"Marcus."

His voice is a warm baritone that just misses being affected. I stand. Alex smiles at me; neither of us offers a hand to shake. As we sit down, he tells me I look well. I return the compliment. He's given up cigarettes, he tells me.

"And I've learned how to eat right. Believe it or not, but it took prison for me to learn about proper diet and self control."

This seems contrary to common rumors about prison food. But I don't bother bringing this up.

"I understand you have a family."

"I do."

Nana was the liaison between me and Alex's wife and kids. Though she had accepted that I had broken off all ties with my Aunt Janice as well as my cousins, she wouldn't hesitate to share with them the details of my life. Alex asks if I have any photos. Not on me, I tell him. This is a lie; there are hundreds on my phone.

"A boy?"

"His name is Cole."

"It's not easy having a son, I'll tell you that."

A story follows. My cousin Joe, Alex's son, is approaching his third divorce. He has two young girls from his first marriage and they are struggling with the split. Jeannine, my other cousin, is a godsend, he tells me.

"She's like her mother. Devoted as hell. It's true. It runs deep with them."

Without missing a beat, Alex tells me he's finally gotten around to reading *The Feminine Mystique*. He points out that this was only after reading *The Female Eunuch*, which he tells me he enjoyed more. As he outlines what he likes and dislikes about both reads, I notice his fingernails. They are clean to the point of transparency. Their tips are thin, white curves. Each nail is the same length and bears not one sign of a cuticle.

After his pro-feminist rant, he tells me about other books he's read in prison. Some recent and some over the years. And all of which have made their mark on him for one reason or another. *The*

Plague by Camus. A book called *The God Delusion*, which he describes as irreverent yet compelling. *A Theory of Justice*. And of course, the *Bible*.

"I owe my education to Cal."

An account of Cal, his cellmate, is then given. He's a friend. A mentor. The smartest person Alex has ever known. Cal, Alex tells me, his voice dropping an octave and his eyes widening to reveal an epic sorrow, is the single reason he's not only alive today, but is *as* alive as he is. This is how he puts it.

Then he tells a too long story about Cal's wife and how she's rejected her husband over the years by refusing to support his spiritual growth. Alex calls her obtuse and says her density is like that of other heathens. From here, he launches into another too long story about a fellow inmate named Jeffers. Jeffers was serving a life sentence for killing a cop at point-blank range. Alex describes him as being a once pitiless man. Orphaned at a young age. In and out of jails for most of his young life. Kept to himself during the first year or so of his sentence. But then Cal got through to him somehow and Jeffers became a changed man. He turned pious and compassionate and scholarly. But this radical change brought with it a faction of enemies. And so it came to pass that just two weeks ago, Jeffers was murdered in the prison yard. In broad daylight, Alex adds.

The rest of the visit is like this. Alex talking solemnly about people I don't know or want to know or even begin to give a fuck about. His conviction in all his anecdotes only adds to my disinterest. My own life, Nana, my father, the murder: None of these are mentioned. It dawns on me that he has not only neglected to ask about my visit after all these years, but that he has expressed not even a sign of surprise over seeing me again after a full decade. He just babbles on as though continuing a conversation we began the other day over coffee.

When there's a lull after his next story—this one is about two men he dissuaded from an escape attempt—I tell him I must be going.

"I understand. Your life awaits you."

Alex and I both stand up. The Latino man looks in our direction. He and his wife are still visiting. The others are now gone.

"You're a good listener, Marcus. A damn good listener. Most people aren't, you know. You're on my list of visitors now. So if you come back, maybe I'll shut up and let you do some of the talking. What do you think?"

He's looking me directly in the eyes with a steady gaze. There is a long pause before I respond:

"I'll be back. You can count on it."

This pleases him. He extends his hand to me. We shake. His skin is smooth and his grip is firm.

"I'm glad you came."

With this, he turns from me and begins to head back towards the double doors at the far end of the room. I swear by God that from behind he resembles my father. His build. His movements. His energy.

"Uncle Alex," I call out to him.

We meet each other halfway.

"I surprised myself by coming here today."

"Then you're lucky. My days are filled with nothing but predictability."

"I didn't know what to expect."

"I understand."

"It's not the easiest thing to do—being here."

"I probably wouldn't be if I didn't have to."

"But I'm going to come back. I mean that. Sometime this summer."

"I believe you will."

"And we'll talk some more."

"That's all we *can* do."

"But before we do—talk some more—I think it's important that you know something first."

"What's that?"

"It's the reason I came here this afternoon."

For the first time today, the aura that has dominated his every gesture, the one of confidence and even mystery, gives way to a sort of unguarded boyishness. His eyes look big and curious. He's actually silent for a few moments, waiting for me to tell him something he can later discuss at length with Cal.

"I wanted to tell you that I forgive you."

It's impossible for me to look at him when I say this. So I turn my gaze upward and focus on a surveillance camera I notice adhered to a far wall. Alex is about to respond when I cut him off:

"Let's not discuss this right now. Let's leave it alone and maybe revisit it this summer when we meet up again."

The look on his face is unlike any I have seen during our visit. There's a glow in his green eyes that seems like some recently added special effect; and his expression has jumped the median and crossed into that rich territory of placid ambiguity. His resemblance to my father is both inspiring and sickening. If I didn't know any better, I'd say Alex has been humbled.

The drive home is a bore. My mind is slow to process much of anything. I feel like I've been anesthetized, but somehow never truly went under. Turning on the radio, I listen to a talk show for a little bit. The DJ, a laconic and pretentious sounding man, tells a story about coaching his son's Little League team one year and how the experience led to estrangement between him and his child. It's a good story, but depressing as hell. Then I switch over to some music. The only clear station plays classical. So I listen to that for a bit before stopping for a bite to eat at a deli just off the interstate.

As I eat a Philly cheese steak sandwich, I call Joanna. She tells me about her day with Cole and asks what time I'll be home. With final exams and the end of the school year approaching, I tell her it will be another couple of hours. When we hang up, I sit and nurse my root beer for a bit. It's an old fashioned brand called Dad's Root Beer and it comes in a retro style glass bottle. Spinning it around on the tabletop, I study my hands for a moment. They are dry and coarse. They are neither the hands of a prig or a manual laborer.

I consider my Uncle Alex's hands and fingernails. They are smooth and polished. Even immaculate. Certainly these are not the hands and fingernails of a convicted murderer. They more closely resemble the hands and fingernails of an executive. It's only 3:00, but I'm too goddamn tired to consider why this bothers me so much. But it does.

By the time I arrive home, I've caught my second wind. It lasts through the evening. Joanna has made pork chops, which I tell her to wrap up for the following night's dinner. Then I take her and Cole out for Chinese food. I order the fried jumbo shrimp and spareribs and Szechuan lo mein and beef chow fun and beef with snow peas. Joanna shakes her head and asks what's gotten into me.

"And a pitcher of beer," I tell our waiter, a handsome, soft-spoken Asian man.

We eat and drink and help Cole draw colorful pictures with the crayons and paper he's been given. I feel lucid and healthy. After dinner, we head to the store where I buy Cole some candy and books and action figures. Joanna whispers that he's having a birthday soon and this is unnecessary. Then she asks again what's gotten into me. Shrugging, I say the only thing that comes to mind:

"It's almost summer."

I don't think of Uncle Alex all evening. This only occurs to me once Joanna and Cole go to bed and I sit down to write. It's close to 10:00 p.m.

My visit with Alex was an absurd exercise of some sort. I'm not exactly sure what type, either. It hardly matters. What matters is that I made the trip. That I faced him. That I was composed as I sat across from him while looking him in the eyes and listening to him ramble before promising him that I would be back for a second visit. This is the truth. I will be back. Sometime this summer. As for now, though, there's only the rush to write and work towards finishing my book.

I've been thinking a lot about this triumvirate I've created in my narrative. A couple hundred pages in, and the book really only has three main characters. William, Enid, and Franco. There're a few minor characters who show up here and there: Jonathan, William's brother, makes a sporadic appearance; William's neighbor, a lonely cuckquean named Katy also breezes in and out of the story; and a few of William's childhood friends stop by to occasionally borrow money from their wealthy companion. But these characters are incidental at best. The true center of the story is William and the colossal machination he has seamlessly woven. This does not seem problematic to me. There are enough internal and external conflicts to move the story forward and keep it interesting.

It's also occurred to me that I'm each of my three main characters. I'm William, the tortured schemer. And I'm Enid, the elusive tramp. And Franco, the earnest, wannabe artist.

Enid has reappeared after a full week. And with the works she made off with in tow. She has studied the two paintings —"Nighthawks" and "The Drinker"—calling them perfect and delicate things, read *Paradise Lost* and *Howl*, both of which she describes as mind-altering, and skimmed *To the Lighthouse*, which she said was simply beyond her.

Such close scrutiny is exactly what she was after. It allowed her to get close to William the only way she knew how. To get inside his head. To try and understand his past and his family and childhood and all the rest of it. And she wished to do this without his consent, of course. Or rather, she knew she had to. William proved his obstinance by refusing to play "Recuerdos de la Alhambra," so she anticipated a lack of cooperation from him.

This was all part of Enid's effort to assimilate to William Walker. She wanted to live with part of him—or what she thought was part of him—for a week and see what it felt like. After a few days, she began telling people—neighbors, friends, family, strangers—that it was she who created these complicated and beautiful works. It felt wonderful. The acclaim. The awe. The adulation. She revealed all of this to William, who saw in the girl's desperation an opportunity for himself.

They sat on opposite sofas in William's living room and discussed the matter. Enid asked for her water glass to be refilled three times. She was talking a lot and was becoming dry as she hurried to get it all out. Such exhilaration over being William Walker for a week. The heavy and wonderful burden of it was more appealing to her than anything she could remember. She told him that she wanted to feel this way forever.

"That's a hell of a thing to say."

William said this with naiveté in his voice. Yet he had already conceived a plan to give the girl what she was after. This plan, of course, would give him what he was after as well. Before he revealed it to her, he was curious about something:

"What did you mean by this?" he said, holding up the brief note she had written and fixed to the vodka bottle just one week earlier.

Enid put her water on the side table and leaned towards the letter to remember what she had written. William recited it as she read:

"I enjoyed our night together. I'll be in touch, but you probably figured as much. PS: Your talents are undeniable. I'd like to think that mine are as well."

Smiling a little to herself, she leaned back on the sofa and folded her hands into her lap. Still and pensive, she appeared on the verge of some deep confession that might send shock waves to her audience.

"What exactly are your talents?" William asked.

The directness of the question seemed to inspire her. She straightened up a little and looked William square in the eyes.

"To forget myself," she said. "To start over completely and build something new out of little bits and pieces I come across. Bits and pieces that seem interesting to me. Ones that are laced with something memorable. Something moveable and elastic. Something that's not mired in the depressing and static energy of this ridiculous universe. It's been this way with me for so long that it's impossible to even remember how it all began. How I began, really. To separate the surface from the foundation."

Her revelation, heavy and pathetic, was troublesome to William. They were very much alike. This clinched it. It's true that he felt some nascent connection with her before, but this was uncanny. Enid was more of a mirror image than he had seen in a long time. And it disgusted him to know they were so similar. If nothing else, it would make handing his life over to her that much easier. So with a deep breath and through bared teeth, he offered her everything he had. The wealth. The celebrity. Not to mention every last poem, painting, song, and story he had ready to deliver to his legions of admirers.

"It's been wonderful," he said, "and inspiring. But it's time to move on to something else. My brother owns a small goat farm in New Hampshire. It might sound silly, but I'm going to work for him. I just need some time for myself. The animals will be a nice distraction."

This was a lie. William's brother in fact rented a basement apartment on a modest farm in the tiny town of Gilmanton, New Hampshire—and had so for close to a decade—but he neither owned the land nor was in the position of hiring his younger brother.

"Why me?" she said, the light in her eyes a bright pool of wonder.

A valid question.

"Because you want this," he said. "And I no longer do."

William told her there was a condition attached to this arrangement. Then he explained about Franco. It's true, he told her, that the young man is handsome and talented, but he is also competition. With Franco alive, he said, Enid will have to share in the praise that is now William's. She will never know the true feeling of what it means to be William Walker. And only when the young docent is dead will she be William's true successor.

"Dead?"

She said the word with great nonchalance.

"That's right."

His plan is simple, he tells her. They will make it look like a robbery at the Institute. Franco is there alone after hours most evenings. No distractions or complications. They will use one of the razorblades the young man has lying around.

"Who will be doing the deed?"

Another valid question. Naturally he wanted her to do it. It was the least she could do for all he was to bequeath her.

"Because I'm fine to do it."

This was said with the same airiness one might reserve for assuming a household chore. William didn't argue. They went to work on the details. Not only for the murder, but for Enid's upcoming endowment.

"Do you think I'll be good as the new you?" she asked.

"I do," he said. "I honestly do. I think you have the right temperament for it. Probably even better than me."

The child within her was gazing out of bright, widened eyes. Absurd, William thought: They were discussing murder only seconds earlier. Part of him wanted to tell her that he was a fake. That they were in fact one and the same. But he couldn't. The awe she felt for him, the idolatry, the way she flitted about, all strange and sexy under his vast shadow, was too much to give up just yet. He pictured himself as an active volcano and her as this flickering little firefly. While he was spewing showers of molten mystery into the air, she was learning some dainty little dance and trying to put on a light show of her own.

He decided that he would gladly consume whatever worship she could offer him from now until Franco's murder. It was likely that he would miss it once it was all gone. This brought about the question of how he would get along in his new life. Whatever that entailed. He had yet to come up with anything in the way of a plan. All he knew was he wanted out of his present life of deception. And that in his new life, wherever it took him, he could worry about redemption for his sins. This would be his charge. Redemption. For the lies and the vanity. And now for the murder. He would have to devote himself to redemption. There were no two ways about it.

For now, he needed to bide his time until the killing of Franco. It was equally important to not think about the murder. This would bring up the looming question that he was trying at all costs to avoid. Why did Franco have to die? That bit that he fed Enid about having to share in the praise did sound almost reasonable. In private, though, he wasn't entirely sure why he wanted the young man dead. Why not just go through with the handoff to Enid and let Franco be? Was it possible that even though William would no longer be an artist that he wanted no one else to be one as well? No one, that is, except another fraud like Enid. There was no denying that he was envious of Franco's talent. It was, after all, real. And perhaps limitless. Perhaps it even had the capacity to destroy William's legacy.

"It looks like we're going to be sharing that secret after all," Enid said, moving over to where he was sitting on the sofa.

He thought on this for a moment. Suddenly he remembered. She was eager to bond with him. And what better way to bond, she had reasoned, than over a secret. There was even some theory of hers about a man's sadness and how many secrets he kept. Odd.

"It looks that way," William said.

"That's all I wanted. To share a secret with you."

"Good."

Enid moved closer to William. He could smell the sweetness of her youth and the lust she had for such faraway stars and spaces. He felt himself becoming aroused.

"That," she said, "and for you to play 'Recuerdos de la Alhambra.'"

There was no doubt that Enid was ideal to inherit William's old life. As for killing Franco, she was ideal for that as well. It seemed that she would be perfectly suited for anything that required an unwavering relentlessness.

The following day marks a ten day countdown to the end of school. A tradition has been established at LSHS that the senior class begins its pranks then. Their goal is one prank per day until graduation. Most classes have met this quota. This has been going on since my first year. Past pranks include some cliché ones: goldfish in the toilets; stink bombs in the stalls. And some original ones: every senior riding their bike to school, and up and down the halls of LSHS. Two years ago, at least three dozen professional looking fliers—on official LSHS letterhead—were posted throughout the halls, stating a mandatory penis and vagina inspection would be a new graduation requirement.

Little teaching is accomplished during these ten days. Most teachers use the pranks as a copout to do next to nothing. The kids love it. It's win/win. As for me, my time is made even easier due to Dan's leave of absence. Not to mention Owen has been skipping my class since the Gertrude Stein incident.

Today's prank is a watergun fight in the cafeteria. It happens to be while I'm on cafe duty. After the kids are dismissed to their classes, I stay behind to help the custodians clean up the wet tables and chairs. Just as I'm about to leave, I'm approached by custodian

Andrew; he's wheeling a mop and bucket towards one of the soaked areas.

Pulling out a slip of paper from his pocket, he tells me he has the information I'm looking for.

"Thank you," I said, not knowing at all what he is talking about.

Because I don't want to be rude, I fold the paper and put it in my breast pocket, leaving Andrew to mop up the puddles of water. On my way back to my classroom, I look at the paper. Even then it takes a minute for me to realize it's Blanch's son's address and phone number in Olympia, Washington.

I keep the paper in my pocket for the rest of the day, not sure what I'm going to do with it. By the time the final bell rings, I've made up mind. My idea is anything but well thought out. It's an idea born out of surrender and even dread. It's lazy and pointless, but it's all I can muster. So I count out ten thousand dollars in cash from my desk drawer and carefully wrap it in loose leaf paper. Then I drive to the post office and ship it, standard mail, no accompanying address or written note, to Olympia, WA.

Chapter 9: The Promise

"He entered the territory of lies without a passport for return."
- Graham Greene

Most of the details I remember about my grandfather's funeral are trivial. There's the image of my cousin Jeannine's new blue Volkswagen, her first brand new car. On more than one occasion, I overheard her talking to her mother about its options and their cost. I even witnessed her stare out the window of L'allegria's to take in the sight of the gleaming vehicle straddling its two parking spaces under the low August sun. Then there was my Aunt Janice's glasses, which were smudged every time I looked at her. I can recall staring at her throughout the day, waiting for her to take them off and give them a proper cleaning.

There's also the image of a young, pretty waitress at L'allegria's named Jody, bragging to one of the hostesses how she had faked a work related injury the week before so she could leave early and go to a concert with her girlfriends. I overheard this conversation as I stood waiting outside the men's room. When my eavesdropping was discovered, Jody looked at me, winked, and walked away. That wink was so beautiful, so visceral, that it almost made me forget where I was.

The funeral was open casket, yet I don't recall Donato's face or what he was wearing or the long, sad goodbye I imagine he and Nana shared. At L'allegria's, there was a heartfelt toast made by Carmine Ricci, who had been Donato's best man; I remember none of it. There was the time my father and I shared together that day. On the car ride. At Nana's house. In the church and then the restaurant. It's all wiped away.

What I do remember is the precise moment I heard the gunshots in L'allegria's parking lot. I was at my table washing my hands with an ice cube from my water. Two older women at the table across from me stopped mid-conversation and clutched their purses. The shots were thunderous. One after another. Five in total.

And I remember holding my father's bleeding body in my arms as people screamed and ran about and called the police. He was already gone by the time I got to him. As we lay there together on the pavement, my mind took hold of some thoughts. They were not complete or linear thoughts with a proper beginning, middle, and end. They were murky and even desperate images that burst into my head, presenting themselves in a sort of still and solemn light. My mother. My Nana. My future children. Me in ten years.

Anger wasn't a part of it. Nor was revenge. It never occurred to me to go after my Uncle Alex and choke the life out of him. This would have meant leaving my father alone there on the pavement.

As time passed, I often caught myself hung up on this anger business. It was staggering to learn that I wasn't angry about what had happened. With anger, your focus turns all blurry as you resort to petty acts of slander and violence that are too transient to ever take hold; they have no staying power. If anything, I became more lucid and self-aware after the murder.

This is not to say there wasn't a lost feeling inside of me. There was. It was like the air I was breathing had become thick with some foggy pollution that wouldn't cease. I was sad for a long time. By the time Joanna and I were together for about a year, her father asked me if I had ever considered therapy.

"Might bring you back," he said.

"Maybe."

He gave me the number of his squash partner who had a private practice. I never called. It seemed too self-indulgent to me. Too emotionally reckless, even. The matter was self-contained in my head. I had a handle on it. I could manage it. Opening it up to a stranger, I reasoned, might turn it into something wild.

Everything changed when Cole was born. I was forced to give up that sadness. You either imbue your children with strength or sadness, and I wasn't about to play the part of the put upon misanthrope. Besides, I knew my abilities as a father would already be somewhat dictated by my misfortune. I was destined to be overly sentimental when it came to my son. This is something I decided I could live with.

Cole's birth had enlivened something in me that my father's death seemed to extinguish. My masculinity. I discovered that it had been dormant for some time. And then it suddenly surfaced. Not in an overt or obnoxious way. It's been more subdued. There are instances where I'll say the phrase "my boy" in public and feel a surge of pride. As in *"My boy* will have a grilled cheese" or "I'm looking to get a haircut for *my boy."* There are times when I stare at him and privately beam over his likeness to me. And there are some darker moments where I ponder the idea of someone hurting him and resolve with absolute certainty that I would do unthinkable things in response.

The countdown to summer vacation has now begun in our house. Seven days left. Cole, who doesn't yet grasp the concept of seasons, knows only that he will soon have his dad at home with him every day. This is cause for some wonderfully elevated dialogue between the two of us. It's mostly in the form of Q and A with the As being fed to him by either me or Joanna.

"What's the plan this summer?" I ask him.

"Fun!"

"Who's going to have fun?"

"You and me and Mommy!"

"What kind of fun?"

"My birthday!"

"What else?"

"The beach!"

"What else?"

"Ice cream!"

"What else?"

"My birthday!"

The past couple of summers have been pleasant. We've

managed some nice traditions of going to the town beach a few times a week. And we once again become regulars at Many Flavors, the old fashioned ice cream parlor. We sleep later and watch more TV and get tan and read and have block parties.

My intention is to maintain tradition. This summer, though, needs to go beyond all this. After my second and final visit to Uncle Alex, sometime around mid to late August, the summer will end with a berserk thud. The least I can do is shower my son with as many spoils as I can manage. So I've looked into a Disney trip. Maybe a week in July. Maybe as a surprise for Cole on his third birthday. My only misgiving is that this will cut into valuable writing time. My book must naturally be finished before my visit to Alex one last time. And even though I'm only pages away from completion, one week in Florida might not be something I can afford. But then there's my boy to consider. And then there's my book. And then there's my boy.

Besides the book, there are other loose ends that need tending to. A new muffler for Joanna's car. Getting the driveway sealed. Replacing the broken ottoman in the family room. Fixing the crawl space door inside my closet. Painting the guest bathroom. After scheduling an appointment for the driveway, and hiring a handyman to fix the crawl space and do the painting, Joanna tells me she's on to me:

"This is a man's version of nesting, isn't it?"

Ignoring my lack of response, she puts her arms around me and tells me how sweet I am. And responsible. Then she tears up a little and says how happy she is that I've come around to wanting a second child.

"This summer's going to be amazing," she says.

Agreed, I think to myself. The first part of it, anyway. The first part will be nice. I'll make certain of that. It will be breezy and memorable. But it might be a hell of a lot better if I had some more pot. There's the matter of my nerves to consider. It's hard to maintain focus on much of anything when I think about the imminence of my visit to Alex in mid to late August. The stash Blanch gave me is gone, smoked up during drives to the grocery store or in the bathroom before late night bouts of writing. A little more would go a long way. Goddamn Blanch for being a fucking pervert.

Amid the all the restlessness and senior pranks at Louis Sutherland High School, I begin making donations to my colleagues. During my lunch one day, I drop off a few boxes in the English office and tape a FREE STUFF sign to them. They are filled with books and movies and posters and binders with lessons plans dating back to my first year of teaching.

"Spring cleaning," I tell them. "Take what you want."

When I'm confronted at the end of the day, intervention-style, I reveal that I will not be returning to teaching the following school year. This is met with moderate surprise. A few head nods and kind regards. I'm not close with these people. They're fine individuals and respectable educators, but this is not emotional for any of us. Jim McArthur asks what my plan is.

"I've got a few things lined up."

"Yeah?"

"For sure."

"That's it?"

"It's all a little up in the air right now."

"Is it your book? Did something happen with your book? Are you publishing that fucker?"

Jim is my only colleague in the department who knows I've been at work on a novel. I told him about *Mister Walker* a month or so ago after an inspiring night of writing.

"We'll see."

Jim eyes me with coyness. Then he laughs a little.

"You sly bastard," he says, "you've got something cooking, don't you?"

The following day I bring bagels and donuts and orange juice for my students. Then I announce to them that I will not be giving them a final examination. This gets me a standing ovation in two of my classes. When they settle down, I search my brain for the speech I prepared the night before. It was filled with bits of humor and wisdom and nostalgia. It was a good speech. Short and not overly sentimental. Roughly the same one for each class. But now it's nowhere to be found. So I extemporize.

"I've enjoyed being your teacher. It's a fun job. I'd much rather work with all of you than a bunch of adults. Adults are a pain in the ass. But you already know this. I'm not sure if I'm a very good teacher, but I do know that through the years I've put a lot of myself into my teaching. This translates into *something*, though I'm not really sure what that is. I strongly believe that only a very specific kind of person has any business teaching a group of kids—the same way that only a very specific kind of person has any business running for office or working with the elderly. And I think I've been that kind of person all the way through my career. Right up to the very end. And I think it's important that once you *stop* being that kind of person, that you step down and let someone else take over. So it's with a heavy heart that I am doing just that. I'm stepping down. And moving on. But please know one thing. It's very important that each of you know *one thing*: Every moment I spent here, with all of you, has been absolutely honest and heartfelt. That's the truth."

By the time I finish speaking, my students raise their plastic cups of orange juice and make a toast to yours truly. Afterwards, some hug me. Some thank me. Some take pictures with their phones. But no one asks for clarification on my speech. Nor do they ask about my plans once I quit teaching. Hell, they're teenagers. They just smile at me, gobble their bagels and donuts, and enjoy their freedom.

Owen continues to miss my class. And *my* class only. Protocol dictates that students be written up with a referral when they cut. Too much paperwork. Besides, since Dan Zinser has also been out, this would mean I'd be giving extra work to Principal Logan. I do end up paying her a visit in her office at the end of the day to let her know my intentions for next year.

"I'm surprised to hear that," she says.

"It's a bit surreal to me as well."

"I bet it is."

"It's taken me a while to reach this point. But here I am."

It's likely that in all the years I've been at LSHS, Dot and I have had a mere handful of conversations. Nurturing and personable though she may be, Dot is not much of an administrator. Rumors have abounded for as long as I can remember that she's on the verge of retiring. For some time now, she and her husband have been renovating a house in one of the Carolinas; its completion, supposedly, will mark her departure from Louis Sutherland High School. In the meantime, she's been prepping Dan for her job.

"It's been a great run," I said.

"I'm glad to hear that."

Dot is a frail looking older woman with stringy yellowish hair and kind blue eyes. She began her career as a middle school math teacher and moved her way up from there.

"I'll miss the kids. That's for sure."

"I wish you came to see me sooner. I may not be privy to the details of what's happened between you and Dan, but I do wish you sought me out. Things might have ended differently."

It's evident that she thinks my departure is due to Dan. I'm okay with letting her think this.

She tells me that Superintendent Freeman has spoken with her; he's assured her that Dan and I will not, and should not, cross paths for the remainder for the school year. He's also informed her about my cancelled meeting with him. She tells me that he would very much like me to reschedule at some point. At the moment, though, Freeman has been besieged—in fact, the entire district has been besieged—with the Hank Blanchard situation.

"Just a shame," Dot says. "And a shock. Who ever would have thought that about him? I don't even know what to say about it. It's remarkable how we take for granted that people are normal until we learn they're not. You see them every week, for years, and you swear they're decent and moral. You have no reason to think otherwise."

My mind flashes ahead to August of this upcoming summer. I picture Dot learning the results of my visit to New Jersey State Prison and thinking the same thing she's thinking right now. That's it's a shame and a shock and how I appeared to be so normal.

My head suddenly begins to ache. The pressure causes me to wince. Dot doesn't seem to notice.

Even though I know I'll never see Blanch again, and though he probably deserves whatever fate has in store for him, I feel a pang of obligation to shift the focus off of him and onto someone else. It seems the least I can do for our friendship.

"I know exactly what you mean. Take Dan. I never liked him all that much. Between you and me, I always found his bravado off putting. But I never figured him to be such a degenerate. It was all pretty shocking to say the least. And sad. Anyway, I've said too much. Best leave it for the powers-that-be to hash it out now."

My book is nearly finished. Its ending has proven to be a source of terrible frustration. One day it presents itself to me clearly and without clutter, and the next it's a knotted mess of implausibility. Yet I feel close to completion. A week or so at the most. This prospect doesn't make me revel in pride the way it should. I feel almost anxious about it. Cranky even. Finishing my William Walker story seems to mark one more in a series of absolute endings.

The point that I'm at has William making his final arrangements to not only turn his life over to Enid, but to have Franco murdered. He is selling off possessions, breaking off ties, and establishing new residency near his brother in Gilmanton, New Hampshire.

There was a constant cycle of both relief and angst in William's life. It was becoming impossible to distinguish the two. Each was fleeting and temperamental. He was looking forward to being a civilian once again, living a normal life out of public view. No more pressure to be a national treasure. No more lies to tell.

The fucking paintings and books and recording. He was tired of them. Mostly, though, he was tired of the pressure that had built up in his head. It was pressure caused by so much deceit. He thought about atonement often. There had never been any religion in his life. Not growing up. Certainly not now. He would need to become a self-starter. That farm where his brother lived seemed the ideal setting for William to find a little enlightenment. Wide open spaces. Clean air. No pretensions. No lunatic fans. All the time in the world to think and work towards untangling the last couple years of his life.

With four days left in the school year, I book a surprise trip to Disney. It's from July 5th to July 9th, so we'll be in Florida on Cole's third birthday. It's a package for four. My idea is to ask the Sandstrom girl across the street to accompany us. This will allow me and Joanna occasional alone time. After booking the vacation, I make an appointment to have the muffler replaced on Joanna's car. The final errand of the day is opening a joint savings account with Nana's remaining money. Seventy-thousand dollars. It's at our usual bank, but with a more aggressive interest rate.

The satisfaction I feel over completing these tasks is pathetic. It's a loopy, greasy kind of high that I've only known through bad pot, cheap beer, and dirty sex. Of course it's a short lived high. That's not the point. Or even the worst of it. The worst of it is the self-awareness that comes with the high. It's dreadful in the way that it's unrelenting. Dreadful in the way that it nearly topples me over like I'm some cardboard cutout. Dreadful in the way that it brings with it loathsome and nearly translucent truths that I know I'll never have the balls to truly deal with. Still, though, we're going to Disney.

Superintendent Freeman's secretary calls and emails me six times in two days. She urges me to reschedule my meeting with her boss. When I finally phone her back, I tell her that will not be necessary. An hour later, I get a call from the man himself.

"I really would have liked to sit down with you," he said.

"I know that."

"But I suppose it was always beyond that."

"I think it was."

"Dan Zinser is as shocked and angry over these allegations as anyone I've ever seen. It's really affected him. I've never known a man as anxious to defend his name. He's truly broken up over this thing."

"That's only natural."

"I suppose it is. But this situation has nothing whatsoever in the way of closure. I'm uneasy about that."

"It's over now. I'm out and he's in. And that's okay with me. Honestly. I don't want to have a meeting with him. God knows I've had too many of those in the past. But my biggest concern is that he is now on someone's radar—that he's monitored."

"What are your future plans if you don't mind my asking?"

"I don't mind."

Then I pause for a moment and tell him I'd like to focus on my family. I know he's curious about how I intend to make a living, but he doesn't press the matter. He ends the conversation by assuring me that Dan and I will not come in contact with one another for the remaining school days.

"It's for the best."

"Agreed."

The last few days of the school year blow by with the surreal energy of a Fellini film. The seniors come to school in their bathing suits one day; on another they play dodgeball in the hallways in between classes. A student band manages to set up and play in one of the courtyards during the first day of exams. Throughout all of this, my headaches seem to worsen. Not to mention that all of the absurdity unofficially becomes the backdrop for my farewell from Louis Sutherland High School. On more than one occasion, I find myself thinking about Blanch and wishing to hell he was here to see me off. Besides *his* absence, Owen has managed to completely avoid me for the remainder of the school year. As a bizarre gesture, I give him an A+ for his final course grade and an accompanying comment on his report card that reads *Student was a valued member of the class.*

Joanna and Cole drive me to work on my final day. Her car is in the shop getting a tune up and new muffler. This day at LSHS is spent cleaning out my classroom and saying my goodbyes. The English department chips in and buys me a Bounty Hunter Gold Digger metal detector. Perfect for the local beaches, they tell me. Not to mention, they add, to find whatever it is I am looking for. Leave it to a bunch of English teachers to buy me a fucking metaphor. Some students see me off by giving me gift cards and flowers.

There are no hugs or speeches on this day. Yet I'm professional towards my colleagues and courteous towards the kids. My focus is on gathering my things and leaving. That's all. But I suddenly find myself mixed-up, in a near panic, breathing heavy, looking over my shoulder, as I take down all of Cole's pictures and drawings from the walls and bulletin boards in my room. There's the baseball scene, done in bright colors, with a one armed pitcher throwing a ball to a red-headed stick figure. There's the faceless Jedi with a green sword twice his body's length. There are photos of Cole at Christmas and at the beach and sitting on his bed surrounded by his beloved action figures.

Collecting all of these, I insert them in the middle of my father's hardbound journal. Then I sling my metal detector over my shoulder, and head to the front of the school to wait for Joanna.

After about five minutes, she pulls up in my car. Cole is asleep in the backseat. I ask Joanna to pop the trunk so I can deposit my things. I've already come up with a plausible story about the metal detector. It's a gift for Cole. A colleague cleaned out his basement and thought my boy would like it for our beach adventures this summer.

Not only does Joanna neglect asking me about the Gold Digger, but she doesn't even look at me. Her expression is statuesque. Even when I get in the passenger seat, she doesn't turn towards me or say a word. I wait until she pulls out of LSHS's parking lot before I speak.

"Freedom. We did it. Got through another school year."

When she doesn't respond, I turn to get a look at Cole. He's snoring softly with his mouth agape. His chubby legs dangle from his carseat and his feet are bare. I study him for a few moments before turning to back towards Joanna. Her expression hasn't changed. I let her know that I called about her car and that it will be ready at around 5:00. Then I ask if everything is okay. This causes her to scoff.

"What is it?"

"Unreal. Absolutely unreal."

"Did I do something?"

"Your selfishness is too much."

"What are you talking about?"

"How are you feeling, Marcus?"

"I *was* feeling pretty damn good until a few minutes ago. The school year's over; it's officially summer. What the hell?"

Reaching around to the backseat, she lifts her purse off the floor and sets it on her lap. With her eyes on the road, she fishes through its contents for a moment before pulling out the thin yellow book Dr. Stewart gave me. Then she asks again how I'm feeling, this time holding the book inches from my face. *Brain Tumors: A Practical Guide to their Ins and Outs* by Dr. Kirby Andrews.

"Let me save you the trouble of another bullshit story: I called Dr. Stewart this morning. Right after I found your little book here."

There's no stopping her. As she drives on through the gorgeous early afternoon, signaling for turns, checking her mirrors, giving other motorists the benefit of the doubt, she tells me what she knows. My last meeting with Dr. Stewart. The results of my tests. The direness of things. Even the contents of that fucking yellow book she found under the driver's seat. That fucking yellow book that I have yet to even open.

"What were you thinking?"

"About what exactly?"

"About all of this. About your diagnosis. About telling me. About your fucking family."

It's rare that Joanna curses like this. It sounds unnatural. Absurd even.

"So compassion is out of the question?"

This is an impulse on my part. She isn't going for it. Compassion, she tells me, is conditional.

"This is not just about *you*," she said.

"Do you have any idea how cold you sound?"

"Spare me, will you? And let me be preemptive by telling you that if you utter one word about not wanting to burden the rest of us with this thing, or about how it was really some noble gesture to suffer in silence, I will drive this fucking car into a telephone pole."

"With your son sleeping in the backseat."

"That's right. I'll kill us all."

"Nice."

"Yup. Just say the word. Begin your assault of bullshit. Go ahead."

We don't speak for the rest of the ride home. By the time Joanna pulls into the driveway, the full scope of this thing is upon me. The summer is ruined. Our two months of sunshine and seafood has slipped into the ether all because a thin yellow book was discovered under the driver's seat in my car. Shutting off the ignition, she turns towards me, her voice softer than before:

"You never intended on having another baby, did you? That was bullshit, wasn't it? Just another act of appeasement."

There it is. The entire crux of her anger. All of it. Tightly balled up into one direct and simple question. A question that brings up a matter that hadn't occurred to me in the last ten minutes.

"That's right. It was bullshit. More appeasement. You got me."

"Well, it's one of the few things you've gotten really good at over the years. What a wonderful way to create distance and mistrust and suspicion."

"C'mon, let me have it."

We sit together for some time before Joanna gets out of the car. Then she leans back in and throws the yellow book at me. It hits the side of my head and falls to the floor.

"By the way, your buddy Officer Walsh stopped by today. He wants you to call him."

There's a different kind of bitterness in her voice when she says this. There's now a twinge of mockery. This makes me wonder if it has something specifically to do with Walsh. I don't even consider asking. Leaning my head against the seat, I close my eyes as Joanna slams the car door and disappears into the house. The inside of the vehicle is warm and safe. I wish I could go to sleep. But since this is unlikely, I settle for resting my body and my brain for a while as the early afternoon sunshine beats through the windows and my boy sleeps soundly in the backseat.

William and Enid were forced to spend a great deal of time together. So much so that William was convinced he would have sex with the girl. It was inevitable, he thought. She was flirty and forward and had that lost quality to her that could so often be assuaged, even if just for a moment, by getting into bed with a stranger. Not that he wanted to admit it to himself, but he even felt that she owed it to him. As the soon-to-be inheritor of a lifestyle she could only dream of, it seemed the least she could do for him. It could be a farewell offering.

But aside from a smoldering look here and there, or occasional innuendo, the girl was absolute focus. There was, after all, the murder to plan. And she had to not only be coached in the ways of celebrity, but she also had to learn about William's latest works she would eventually claim as her own. The manuscripts and recordings and paintings. There were piles of them. Enough for many more years of fame. And they were all ready to go. They were nameless, anonymous entities, ready to be welcomed into the world, one by one, and marveled over by adoring fans.

"I can't believe how prolific you've been," she said.

"It's been pretty consuming. That's for sure."

"I'll bet you're looking forward to having some time for yourself."

"Absolutely."

They went over the art of how to do a public reading. He worked with her on posture and elocution. They did run-throughs on a poem entitled "Kubla Khan" and a chapter excerpt from My Antonia. She was hardly a natural, but she showed an eagerness to learn. Then they talked about the paintings.

"Not much is required for this particular medium," he explained.

"*There's a lot of room for improvisation. Not to mention the piece should speak for itself. Unveil it, say what it is, and sit back and enjoy the accolades.*"

"*I can do that.*"

"*I have no doubt.*"

"*This has to be the world's most important job,*" she said. "*Making all these beautiful things that give people so much pleasure. Thank you for trusting them with me.*"

"*It is important, I suppose. But then it's not. And then it is again. It changes all the time. And it's difficult to keep up with it. It's like trying to predict weather.*"

She had provided him with a fitting opportunity to be introspective. For this he was grateful. It was essential that he come across like a man filled with both pride and doubt.

"*What about the music?*"

"*What about it?*" he asked.

"*I don't play a single instrument. How will I appear as a skilled musician and composer?*"

He felt his body temperature increase a little.

"*The beauty of this role is that it's self-made. You make the rules. You decide what you're willing to do. And then you stick to that.*"

"*Just like you've done.*"

"*I suppose.*"

"*Don't be modest. You have unsurpassed conviction as far as I'm concerned.*"

"*If you say so.*"

"*Don't try to soften now. It's too late. I know you.*"

"*What exactly are we talking about?*"

"*Only the most beautiful song ever.*"

William sighed. Then he flashed a smile—the kind with equal parts fatigue and amusement.

"*Let's get back to this,*" he said, holding up an oil on canvas of a man rowing a woman and baby in a rowboat.

"'*Recuerdos de la Alhambra,*'" she said.

"*C'mon.*"

"'*Recuerdos de la Alhambra.*' '*Recuerdos de la Alhambra.*' '*Recuerdos de la Alhambra.' 'Recuerdos de la Alhambra.' 'Recuerdos de la Alhambra.'"*

"Aren't you forgetting about something much more important than that?"

"What?"

"A young docent named Franco."

She deflated a little. Then a frisky grin began to make its way across her face. After a moment, she began to whisper. Inaudible at first, it grew louder until it became a breathy chant:

"'Recuerdos de la Alhambra.' 'Recuerdos de la Alhambra.' 'Recuerdos de la Alhambra.'"

Joanna's parents, Will and Aimee, become sudden fixtures in my house over the next few days. This is foreign to us all. I've grown more accustomed to socializing with them at restaurants than in either of our homes. And since Cole was born, they are more apt to pick him up for an afternoon outing than to visit with him on his own turf. This has caused most of my conversations with them in the last couple of years to take place either in my driveway or at my front door.

Now, though, they are at my home. And like me, they opt to ignore the cause of this aberration. They bring with them beer and ziti and breads and cupcakes for Cole. Sitting on the back patio, they watch their grandson play in his sandbox while they eat and drink. They regard me with a sort of remote pity. Especially Aimee, who regularly tells me to sit down and take it easy. Will, who can be chauvinistic at times, even offers to take out the trash and do a few dishes.

Will and I are left alone one evening after Joanna and her mother take Cole into town for ice cream. Sitting outside with beers in our hands, we make small talk as our food digests. He comments on my newly sealed driveway and freshly painted guest bathroom.

"A greater man would do those projects himself," I said. "Not me. I'll write a check any day of the week if it means I don't have to break a sweat."

Will laughs. Getting me off the hook, he points out that I have a family and a job.

"Yeah," I said. "At this stage in life, hiring someone does seem to make the most sense."

"What stage is that?"

"Pardon?"

"What stage would you say you're at exactly?"

"This," I said, sweeping my arm wildly in the air. "This is my stage."

"I'm just wondering how you'd define it."

"You just did, Will. Family. Job."

Will sets his beer down and straightens up. His eyes look tired under the twilight. It occurs to me at this very moment that I don't know his age. Probably early sixties. He's still got some time left in this life.

"You know what I'm talking about."

"I sure as hell do."

"We're worried," he said.

"So am I."

"We want to help."

"I imagine you will. Soon enough."

"Don't talk like that."

"What was Joanna like when she was a child?"

"Where did *that* come from?"

"I want to know."

Unable to resist, he threads together a nonlinear string of memories. Joanna in Girl Scouts. Joanna in Christmas plays. Joanna the artist. Joanna the do-gooder.

"You were outnumbered, huh?"

He admits to this, confiding in me that he loved being the only male.

"For selfish reasons, I should add. I was the outlier. This meant I could embellish the hell out of my hero status. It was very rewarding."

Without meaning to, I obliterate his nostalgia by announcing that his daughter hates me.

"It's true that she's a little pissed."

"Nothing I can do."

"I think she's feeling duped."

"Well, maybe. But I believe I'm entitled to that feeling as well. Granted, for different reasons."

Because I don't want the moment to lapse into oblivion, I tell him I have something for him and Aimee. Then I excuse myself for a moment and return with the Disney pamphlets.

"I thought it would be nice to even things out a little for you. Two boys, two girls. Five days. Perfect."

"This is anything but perfect," he says upon studying the literature.

"I think this is as perfect as we're going to get, Will."

"It's not my place to do this."

"It will be soon. A little advance practice couldn't hurt."

"What does Joanna think about this?"

"It's a surprise. From *you*."

"From *me*?"

"Call it an impulsive gesture—born out concern for your daughter and grandson."

"C'mon."

"Take a survey, Will. Given recent developments, I'd say this trip is warranted."

"Leaving you home alone, at this stage, is warranted?"

"I'll be fine."

"Joanna is not that selfish."

"Sell it to her."

"You'll miss Cole's birthday."

"Space and time. Joanna needs these right now. It's five days."

Just then, Joanna's car pulls into the garage.

"Do we have a deal?"

"I'm not sure."

"I need to know."

"Let me talk to Aimee."

"Forget Aimee. Think about your hero status. It'll skyrocket."

The front door to the house opens and Cole calls out for me.

Will folds the pamphlets and hides them in his back pocket. Making my way inside, I turn to Will and ask him to bring me back a souvenir. Then I meet up with Cole in the living room where I pick him up and roughhouse for a bit. After a while, I go off by myself and lie down in the cool dark of my bedroom.

The next few days are languid meditations of hot summery bliss. Cole and I spend more time together than we ever have before. While Joanna labors away on a new painting, Cole and I go to the beach and arcade and out to lunch. As an early birthday present, I buy him a blue Fisher-Price Jeep with chrome pipes and rims and a jet black roll bar. Joanna, upon learning of my purchase, accosts me at the bottom of the staircase the afternoon the Jeep is delivered.

"One more secret," she says, shaking her head. "Perfect."

"What's secretive about it? It's right there on the front lawn."

"You didn't even ask me. It's no less a secret than anything else of yours."

"I can't buy my son an early birthday present?"

"We're never talking about the same things anymore, are we?"

"I suppose we're not."

After a moment's hesitation, she tells me that she and Cole and her parents are going to Florida in a few days. The trip, she says, a lilt of arrogance in her voice, is a gift from her parents.

"The timing is good and bad."

"I understand," I tell her.

"Thank you."

When she turns from me and starts up the stairs, I ask her if all of this is really about having a second child.

"That's a good question."

"Well, is it?"

"I don't know."

"Then what *do* you know?"

"I know that right now I feel lonelier than I've ever felt before. I know that I feel like my husband is a complete stranger to me. I know that he and I are about as different from each other as goodness and luck are different."

"Which one would I be: goodness or luck?"

"Now *that's* an even better question," she said before turning from me and disappearing up the stairs.

Two days before they planned on murdering Franco, William decided on his final statement. It was a Willa Cather story entitled "Neighbor Rosicky." The story's protagonist is Anton Rosicky, a Czech farmer, whose love and devotion to farming and to his family inspires everyone he knows. A simple, salt of the earth man at heart, Rosicky is warned by his doctor to retire and rest his heart. He ultimately ignores this advice and dies in the end, but not without leaving behind a tremendous legacy of love, compassion, and hard work. The narrative, William reasoned, combined with the John Keats sonnet, serves as a fitting epitaph to his own story. It's an allegory, really. Rosicky's hard work would symbolize William's own toil as an artist. Rosicky's family and friends and doctor would symbolize William's fans. Rosicky's death would symbolize William's retirement to the country. Perfect. The last lines, depicting the family doctor driving past the cemetery where Rosicky was buried, read, "Nothing could be more un-deathlike than this place; nothing could be more right for a man who had helped to do the work of great cities and had always longed for the open country and had got to it at last. Rosicky's life seemed to him complete and beautiful."

The comfort William drew from these line—lines he admittedly never could have written himself—was enough to bring him to tears. Enid, thankfully, did not witness this. Lately she was off on her own, most likely putting her affairs in order. Not that she was saying goodbye to all that much: a cheap rental apartment with cold, uneven floorboards; a minimum wage job as a salesgirl in a second rate department store; a few friends she barely saw these days.

"I'm ready for this," she said one night at William's house.

"I'm sure you are."

"Are you nervous?"

"A little."

"I'll bet."

"Are you? You've got the difficult job. All I'm doing is a disappearing act."

"I'm looking at what I have to do as though it's a sacrifice. That's what I've been telling myself. And I believe it to be true. It is a sacrifice. A sacrifice for you and for me and for this life I so want. The victors outweigh the victims. It's as simple as that. Do the math yourself. It's funny—I keep thinking about what the Bible says about murder and I suddenly stop in my tracks. And then I remember what it says about sacrifice and I can move again. I suppose we can use the Bible to justify almost anything. I suppose it's the same way with art, too."

In an effort to process all that she had said, William poured himself a drink, something he was doing more of these days. Thanks to Enid.

"Christ," he said, "you really are ready for this."

The night before Joanna leaves for Florida, I climb into bed with Cole and lay with him for awhile. His room is lit by two nightlights, which makes it easy to see his face as he sleeps. There's a slight flutter of his eyelids that makes me think for a moment that I've awoken him. But he continues to sleep. So I speak to him in a whisper, telling him some of what's on my mind:

"You look just like your Daddy, Cole. Do you know that? For better or worse, you look just like your Daddy. This will someday sadden your mother. Not to mention infuriate the hell out of her. But you'll understand why and you'll take it easy on her. She's very sweet, your mother. Probably too sweet. I see a lot of that sweetness in you. And that makes me happy. You should strive to be more like your mother than like me. We don't know how much control there is over this, so all we can do is hope.

You're so young. You've got years and years and years left to this life. I suppose this is a blessing as well as a curse. I never meant to saddle you with any type of burden. But I guess me being your father pretty much made that predetermined. I don't know exactly what I've given you these last few years. And it will destroy me right now to think about that. So I have to be selfish and say that it will be up to you to figure that part out. And you will. In many years from now you'll figure it out. Your mother will help you with that. She knows me. Better than I thought, actually.

There's this book that I wrote. I'm nearly finished with it. I really don't know if it's any good. It might *not* be. But I think there's some good stuff in it. Somewhere there is. You might need to search for it. But I'm almost certain it's there. All those good parts —the true parts—those are for you.

You'll read it someday. And you'll decide for yourself. But for now, my boy, just sleep in your nice bed. Your big boy bed. So warm and comfy. You're lucky, my boy. Damn lucky."

There isn't much interaction between me and Joanna the following morning. Even though she packed during the previous night, she runs around and tidies the house and waters the plants and obsesses over travel plans, all the while waiting for Will and Aimee to arrive at 8:00 a.m. in a rental car Will has arranged. I make a big breakfast of scrambled eggs and sausage. Joanna barely eats a thing.

I'm working up the nerve to talk to her, to say something meaningful. About a thousand thoughts run through my head, but none of them seem fitting. It's only when I find her in Cole's room, making his bed and clearing the floor of his toys, that I find my voice:

"Can you promise me something?"

"What's that?"

She avoids looking at me.

"That you'll teach Cole how to paint. I'm not saying next week or even next year, but just someday. I think he'd be good at it. And it'd be a nice thing for the two of you to share. I can envision long talks between the two of you where you discuss brush strokes and canvas preferences and art history."

Now she is looking at me.

"Where did that come from?"

"Can you just assure me?"

"Yes. Fine."

"Do you mean it?"

"Yes, I mean it."

"Good."

Once the car arrives and the luggage is loaded, we say our goodbyes. Aimee hugs me and tells me to rest and take it easy. Will shakes my hand and gives me a secretive wink.

"Do you want to come, Daddy?" Cole says to me.

"You go. I'll be here when you get back. I promise."

The sound of these words makes me cringe a little. Joanna seems to notice because she asks if I'm okay.

"Fine."

Then I pull her towards me and kiss her and tell her I love her. Her eyes look almost colorless, like something within her has been defeated for the final time and she knows it and accepts it, yet mourns for it with all the poise a good, honest woman can muster. Something needs to be said. We can't end on such a sad note. So I say the only thing I can think of that makes me hopeful:

"Do you know I've been writing?"

"What?"

"I've been writing. Steadily, too. For a couple of months now. I don't know if you knew. It's been going very well."

"I'm glad."

"It's a novel. Kind of a magical realism thing. It's actually close to being finished."

"Great."

"I just wanted you to know."

When the car pulls away, I hunch over in the street outside my house and dry heave for a few moments. Nothing comes up, so I head back inside and sleep on the sofa until noon.

The ring of the doorbell wakes me up. When I peer out the living room window, I see Walsh's burgundy Ford pickup truck. Resuming my position on the sofa, I listen to him ring the bell a couple more times. This is followed by loud knocking. I don't move. After some time, I listen to him get into his truck and drive off.

The rest of the day is spent writing. I take only a few breaks. Mostly to eat and take quick powernaps. During one such break, when the feel of finishing my book is too much to take, I get antsy and head into Joanna's studio. Her latest painting, a work still in progress, is of a city street that's being submerged in water. The street, which looks European, has a span of multicolored houses that are up to their front doors in gorgeous blue and white water. Details in the painting include swaying clotheslines, broken windows, scattered birds overhead. There's no doubt that this is her best work ever. It has a mature and even dark quality to it that I'm not sure I've ever seen in her painting. It seems to me like it's her first painting that has real meaning and substance to it. It's so good that it must be personal. And I'm glad she's not here to explain it to me.

I finish my book eight hours later at 3:00 a.m. There's no fanfare. No music or champagne. Just the heaving early hour silence of the Connecticut suburbs. The book ends with some last minute plot twists. Enid, as per her plan with William, heads to The Institute late one night to do away with Franco. The plan calls for William to keep his distance so as to have an alibi. Upon receiving Enid's call, William will show up at the institute, find Franco's body, and call the police. He will then declare to the public that the murder had caused him enough distress to call it quits and disappear from the public eye.

This is not what happens. Enid lures William to the Institute where she and Franco end up double-crossing him with an ultimatum: play "Recuerdos de la Alhambra" on the guitar they have for him or be killed with Franco's razorblade. Upon William expressing shock to Enid over the treachery, she tells him she discovered him to be a phony from the beginning. A scuffle breaks out and William is killed by Franco. Enid and Franco, who were actually in cahoots for weeks, embrace and celebrate. When the young docent tells her he has an original painting for her as gesture of their alliance, he disappears to retrieve it. His plan, we find out, is to do away with her and make it look like a lovelorn murder/suicide.

Her plan is similar. Minus the lovelorn part. Franco ends up dying when Enid shoots him in the chest. Then she plants the gun on William, raids Franco's stash of finished pieces, and flees into the night. A short while later, Enid is hailed as a worthy successor to William, whose secrets of duplicity she guards out of respect for his misguided ambition.

I reread the last couple of paragraphs over and over. I read aloud and silently. Sitting and standing. I read them monotone and with bombast.

The funeral was like a capsule of liquid sorrow that flowed up and down in slow motion. People came and paid their respects and said kind words. They laid striking bouquets of flowers on the casket before uttering a prayer and walking away forever. Of course it was sad. Of course the mourners spoke about the sudden and violent death.

But how could they have known that when his life spilled out of him, drenching the sacredness of the place he helped to build, that he must have had thoughts about all the times when men before him were certain that the world was coming to an end. Not just their world, but the vast universe in all its bright mysteries and wild, rootless schemes. How could they have known that gazing upward through the haze he would have groped at the sad, winged night, pleading with his own memory for it to lift him up and save him, give him more breath, or, at the very least, keep his spectacular secrets in a place where they could survive and be safe and set to a spellbinding music infused with magic and madness.

There isn't a doubt in my mind that this is a grandiloquent ending. Shit, it borders on nonsense to me the more times I read it. Yet something about it is greatly appealing. It's true that it pleases me how William more or less gets away with his con; after all, aside from Enid, the only other person who knows he's a fraud is dead. But there's something more. It might be how Enid's discretion over

William's sins allows his legacy to remain intact. The reverence felt for him by his adoring public is not at all compromised in death. If anything, his stock increases. He thus garners sympathy by someone, if not the reader.

I was rooting for William. Sure he was a shitbag to some degree. Maybe even to a large degree. But he was given a chance and he took it. It's not like he was devoid of humanity or compassion. He was often contrite about his actions. Often he wanted to stop. But he found, as most people do, that if he stopped, life would slow down enough where the mirrors would no longer spin and his reflection would come into focus to the point where he'd have no choice but to take a look. This would be too much. It would have overwhelmed him, thrown him off course so much that he would have found himself in the absurd position of starting over. And starting over when you're already lost can be jarring.

The next two days are spent typing and editing the book. It goes by quickly. When I finish, I am left with an eight chapter, two-hundred-and-forty-one page manuscript. After I compose a terse dedication page to Cole, which I add after the title page, I secure the novel in a shoebox and store it on the floor in my closet next to my father's journal. The completion of the book happens to be on Cole's birthday.

My next project is a bit different. It's one I thought I'd be doing sometime in August, but it hasn't worked out this way. The time is fitting right now. The summer is spoiled. There's nowhere to go and nothing to do. So I pour myself a glass of beer and track down one of Joanna's razorblades; she stashed a few of them inside a mason jar she put in one of the kitchen cabinets. Then I take a brown leather belt from my closet and go to work. Like some wannabe mastermind idiot, I sit at the kitchen table, drinking, humming to myself, and outfitting the belt with a secret compartment next to the metal buckle.

It proves to be easy work. All I do is tear some stitching off by the loop on the belt, make a clean incision underneath it that's wide and long enough to conceal the blade. Then I slide the blade in. It fits well. Perfect, actually. It's snug, but not overly so. The true test is to wear the belt and see how easily I can draw the blade. I find that if I keep it loose, it's manageable.

Getting drunk allows me a good night's sleep. By the time I wake the following morning, I can't recall any of my dreams. This is for the best. They were probably wasted and fragmented episodes of desperate consequence.

After a shower and quick breakfast, I walk through my house, running my hand over random items. Pictures and artwork on the wall. A pewter key holder I bought for Joanna in the Cape. A sofa table I stripped and refinished the year we were married. Cole's bed. The brown leather belt that I end up looping though my jeans.

At a few minutes after 9:00 a.m., I head out the door and get into my car to make the trip to Jersey. It's a lovely morning. The warm sun beams through a few sheer, lacy looking clouds. The drive is pleasant. Very little traffic. Taking my time, I stop at a diner just outside of Trenton, where I order a coffee and a bagel sandwich.

I manage to psych myself into making the phone call I've been thinking about for days. The purpose of the call seems fickle even now. I initially told myself it was out of moral obligation. Then I resign to it being mainly a matter of my ego; part of me desperately wants to tell Walsh to go fuck himself.

He answers on the third ring.

"How does it feel to be footloose for the summer, Mr. English teacher?"

"Not bad."

"I'll bet. You can put me down for two months off anytime."

"I heard you've been looking for me."

"I did stop by the other day. That's true."

"Let me guess: more good cop bad cop? See if you can beat a confession out of me before inviting my family out on your boat again."

This makes him snicker.

"How *is* the family by the way?"

"They're in Florida."

"But not you?"

"Not me."

My waitress checks on me with a pot of steaming coffee in her hand. I smile and motion for a refill.

"That's some arrangement."

"How do you mean?"

"I just can't remember my wife giving me the house to myself for any extended time. I guess I'm jealous."

"Well, Joanna figured I needed some alone time to plan my next crime."

"That's support for you."

"What can I do for you, Officer?"

"*You* called *me*."

"What can I do for you?"

"Rumor has it you're calling it quits over there at LSHS."

While making another inquiry about me, Walsh discovered that not only did I leave my job, but that I wrote a letter impugning the vice principal of some lurid charges.

"You're fucking relentless."

"I revealed none of this to Joanna when I stopped over the other day. I didn't quite know what you had told her."

"Am I supposed to be grateful to you for this?"

"A little bit, I think."

"Why are you so interested in me?"

"That's actually a good way of putting it. It's true: I am interested in you. And I find that the more I learn, the more intrigued I become."

"Why are you bothering to learn *anything*?"

"It started out as matter of the law. That's absolutely true. It wasn't personal."

"And then?"

"I knew from the beginning that your statement was a lie. No two ways about it. I knew you were lying. And it intrigued me. But I was doing my job. But doing my job seemed secondary to the growing curiosity I felt over the matter. It just evolved into something personal."

"Why?"

"I think because we're so similar."

"Similar?"

"We both have families. We're both around the same age."

"Don't forget the civil servant thing."

There's a pause. I motion for my waitress, who brings me the check. Dropping some cash on the table, I collect myself and head outside.

"Call it strange if you will, but I felt some connection with you. Like maybe even in another life we could have been friends. And it was that connection that sparked my imagination. I thought, here's a guy who has pretty much what I have—security, stability—and he's putting it all at risk. And for what? What's he up to? As I said, I was intrigued. And I still am. Intrigued."

There's a brief moment of static on the line. After confirming that Walsh is still there, I offer him the closest I can come at this point to any type of redemption:

"I think there's a moment in a man's life when he becomes aware that his dreams are not going to come true. It's a singular moment. Yet that moment is long and pressing and revealing as hell. And it rams into him like some wild goddamn animal. Over and over. And where it finally knocks him is where he knows he'll remain, for better or for worse, for the rest of his days. I approached that moment a while back. I can't even recall exactly when. It might have been as far back as when my father died. Who knows? The point is that I got there. And I knew fighting it would be futile. I'd just look foolish to myself. Maybe no one else would have ever noticed, but I'd look foolish to myself. And to tell you the truth, I always wanted to keep from looking foolish to myself. If I think about it hard enough, I can even convince myself that not looking foolish has always in fact been my dream. But the truth of the matter is there has always been more. But that hardly matters right now."

No response. I wait.

"You can call that my 'I have a dream' speech if you want."

Still no response.

"Hello?"

"Hello?"

"Are you there?"

"I didn't catch that. You were breaking up."

"Can you hear me?"

"Hello?"

"You're breaking up, too."

"Can you hear me?"

"Hello."

Then nothing. Walsh is gone. The line is dead. So I decide to follow one dramatic gesture with another. Turning off my phone, I drop it under my rear wheel before climbing into my car and backing out of the parking lot.

By the time I arrive at the prison, my mind is in an almost militant state. There's a stark quality to my thoughts. They are lucid and orderly, laying out a careful trajectory of what will occur in the next hour or so. It's all so meticulous that it makes me wonder for a moment whether I'm envisioning scenes that have already happened.

This changes almost the instant I enter the building. I suddenly blank. And with a foreign sense of reserve, I go through the necessary motions. The sign in. The paperwork. Identification. Waiting in the lobby. Waiting with me is a lone man, probably in his fifties, as well as a middle age woman and her teenage son. The man leaves first, ushered from the room by a corrections officer. A short time later, the woman and her boy follow. Sitting in the room alone, I begin to fidget with my belt. It's loose around my jeans, and my fingers easily slide underneath it.

By the time I reach the metal detection area, I am lightheaded to the point where one of the officers, a stout man I recognize from my last visit, asks if I'm okay. Handing him my belt and car keys, I nod and tell him I'm hungry. He responds, but I don't hear him. His words sound like white noise and the room begins to spin. Then I'm scanned with the wand. My stomach suddenly feels nauseous. The stout officer continues to talk to me; another one joins in. He's handsome. I don't recognize him from my last visit. I'm told to walk through the metal detector. The two men keep talking. To me. To each other. It's too much. The fucking room continues to spin.

"Want these?" the officer asks, holding up my belt and keys.

Nodding, I take them from him before being led into the all-purpose room. Alex is waiting for me. He sits in the same area as the last time we met. With his legs crossed under the table and his hands folded on his stomach, he appears to be at ease. Seated nearby is the man from the lobby; he's visiting an inmate with short curly hair and tattoos up and down his skinny arms. The woman and her teenage son are across the room with an inmate whose back is to the rest of us. A corrections officer paces the floor with slow, drawn out steps.

"My nephew returns," Alex says. "And so soon."

Putting my belt on allows me to avoid a handshake. I can feel Alex watching me. Looking past him, I take in the vastness of the room. It somehow seems bigger than before.

"I hope you'll pardon another impromptu visit."

"Absolutely."

"I've never been much of a planner."

"I don't mind."

"I suppose you could refuse the visit if you wanted."

"I could."

"Ever do that?"

"No."

Taking a seat across from him, I can't help but overhear the two men at the nearby table. They're talking about someone's retirement party and laughing about a mishap that occurred. They share the same laugh, which leads me to believe they might be father and son. It suddenly strikes me that they could surmise the same about me and Alex.

Looking past my uncle, I spot the surveillance camera on the other side of the room. Staring straight into it, I can't help but wonder if we're being watched at this very moment. And if we are, is anyone interested in figuring out what we're saying? It's astonishing to think about all the talking that has happened in this room throughout the years. Talk filled with anguish and disappointment. Talk born out of pure obligation. Talk to simply pass the time. Talk of amusing retirement parties.

"This is a hell of a place."

"You don't know the half of it."

"True."

"The kind of strength needed to thrive in a place like this is beyond any civilian."

"I studied martial arts from this lesbian woman. For just a short time. It was hardcore shit, really. Very impractical, but cool at the same time. What a rush. I'm thinking now that it gave me the strength to come here and face you."

"That's a different kind of strength."

"How so?"

"It's the difference between walking on hot coals and lighting yourself on fire. Right now, I'm on fire. But you can't see that."

His bullshit letters to Nana suddenly flood my brain. Holier-than-thou rants on strength and forgiveness and revenge. My focus veers off to the mother and her teenage son. Their visit is subdued and even secretive. The inmate they are meeting is fidgety. He leans forward in his chair and scratches his side before sitting back and rotating his head around. He then repeats this, but in a different order.

"What do you think they're talking about?"

Alex turns to regard the threesome. Then he shrugs.

"It hardly matters. But there's a good story there, don't you think? There must be."

"Maybe."

"This place must be filled with good stories. Don't you think? What am I saying? You probably know a lot of them, don't you?"

"You could say I know a fair share."

"We've got ourselves one, don't we? A good story."

Considering this for a moment, Alex seems put upon. He mumbles for a moment before agreeing with me that we do indeed have a good story.

"I'm very interested in stories. I find them easier to understand than real life."

"What's on your mind, Marcus?"

"This room. This very room is on my mind. It has a story all its own. Can you imagine all that has happened in here? Families destroyed and deceived and in denial.

Think about all the tears probably shed in here. The lies told. The divorce papers served. This room is a fucking goldmine. Stories and secrets and stories and secrets—more than anyone can imagine."

My rambling has turned Alex into a dumbfounded waif. The lost look in his eyes is comical, even cinematic; it's from another time and space compared to how he looked when we last met. I suddenly remember that he is bipolar, a fact that emerged shortly after his arrest. Today he looks it.

"Is that why you came here this afternoon? To talk about our story?"

Looping my fingers under my belt, I work at prying the razorblade from its hiding place. As I dig into the leather with my nails, I force myself to smile at my uncle. He maintains the stunned look of a man whose grip on himself is slowly loosening.

"Not at all. I have no interest in talking about our story."

"Then what?"

I'm struck with an urge to ask him a personal question I already know the answer to:

"Do you meet with your son in here? My cousin Joe."

"Of course I do. He's been coming for years. Jeannine, too. And your Aunt Janice."

Alex's voice is full of pride when he says this.

"I don't think I could do that: meet with my son in a place like this. No way. It would destroy me for sure."

"You don't know that. You don't know the first thing about that. Until you're in here, breathing these fumes, day in and day out, you can't say what you would or would not do. This place makes your mind up for you. You don't have choices when you're in here. You have time. All you have is time."

All that bravado from our last visit is completely gone. Alex has been reduced to nothing more than a man with years of sorrow and regret. Probably the way he was when my father was still alive.

Neither of us says a word for a while. We sit and listen to the man from the lobby talk to his inmate son about some car show he attended the week before. I continue to work on loosening the blade.

"Say something," he said.

All I can do is look through him. Lines from that John Keats poem I used in my novel come rushing into my thoughts. Lines about never being able to write all that's in one's mind. Such a tragic sentiment. This Uncle Alex story would for sure make one hell of a book. It's got a little bit of everything: love, violence, flawed characters, truth and lies, goodness and luck. And who better to tell it than me? It would have been my masterpiece, my life's work.

"Marcus."

Taking a breath, I brace myself for what's to come. Without meaning to, I launch into the same 'I have a dream' speech I gave to Walsh earlier in the day. Walsh had missed it. And I thought someone needed to hear it. And what better place to say it than in this place? This place where such talk might be rampant. Where it comes to be uttered for the sake of God knows what, to breathe out its short, meager existence until time runs out or exhaustion sets in, only to survive as some strange silent film on surveillance footage.

Alex is tuned in, yet it's clear he's through with me. The blade is suddenly pried loose and rests easy in the center of my fist. The feel of it causes me to pause, mid-sentence. Looking over to the father and son, I attempt to eavesdrop on their conversation. But they appear to me only as two animated bodies, moving their mouths, throwing their heads back and forth, teasing out wide, brash smiles in the other. Then I look up at the surveillance camera before turning my attention to the mother and her teenage son. They seem bored and on the verge of leaving. When I finally face my Uncle Alex again, he is slouching in his seat, a sad and weary expression turning his features into something far removed from any family member I've ever known. Looking him dead in the eyes, I offer an apology for being so easily distracted.

"Now, where was I?"

Purchase other Black Rose Writing titles at <u>www.blackrosewriting.com/books</u>
and use promo code PRINT to receive a 20% discount.

CPSIA information can be obtained
at www.ICGtesting.com
Printed in the USA
FFOW01n1057081214

312FF